Midnight Unchained

Georgina Stancer

This book is dedicated to my Mum and Dad.
They are the best parents a girl could ask for.

Contents

Prologue

Three days she waited, plotting her escape. Now the time was here, Nessa didn't know if she was strong enough to make it out on her own. Lack of food and water made her weak. But she had to try, she couldn't stay here. It wasn't safe.

When she first woke up in this dark dank cell three days ago, she thought she must be stuck in a nightmare. It wasn't unusual for her to have this nightmare, but normally she woke up when the bad guys came for her. This time she hadn't.

When the bad guys came for her, she had gone to sleep instead. Minding her own business as she made her way home from work late one night, two men and a woman had appeared out of nowhere. The men had grabbed hold of her arms so she couldn't get away.

If Nessa had expected the woman to help her, then she had been sorely mistaken. Instead of helping, the woman blew some powder into her face that knocked her out cold within seconds. Later on, when she finally woke up, she found herself locked in this god-awful place.

The stench of rotting meat permeated the air. Scurrying sounds were constant as rodents ran rampant, not only around the building but the room she was occupying as well.

Every time her captors had brought her food it had been crawling with cockroaches. Nessa knew she needed the sustenance if she stood any chance in escaping, but no matter how hungry she was, she couldn't bring herself to eat any of it.

It was bad enough drinking what passed for water around here. She was sure it was more mud than water, and the smell alone was enough to make anyone want to vomit. Pinching her nose whenever she had to drink any of it so she didn't have to smell it at the same time, then fighting to keep it down when it wanted to come straight back up again.

There wasn't much in the room she could use to aid her in escaping this place, but she would not let that stop her either. One way or another, she was getting out of here today.

The few items in the room she could choose from were a metal bed with a mattress that had seen far better days, a paper-thin pillow and a rough blanket. Plus, there was her personal favourite… a bucket in the corner of the room for her to use as a toilet. Yeah, it was definitely no five-star hotel.

When she had spotted the screws holding the bedposts in place, she could've jumped for joy. It was the perfect size and shape to use as a bat. And that's exactly what she would use it as. Not wasting any time, she had set to work on one of the posts.

Choosing the post that was wedged in the corner so it wasn't visible to the guards, she carefully pulled the bed out a little so she would have better access. Using her fingers and nails until they bled, she coaxed the screws loose with no one being the wiser about what she was doing.

Whenever she heard movement in the hallway, she quickly returned the bed to its original position as quietly as she could. The last thing she needed was for them to figure out what she planned before she had a chance to carry it through.

Finally, after days of trying, the last of the screws were out and the post was free. Now all she had to do was wait for the guards to return. All the hairs on her body stood on end as she listened to them walking past her door.

It was the same every day. Like clockwork, two guards walked along the corridor. Starting from the far end, they stopped at each room, handing out food and water to the occupants. Hers was somewhere around the middle. She didn't know if every room had someone inside, and she didn't know how many rooms there were, but she assumed that most did.

Ready to pounce the moment they opened the door, holding the metal post above her head, she didn't hesitate when the first guard stepped inside. Swinging the metal post in a downward arch with all her strength, she whacked him on the top of his head. As he doubled over, she lifted her knee, connecting it with his face.

Ignoring the throbbing pain radiating from her knee where it made an impact with the guard's face, she turned her attention to the other guard. It took the second guard a moment for it to sink in what had happened to his comrade, which gave her the advantage she was counting on.

Before he could react, she pulled back her arms and then swung the metal post straight into his face. Blood instantly squirted from his nose as the post made contact. When he lifted his hands to his face, she kneed him between the legs, dropping him instantly to the ground.

Nessa hit him over the head for good measure before grabbing the keys from where they landed on the floor and made her escape. Using the door to push the second guard further into the room, she quickly locked it behind her so they couldn't follow her straight away.

She didn't bother stopping at any of the other rooms. If she was going to get away before the others noticed she was missing, then she couldn't stop to help anyone else. The best thing she could do for them now was to escape and get help.

With a rough idea of the layout of the building, she was as prepared as she was going to be. Sending up a silent prayer, she took a deep breath and crept along the corridor to the door at the far end.

There was a stairwell on the other side of the door. She knew what was downstairs, it led further into the building and that was the last place she wanted to go. They had taken her down there not long after she arrived here.

Nessa shuddered at the memories of what they did to her while she was down there, she definitely didn't want a repeat of that experience.

No, she wanted to go up. That was the only way she hadn't been, at least not that she could remember, so she assumed that it was the way out. She didn't even care if it took her to the roof, as long as she wasn't in this building anymore. Nessa would shout for help from the rooftop if it came to it.

The door at the end of the corridor creaked as she opened it. Nessa froze, listening for any sounds. Only when she was certain no one heard it did she open the door further, just enough for her to squeeze through, then she closed it again as quietly as she could.

Making her way up the stairs, she listened intently for any sounds coming from either direction. Nessa didn't bother stopping to look through each door on her way up the stairwell; she didn't care what was behind them. It was only when she reached the top that she finally went through a door.

The bright sunlight blinded her momentarily. When her eyes adjusted to the light, she looked around at an empty rooftop.

Typical, she thought, *but at least I'm finally outside.*

It may be a small victory, but she was going to take it as a good sign that nobody else was up here. Now she just needed to find a fire escape to climb down.

Taking a deep breath of fresh air, she stepped outside, closing the door behind her. Nessa walked the perimeter of the building as she looked for the fire escape.

She sighed in relief when she found it. Even though it was only a few metal bars sticking out of the wall, it was still a way off this roof, and she was going to take anything she could to get away from this place.

Without a second thought, Nessa carefully maneuvered over the side of the building and climbed down the ladder. The cold metal bars, rusted with age, froze her bare hands and feet. Wishing she had more clothing on than just a pair of shorts and a vest top, she tried not to let the cold slow her down.

Reaching the bottom of the ladder, Nessa looked around to see which direction to go. All she could see was woodland. She couldn't even see a road leading through the woods from where she stood.

Not letting that stop her, Nessa picked what she hoped was north, then raced off into the woods. Sooner or later she was bound to come across civilization. Nessa just hoped it was sooner rather than later.

With what little energy she had left in her, she didn't think she would make it very far on foot.

Howling came from the building behind her, along with the sound of people shouting. They were trying to find her. She knew that it wouldn't take them long to realize she had escaped and to send out a search party to find her, but she hadn't thought it would be that quick.

Digging deep, Nessa pulled up the last of her energy reserves and ran as fast as she could. Not expecting it to have much effect, she was surprised with the speed and agility she could pull off with what little energy she had left.

Before she knew it, she broke through the tree line and was next to a busy dual carriageway. She risked looking back to see if anyone was following her. She could just about make out movement in the woods as they headed in her direction.

With no time to spare, Nessa started waving down cars and shouting "Help!" as she walked backward along the side of the road. All the while she kept trying to gain more distance between her and the bad guys.

It seemed like forever before one car finally pulled over. She raced over to it, praying it wasn't one of the bad guys. Luck was on her side for once as she looked through the open window and saw it was a little old lady behind the wheel.

"Are you okay?" she asked.

"No, nowhere close to being okay, but I'm hoping you can help remedy that," she said honestly. "Could you please give me a lift?"

"Of course," the lady said with a smile.

"Thank you so much. You don't know how much this means to me," Nessa said as she climbed in the car.

"Where would you like me to take you, dear?" the lady asked. "Do you need to go to the hospital?"

"No, could you drop me off at the closest police station please?" Nessa asked.

"Are you sure you don't want a hospital?"

"I'm positive. Please, just the police station, as soon as possible."

Nessa knew they were getting closer, and the longer she sat here talking, the more chance they had of catching her before she could truly get away.

The little old lady looked her over, concern showing on her face, but without another word, she put her foot down and they sped off.

Nessa looked back just in time to see the bad guys break through the tree line. She hoped they hadn't seen her getting into the car.

Chapter One

"Tell me why we're here again?" Aidan asked for the umpteenth time.

"Because we are," Kellen snapped.

Aidan knew exactly why they were here. They were trying to find the people responsible for turning Anya from a normal Human into a wolf shifter. Until that moment in time, everyone thought it was impossible to turn a human into one of them, but they had been proven wrong.

Well, everyone except Rush, the Alpha of their pack. He seemed to know it was possible all along. It would have been nice if he had shared that bit of information with the rest of the class, but being the Alpha meant he didn't have to tell them jack shit.

They still didn't know all the details about how it

happened, that was one of the main reasons they were out here searching a caravan park in the Human realm.

From the description Anya had given when she was being held captive, and from what Connor had picked up with his enhanced sense of smell when he rescued her, they knew it was a male Wolf Shifter and a female Witch they were looking for.

The Shifter gave Anya a fake name, trying to pass himself off as a Mr Smith, but Anya didn't buy it. She told him she didn't believe him and that's when he admitted it wasn't his real name. So, they were still none the wiser of who he is, and they only had a basic description of what he looked like as well.

She had given a partial name and description for the Witch though, not that it helped much but it was still a start. Anya told them that she had been kept asleep for some time, and it was the Witch that kept putting her to sleep by blowing some kind of powder into her face.

Kellen wanted to get hold of some powder, so he could use it on his sister when she pissed him off. He could see it coming in handy when he wanted a couple of hour's peace, knowing she was exactly where he left her.

"No need to snap," Aidan said. "I just don't get why we have to search this shitty campsite in the pissing rain. Why can't we wait until tomorrow, you know, search in daylight? Might be easier."

"It might also be too late," Connor said, coming up behind them with Anya in tow.

Since they mated a few months back, they haven't

strayed too far from each other for long. Nowadays, wherever Connor was, Anya was close by.

Kellen missed the days when he could pop round to Connor's house and bitch about his sister, Kayla. Now Anya was living there, he couldn't do it anymore. Well, he could, but Anya always stuck up for Kayla.

He would like to see how Anya would cope with having to deal with Kayla permanently. She was a handful at the best of times, but she was always an angel when Anya was near.

Kellen couldn't wait for Anya and Connor to have pups of their own. He was looking forward to seeing how they are going to deal with unruly teens, especially if they turn out anything like Connor when he was younger.

Kellen didn't know what Anya was like growing up, but if she got into the same amount of trouble Connor did, then they were in for a bumpy ride with their pups, and Kellen was going to sit back and enjoy watching every minute.

"We can't let him do the same thing he did to me to someone else," Anya said. "Plus, he might know what happened to Sasha."

Sasha was Anya's best friend. She also played an instrumental part in aiding the Wolf Shifters in locating and retrieving Anya from the bad guy's clutches. They might not have been able to reach her in time if it wasn't for Sasha's ability to teleport, not just herself, but others as well.

Unfortunately, no one has heard from her since the

fight ended between the Shifters and the Demons. As far as they knew, she was still unaware that Anya was now safe.

"Don't worry, we'll find Sasha, I promise," Connor told her, pulling her under the protection of his arm.

"I know. I just wish we knew what happened to her," Anya said.

"I wish we knew what she was," Aidan said. "You sure she never told you?"

"No, I thought she was Human like me."

It wasn't the first time Anya was asked that question, and it probably won't be the last either. They were all intrigued to find out what Sasha was. Kellen and some others thought she might be Fae, but Aidan thought she was a Witch. Connor was keeping his opinion to himself over what he thought she was, probably because he didn't want to upset Anya by thinking her friend is something she's not.

"You two finished searching your area?" Kellen asked them.

"Yeah," Connor said. "How about you two?"

"We have this bit left and then we're done," Kellen said as he indicated a row of caravans.

"Did you find anything?" Aidan asked.

"Don't you think we would have told you as soon as we walked up if we had," Connor said.

"Yeah, I suppose," he conceded.

"The only thing I could pick up was the rain," Connor said.

"Yeah, same," Kellen said as Aidan nodded in agreement.

"I don't think I'll ever get used to how loud the rain is now, or how much it smells," Anya said.

Kellen couldn't help but smile at her. Aidan burst out laughing, while Connor just shook his head as he leaned down to place a kiss on her forehead.

"What?" she asked.

"I can't believe you said that rain smells," Aidan said, still laughing.

"Well, it does. In a good way, of course," She said, blushing. "I just didn't realize before that it has a smell. I like it, but it doesn't help when you're trying to track someone's scent. But then, I've never needed to do that before either."

"Don't worry, you'll get used to it eventually," Connor assured her.

It amazed Kellen how swiftly Anya had taken to her new life. Everyone in the pack thought it would have taken her longer to get the swing of things, but she picked up everything pretty quickly.

"I know," she said.

"You've done really well so far," Aidan said, copying Kellen's thoughts. "You'll be a pro in no time."

"You think?"

"Yeah, I do," Aidan told her honestly.

"See? What did I tell you?" Connor asked.

"Shall we get finished here so we can go back to the hotel and dry off?" Kellen asked, getting everyone back on track.

The wind and rain were starting to pick up momentum, and Kellen didn't know about the others, but he would rather not stay out longer than necessary in this weather.

"Sounds good to me," Connor said.

"I second that," Aidan added.

"We'll help you check this area," Connor said.

"There's no point in us all staying and getting soaked through. Why don't you two go back and sort some food out for when we're finished?" Kellen said.

"Yeah, I'm starving," Aidan said as he rubbed his stomach. "That sounds like a better idea."

"If you're sure," Connor said.

"Yes," Kellen and Aidan said in unison.

"Okay then, we'll meet you back at the hotel," Connor said.

"See you soon," Anya said as she walked away with Connor.

Kellen didn't wait for them to disappear; he walked down the last stretch of caravans, Aidan hot on his heels.

"I don't think we will find anything," Aidan said.

"Maybe not, but it's always worth checking," Kellen told him. "We don't have much further, so we might as well finish looking."

"Fine," Aidan said reluctantly. "I suppose you're right."

"You can go with those two if you're that bothered," Kellen told him.

It wouldn't take them both to finish checking the caravan site, and Kellen was more than happy to do it alone if it meant he wouldn't have to listen to Aidan moan about it.

"Nah, I'll stick with you."

"You just don't want to be left alone with the two lovebirds, do you?" Kellen asked, knowing what the answer was going to be.

"What? And feel like the third wheel? No, thank you. I would rather stick red hot pokers into my eyes."

Kellen laughed. It was just like Aidan to come up with something like that.

"It's not so bad when we're both there," Aidan said. "I don't feel like the odd one out."

"You'll always be the odd one out," Kellen told him, still laughing.

"Thanks," Aidan said sarcastically. "You know what I mean though, right?"

"Yeah, I know what you mean," Kellen agreed.

He couldn't deny he felt the same. Not that Kellen felt unwelcome in their company, just a little like a third wheel when he was alone with them. He knew it was because their relationship was still new and that they didn't even realize they were doing anything, so he didn't take it to heart.

"To be honest, we'll probably be the same when we find our mates," He told Aidan.

"Yeah, I suppose," Aidan agreed.

Kellen sniffed the air. "Do you smell that?"

"Smells like a panther," Aidan said.

"That's what I thought."

"But they're not native here, are they?" Aidan asked, frowning.

15

"No, they're not," Kellen said, shaking his head.

"I didn't think so. Where do you think it's coming from?"

"I don't know, but it's around here somewhere, or it has been recently."

"Recently by the smell," Aidan added.

Kellen agreed. From how strong the scent was, they must have only just missed the animal. Or Shifter, which was more likely give the location they were in. As far as Kellen knew, they do not have any wild panthers in the UK.

"Should we go looking for it?" Aidan asked.

"No, we're not here to look for a panther," Kellen reminded him.

"What if it's a Shifter?"

"It more than likely is a Shifter, but unless they're working with the bad guy, they're none of our concern," Kellen told him, knowing they were being watched at that very moment, and it was probably the feline Shifter.

"We should at least check them out."

"Aidan, I'm soaked to the bone," Kellen told him. "So unless they have anything to do with the people we're after, I don't give a shit."

Which wasn't technically true, but he didn't want to let on to the Shifter that he knew they were being watched from the shadows. Kellen had spotted the panther just after they picked up on the scent.

Luckily enough, Kellen could speak with Aidan without the other Shifter hearing a word they said. One of the many benefits about being a Shifter was the fact they could communicate telepathically.

So instead of saying anything more out loud for all to hear, Kellen opened a link with Aidan before he could say another word.

"Whoever the panther is, they are following us as we speak. I would rather go back to the hotel and make out everything is normal. Then later…when we know we are not being watched…one of us can sneak back to find out what we can."

"Good plan, Batman," Aidan replied before adding out loud "So, what do you think those two have got us for dinner?"

"Smooth move, dickhead," Kellen said.

"There's no need for name calling. Did I call you shit-for-brains? No, I didn't."

Kellen just about stopped himself from bursting out laughing, but he couldn't stop the smile though.

"There's no need to shout either," Kellen told him.

"I don't know, but I'm fucking starving," he said, trying to hide the fact he was smiling.

"Me too," Aidan added.

"Come on then, let's go back to the hotel," Kellen said, changing direction and heading for the exit.

Just as Kellen assumed, the panther followed them as they headed out of the caravan site. He hadn't been sure if it would turn back once they were off the site, but he wasn't surprised to find that it was following them all the way back to the hotel.

"So, what's the plan?" Aidan asked after a few minutes.

Kellen wasn't sure yet, but there wasn't any point standing around in the rain. Plus, it would be a good idea to lose the Shifter before going back out. Hopefully, the Shifter won't hang around for too long after they go inside.

"I don't know, but we'll figure something out when we're with the others."

Next time they head out, they need to make sure that no one watches them as they searched the area. Until they know for sure, this Shifter could be involved with the bad guy in some way, so they needed to be extra vigilant just in case.

As far as they know, the bad guy they were after was a wolf Shifter and he was working with a Witch and Imfera Demons, but that didn't mean he wasn't working with others. Kellen just hoped that no other Shifters were involved with him.

Chapter Two

Six weeks had passed since Nessa escaped from the bad guys, and yet, she was still running for her life. They hadn't given up searching for her, even after she reported them to the police.

Not that the police were much help either. They hadn't believed a word she told them. Especially after they checked out the place where Nessa had told them she'd been held, and that there were other people still being held there, only to find the place completely empty.

Nessa didn't have a clue how the bad guy's had completely emptied the place in under an hour, leaving not a single trace that anyone had been there in years, but that is exactly what they had done.

After that, the police thought she was a crazy person and tried to have her sent to a secure ward in the local hospital. Nessa wasn't having any of that. So, at the first opportunity she got, she made a run for it.

Nessa wasn't only running from the bad guys anymore…who seem to still want her…but she was also on the run from the police. She didn't know why the bad guys wanted her, but at least she finally knew what they had done to her.

She found that out the hard way. Until then Nessa hadn't paid much attention to the phases of the moon, but come the following full moon after she escaped, her life had been turned upside down and inside out, in more ways than one.

It had started with a headache that quickly turned into a fever. The pain had been so intense she thought at one point that she was going to die. Luckily enough, that hadn't been the case.

Nessa would have sworn she had been hallucinating through some of it, seeing black fur cover her skin and her hands turn into paws, she had even glimpsed a flick of a tail. But she hadn't been hallucinating.

The next morning when she woke up, she had scared herself half to death when she first opened her eyes and caught sight of herself in the mirror next to the bed. Nessa had never leapt out of bed so fast in all of her life. She was a fully-grown panther.

Yellow eyes stared back at her as she took in her new appearance. Huge paws with razor sharp nails, a long slim tail, and pure black from head to tail.

Her dark fur had come in handy many times since. Even now she was using it to her advantage as she watched the strangers search the caravan site where she had been staying for the last couple of nights.

Nessa knew she couldn't stay anywhere for long now the bad guys were after her, but so far, she has stayed in one place for at least a week before they got too close to her. This time, however, they have found her a lot quicker, and have come a lot closer to catching her.

If it wasn't for her new skills, Nessa was positive they would have caught her by now. Luckily enough, tonight she had been out on a run when she spotted a couple of shady looking men.

Nessa followed them, silently watching from the shadows as they made their way around half of the campsite before meeting up with another man and a woman. She assumed the man and woman covered the other half of the campsite, but she had been too preoccupied with the first two to realize there were any others.

Who could blame her though? It wasn't every day that two gorgeous men with well-built bodies came wondering around. Even if they were bad guys, they were fucking hot.

Nessa found it amusing that the taller of the two men seemed to be getting annoyed with the other one. There had been a couple of times she had laughed in her mind at how easily he was wound up.

She listened as the group talked amongst themselves. From what they were saying, it appeared they were looking for someone, but not her.

Nessa couldn't help but sigh in relief when it turned out they were looking for a man. It appeared the person they were after had done something to the woman they were with. Nessa couldn't imagine what might have been done to her; the woman looked perfectly fine.

Well, whatever it was, it hadn't affected the way she looked. The woman was beautiful. Her long strawberry blonde hair was pulled up into a ponytail, but Nessa could tell that it would nearly reach her bottom if it was down.

Even soaked through with no make-up on she was stunning, Nessa, on the other hand, would look like a drowned rat. So it was no surprise that the men she was with were also drop dead gorgeous. Nessa could tell from the size of them they were all well-built underneath their layers of clothing.

She had to admit though, her eyes kept being drawn to the tallest of the men. There was something about him that had caught her attention from the moment she first set eyes on him.

He was slimmer than the other two men, but Nessa had a feeling he was just as dangerous as them though. It was one of the things that made them stand out to her, the reason she had decided to follow them. They were up to something, she just didn't know what.

The man and woman didn't stay for long, after talking for a couple of minutes they parted ways, heading back to where they were staying. Nessa left them to it; she was more interested in the other two anyway… well, one of them.

As much as she told herself that he was bad news, she wanted to learn more about them, about the people they were after. Because if big burly men like these were looking to stop someone from hurting others, then she wanted to make sure she knew who to avoid if she crossed their path in the future.

Nessa closely followed the men, listening intently to their conversation, but they didn't mention the person they were after again. What they mentioned, however, froze her to the bone.

Just as they were coming up to her caravan, the taller of the two lifted his head and sniffed the air. Now, normally that wouldn't have made a difference to her, but when the other man said that it 'smells like a panther' while she was in panther form following them, that was definitely a cause for concern.

Her heart skipped a beat before going double time, making it harder for her to hear what they said next. Nessa didn't miss the part where they were talking about shifters. Is that what she was now? A shifter?

Nessa supposed it made sense, she could shift forms from a Human to a panther. But how did they know?

There was definitely more to these men than she originally thought, and they were definitely more dangerous than she first gave them credit for, especially since they seemed to know about her abilities.

Nessa didn't know what she was expecting them to do next, but it wasn't for them to just give up and leave the campsite. But that is exactly what they did.

Complaining about the wet weather and being hungry, they left without a backward glance. Nessa stayed with them, just with a little more distance between them this time, as they made their way to the local hotel.

She assumed that their friends were already waiting inside for them. Nessa didn't think it would be a wise idea to follow them in, especially since she was still in panther form, so she waited outside for a few minutes to make sure they didn't turn around and come straight back out again.

When she was certain they weren't coming back out, Nessa quickly made her way back to the campsite.

She wasn't stupid enough to go straight to her caravan; she needed to make sure that there were no other strangers snooping around first. Only when she was satisfied that she was alone again did she finally return to her caravan.

Nessa had left one of the bedroom windows open when she went for a run earlier, so she could enter the caravan without the risk of being seen as she shifts back into Human form. She could easily jump through the window and then shift when she was safely back inside.

Without wasting a single second, Nessa quickly set to work collecting up all her belongings. She needed to leave tonight, she couldn't stay here any longer, the newcomers had made sure of that.

Chapter Three

Aidan knocked on Connor's bedroom door when they arrived back at the hotel. They didn't see the point in hanging around, they wanted to update Connor and Anya on what they had come across in the campsite.

It wasn't every day they came across a Shifter, of any breed, living outside their realm. So, they needed to check them out to make sure they weren't working with the bad guy. Because if they were, then Kellen and the rest of the wolf Shifters wanted to find out all that they knew about him.

"You two are back early," Anya said as she opened the door for them. "I thought it would've taken you longer to finish."

"I told you it wouldn't take them long," Connor told her.

"Yeah, I know, but I still thought it would take them longer. We've only been back a couple of minutes ourselves."

"There was only one row left to check," Kellen reminded her, smiling gently.

"Did you find anything?" Connor asked.

"Yeah, you could say that," Aidan said.

While they ate, Kellen and Aidan filled them in on the feline Shifter.

Anya waited for them to finish. "What are we going to do about her? If it even is a female."

"Oh, it's definitely a female panther," Aidan told her.

"How do you know?" she asked.

"Because we can tell by her scent," Connor told her. "You'll be able to easily tell the difference once you're used to it."

"Oh yeah, sorry, I keep forgetting about that," she said as her cheeks turned a rosy shade.

"No need to apologize, you're still learning," Kellen told her.

"Yeah, but I should at least know that by now."

"Considering how much you've already learnt in such a short amount of time, I think you're doing extremely well," Connor told her as he pulled her on to his lap and wrapped his arms around her waist.

"We all think you're doing great at picking everything up," Kellen told her, Aidan nodded his agreement.

"Thanks, guys," she said with a smile. "I honestly couldn't have done it without you all teaching me."

"You're more than welcome," Kellen said. "After all,

you're part of the family now."

Even though none of them were related, Kellen, Connor, and Aidan were as close as brothers. They had been best friends since they were young. So, when Anya mated Connor, she became their adopted sister, especially since she didn't have any family of her own.

"I'm going back to the campsite in a minute on my own to see if I can find out any information about her," Kellen announced.

He'd been thinking about it the entire way back to the hotel. They stood more chance of finding out who the Shifter was if only one of them went back out.

They probably already scared her off, which was the last thing they wanted to do, especially if she has any useful information on the people they were after.

"When did you decide that?" Aidan asked.

"On our way back here," Kellen told him. "I thought it would be best if only one of us went back out, less likely to be seen then."

"Yeah, but why is it you?" Aidan asked.

"Because I call dibs," he said, sticking out his tongue.

"Seriously?" Aidan said. "You're such a child at times."

"That's the pot calling the kettle black, don't you think," Kellen said as he burst out laughing. "You're always acting like a child."

"No I'm not," Aidan said stubbornly.

"You do," Connor said, agreeing with Kellen.

"Is that how you feel as well," Aidan asked Anya.

"Sorry," she said with a guilty smile.

"Oh, wow…just wow," he said, throwing his hands up in the air. "Well, now I know how you all feel."

"You've always known how we feel, stop pretending you didn't," Kellen told him.

"Yeah, I know," He said smiling. "I was just pulling your legs."

"Well, don't do that," Anya scolded him. "You had me feeling bad about it."

"Sorry," he said sheepishly.

"So you should be," she said, pointing a finger at him. "It's not nice to trick people like that, you know."

It was Aidan's turn to look guilty. "I promise not to do it again."

Kellen didn't know how Anya had kept a straight face for so long, but he could see the corners of her lips turn up just before she burst out laughing.

"You're mean," he told her, then turned to Kellen. "Can you believe that? I thought I had really upset her then, I felt terrible," he said as he shook his head. "Then she burst out laughing. She's mean."

Aidan looked like a two-year old that had just been scolded by his parent. Bottom lip pushed out and everything. Kellen couldn't help but laugh at him.

"I like her. She put you right in your place," Kellen told him.

"That's my mate," Connor said proudly as he hugged her tightly.

"Anyway, we're getting off topic here," Kellen said, bring them back to the problems at hand.

"Yeah, we were going to decide who goes snooping

around the female Shifters caravan," Aidan said.

"I've already told you I'm going," Kellen said. "If you've got a problem with that then tough shit."

"No..." Aidan said, dragging out the word. "I'm going."

"We need someone who isn't going to be seen, or heard, you can't do anything without giving yourself away," Kellen pointed out.

"That's not true," Aidan said. "I can do lots of things without being seen or heard."

"Sleeping doesn't count," Kellen told him.

"I don't have a problem with you going back out," Connor said. "Have you seen it out there? It's pissing it down."

Kellen gave Connor an irritated look at the comment. "Of course I've seen it; we were just out there, dick-head."

Connor shook his head. "There's no need for name calling."

"Yeah, on second thoughts, you can go," Aidan gave in.

"Why, thanks," Kellen said. "That's so generous of you."

Aidan smiled. "You're welcome."

"Do you think she has anything to do with the guys who did this to me?" Anya asked.

"We don't know," Kellen said honestly. "It is a possibility, but we won't know for sure until we find out who she is."

"Well, what are you waiting for then?" she said. "Go

and find out."

"I love your enthusiasm," he said, smiling. "But can I at least finish my coffee first?"

"Yes, of course. Sorry, it's just, I want them caught before they can do it to anyone else," she told him, not that she needed to.

Kellen was more than eager to catch them as well. The more time that passed until they were caught, the more chance they could do the same to too many other people. It was bad enough that Anya's life had been irrevocably changed, nobody else deserved to have the same thing happen to them.

"I know, we all do," he assured her. "And we will catch them, I promise."

"It's not that I don't love my new life, but…" Her eyes filled with tears as she recalled what had happened to her.

Connor pulled her closer to his chest as he spoke softly into her ear. Kellen couldn't hear what he was saying to her, but he knew it would be words of comfort because that is exactly what he would say if it was his mate that needed soothing.

"Don't worry, we won't let it happen to anyone else, I promise," Kellen told her when she looked in his direction.

"You can't promise that," she told him. "At least, not yet, not while they're still out there."

Kellen knew she was right, he shouldn't promise things he had no control over, but he couldn't help it. He cared for Anya like she was his own sister, so he wanted to make everything right in their world, which sometimes made him make stupid promises.

"I'm sorry," he told her. "You're right, I can't promise that, but I can promise that we'll stop them. We won't give up until they have all been caught."

"I know you won't," she told him.

Kellen downed the rest of his coffee and stood. The sooner he checked out this Shifter, the sooner they'll know if she has anything to do with the bad guys.

"Right, it's time I get going," he said.

"You didn't need to drink your coffee so fast," Anya told him.

"I know," he said with a smile. "But you're right, if I'm going to find out anything useful, then I need to get going. She knows we were there, so she could be planning on leaving pretty swiftly, especially if she does have anything to do with them."

"You sure you want to go alone?" Aidan asked him.

Kellen knew that Aidan was only offering to go with him because he didn't want to feel like a third wheel around Connor and Anya, but Kellen wasn't lying when he said it would be better if it was only one of them.

"Yeah, I'm sure," he told Aidan. "I'll report back as soon as I have something."

"Don't leave it too long before checking in," Connor said. "Don't forget we only have these rooms for a week."

"How long do you think it's going to take me?" Kellen asked. "Because I don't plan on being that fucking long, and if I am, then you best be coming to look for

31

me."

"I was just reminding you," Connor said.

"Yeah, well, I know how long we're here for," Kellen said. "But I can definitely promise you that I won't be out for that long. In fact, I'll more than likely be back before you're up in the morning."

"You best be," Aidan said.

"Yes, dad," Kellen said, rolling his eyes.

"Stay safe out there," Anya told him.

"I will do," he told her as he headed to the door. "Catch you all later."

Kellen didn't wait for a reply. He shut the door behind him and walked down the corridor to his room.

It didn't bother Kellen that it was still raining. In fact, it worked in his favour, drowning out his footsteps and washing away most of his scent. Even knowing he was going to get soaked through again, he still needed to change his clothes before going back out.

With a white t-shirt and blue jeans, he had easily been seen last time. So, this time Kellen dressed all in black, so he could blend into the darkness. After all, there was no point in sneaking around if he was going to be spotted easily from a distance because of his choice in clothing.

Once Kellen was dressed again, he wasted no more time. Instead of leaving through the front entrance with all the other guests, Kellen navigated his way out through the kitchen to exit at the rear of the building. That way, if the female from early was still watching the front of the building, then she wouldn't notice him leaving.

Kellen hoped she was still watching the hotel, it would mean that he could search her caravan unhindered, but he should have known he wouldn't be that lucky. She was already inside by the time he reached her caravan, and from the sound of it, she was packing up her belonging. No doubt ready to make a run for it.

Kellen couldn't let that happen. Not before he knew if she was working with the bad guys, or even if she knew anything about the people they were after. So, before she could finish packing, he ripped the door open and stepped inside.

Chapter Four

Just as Nessa was packing the last couple of items into her bags, she heard the door of the caravan being ripped open. Without a second thought, she shifted into the panther and leaped out the bedroom window.

At that moment in time, Nessa was grateful she had left it open after she returned earlier. She had a feeling she might need a quick escape after seeing the strangers, and she had been right.

Nessa hid under the caravan next to hers and waited. She wanted to be sure it was the same people as earlier, and it didn't take long either.

"Fuck!" a male voice came from the bedroom a moment before he stuck his head out of the window.

The taller of the men from earlier, the one that captured her attention more than he should have, was now in her bedroom.

What the fuck do they want with me?

Nessa didn't know, but it couldn't be anything good. A shiver raced down her spine at the thought of them catching her and dragging her back to the bad guys who had turned her into a panther.

Not going to happen, she thought, *I would rather die first.*

There was no way Nessa was ever going back to that hellhole, even if it meant a fight to the death. She was prepared to do whatever it took to stay out of their reach.

"Fuck!" he said angrily when he didn't see her, banging his hands against the window ledge before disappearing back inside the bedroom.

Nessa was about to creep over and peek inside, but she caught movement out of the corner of her eye that froze her in place. The second man walked straight passed her hiding spot, heading for the now wide-open door no doubt.

A moment later, Nessa heard the two men talking from inside. From what she could make out, the taller one wasn't happy about the other man being there.

What the fuck has he got to be annoyed with, it's not like it's his caravan.

Technically it wasn't hers either, but she's the one that's been staying there, not them.

At least she knew what all their names were now. The taller man was called Kellen, and the man he was bickering with was called Aidan. She still didn't know the names of the other two, but she didn't really care either. They weren't the ones now rummaging through her belongings.

Nessa fumed as she listened to them, banging around and no doubt making a complete mess of the place. Even after they finished searching inside her caravan they didn't leave.

Nessa knew she couldn't stay in her hiding space all night. The longer she stays huddled under the caravan next to hers, the more chance she had of being seen. If not by them, then by a holidaymaker taking their dog out for an evening walk.

It didn't appear as if the men were going to leave her caravan anytime soon, so she decided to camp-out in one of the caves near the campsite.

Making her way along the shore, Nessa picked out the least accessible cave she could find, that way she was less likely to be seen if she somehow overslept. Especially since she would be sleeping in her panther form.

Using the panther's agility, Nessa easily climbed to a small outcropping that hid the entrance to one cave. It wasn't the largest, but it would do for the night.

Crawling through the entrance, Nessa curled up at the back of the cave. It wasn't the most comfortable of places to sleep for the night, but at least it was shelter from the weather.

As she lay there, she went over everything that had happened tonight. She still wasn't convinced those people weren't working with the bad guy she was running from.

Nessa had to admit though, that the taller of the men was extremely hot, like pantie melting hot. Not that any of them were exactly ugly, but there was just something about the man that caught her attention more than the others.

From the way one of the men was with the woman, she assumed they were a couple. Nessa couldn't remember the last time she went on a date, let alone when she was last in a relationship. It wasn't exactly the easiest thing to do when you're on the run.

Even before Nessa had been held captive, she didn't have much of a love life. For that matter, she didn't have much of a life either.

Nessa wasn't what you would call a social butterfly, more like a hermit. Apart from work, the only time Nessa went out was when she needed to go food shopping.

It hadn't bothered her that she never had a life outside of work until she escaped the bad guys, she could have done with a friend to turn to in her hour of need. But no, there were no friends or family that she could go to for help, and it had been that way since she left home at fifteen.

Nessa shook her head. She knew where her thoughts were going and she didn't want to go there. It was bad enough she had to live through it, but she sure as hell didn't need the mental reminder.

Looking out of the cave, Nessa watched the wave's crash against the shoreline as stars twinkled in the night sky. She couldn't change her past, but there was nothing stopping her from changing her future.

Closing her eyes, Nessa listened to the sound of the sea as she drifted off to sleep.

***

"I have good news and bad news," one of the mercenaries he employed said as soon as he answered the phone.

"What's the good news?" he asked.

"We've found the female."

Well, that was good. It had been six weeks since she escaped, so it was about time they found her. Six weeks with not a single sign of where she had gone.

"What is the bad news?" he asked, dubious of what the answer was going to be.

"We're not the only ones who found her, the wolf Shifters have been snooping around and found where she was staying."

"Was?"

"Yes, I think they scared her off," the mercenary said. "We spotted her running towards some caves."

Now, that was interesting. Why on earth would she be running away from them? Unless she thought they had something to do with him. It was the only reason he could think of for her running away from them.

"What would you like us to do?" the mercenary asked.

He thought about it for a moment before saying. "Call animal control."

"Huh? What for?" he asked.

"Tell them that a large black cat has been seen. Tell them it looks like it might have escaped from the local zoo," he said with a smile.

If she was staying in a cave overnight, it was highly likely that she would still be in animal form. After all, it was the best way to stay warm. Ultimately though, it was going to be her downfall.

"Consider it done," the mercenary said before hanging up the phone.

Good, he thought as he placed the phone back on his desk. *If I can't have her, then nobody can.*

Chapter Five

"Fuck!"

Kellen could have kicked himself for letting the feline Shifter get away, but he hadn't expected her to leap out of a bedroom window. If he had known she would pull a stunt like that, then he would have brought Aidan along with him. Instead, Aidan turned up after she had already disappeared.

"Fuck!"

"What's happened?" Aidan asked as he walked inside the caravan.

"She fucking got away," he said, fuming with himself.

On the upside, at least he caught a glimpse of her this time. It was no wonder they hadn't seen her earlier, her sleek black coat blended seamlessly into the darkness.

"How the hell did that happen?" Aidan asked.

"She jumped out the fucking window as soon as I opened the door," Kellen said angrily.

"Didn't you check that the windows were closed before you opened the door?"

Kellen growled at Aidan, but it was only because he hadn't thought to check and he should have. Normally it was one of the first things he did, was check the perimeter. He knew she was on edge when he heard her packing, but he had been so preoccupied with stopping her from leaving that it hadn't even entered his mind.

"I take that as a no," Aidan said. "Have you checked outside the caravan?"

"Not yet."

"Why not?" he asked.

"Because I turned around and you were walking in," Kellen told him before asking. "Didn't you see anything before you came in?"

"No, but I wasn't looking," Aidan said as he shrugged his shoulders.

"Well, you should have been," Kellen snapped.

"Whatever, you're just pissed because she got away from you," Aidan said, and he was right.

The only person Kellen was pissed off with was himself. It was a rookie mistake not to check outside of a building, any building, before going in after someone.

"You're right," Kellen admitted. "I'm sorry."

"No problem," Aidan said. "Just don't do it again."

Kellen nodded his head and then turned to inspect the caravan. A couple of bags were in the living area, while another one was open on the bed.

"Since you're here, you can help me search the place," Kellen told him.

"Okay…" Aidan said, dragging out the word. "What we looking for?"

"I don't know," Kellen told him honestly. "Just look for anything that'll tell us who she is. If you find anything to link her to the guys we're after, then all the better."

"Okay, I'm on it," Aidan said, rubbing his hands together as he walked over to the pile of bags.

Aidan grabbed two of the bags and took them over to the sofa, while Kellen picked up the last two and carried them into the bedroom, so he could search the one in there at the same time.

Emptying all the bags onto the bed, he rummaged around looking for anything that might be of interest. When he found nothing except clothes in the bags, Kellen checked the rest of the room before joining Aidan in the living area.

"Have you found anything?" he asked.

"Nope, not a damn thing," Aidan said, shaking his head. "How about you? Any luck in the bedroom?"

"Same," Kellen said. "Absolutely fuck all."

"So, what do we do now?" Aidan asked.

"Wait here while I go search outside," Kellen said. "You never know, we might get lucky. In her haste to get away, she might have left some tracks to follow."

"You probably should have done that while I searched the caravan," Aidan pointed out. "We could have saved time."

42

"Well, why didn't you say something earlier?" Kellen asked.

Aidan shrugged his shoulders. "Didn't think about it until now."

Kellen couldn't say anything because he hadn't thought about doing that either, but it would have been a wise idea. That way, they might have been able to catch her.

"Fine," Kellen said on a sigh. "It's better late than never, I suppose."

"While you're gone, I'll let the other two know what's going on."

"Sure," Kellen agreed. "Just keep a listen out for if she returns as well."

"Will do," Aidan said.

Kellen left without saying another word. Once outside, he jumped up onto the roof of the caravan, checking for any footprints that shouldn't be there. He spotted a couple, but they weren't fresh.

Jumping back down, Kellen checked underneath the surrounding caravans. Not expecting to find anything there either, he was pleasantly surprised to see a lot of paw prints and scratch marks in the mud. He even noticed a spot under the caravan behind hers that looked as if she had been hiding there recently.

If it turned out this was where she had been hiding after jumping out of the window, then he was surprised he hadn't seen her. Not that he had been paying any attention to underneath the caravans when he looked out the window. In hindsight, he should have done, but then he should have done a lot of things differently tonight.

"I think I've found where she was hiding," Kellen told Aidan.

"Is it far?" Aidan asked in return.

"No," Kellen said. *"It's right next door."*

There was silence for a moment before Aidan said *"You're joking."*

"I kid you not," Kellen told him. *"If you don't believe me, then look out the side window."*

A second later Aidan's face appeared at the window.

"Fuck sake," came his muffled voice from inside.

"Tell me about it," Kellen said, even more pissed off with himself than he had been. *"We could have found her if we had just looked outside properly."*

Kellen had said 'we', but he knew it was his fault. He didn't have a clue what was wrong with him tonight. It wasn't like him to make so many mistakes in one month, let alone in one night.

Something was throwing him off his game, he didn't know what it was, but he certainly didn't like it.

"So, what are we going to do now?" Aidan asked.

"I'll keep looking," Kellen told him. *"I'll see if I can find any fresh tracks anywhere else around here."*

"What about me?" Aidan asked. *"Do you want me to help?"*

"No, stay here just in case she returns while I'm out here looking."

"Okay," Aidan said. *"Good luck."*

"Thanks," Kellen replied before closing the link.

Crouching down, Kellen checked under the caravan

before walking around to the other side. There were a few paw prints in the mud, but other than that, there was nothing.

Expanding the search area, he paid more attention underneath the caravans as he passed them, but there was nothing. It wasn't until he checked the beach that he finally found more paw prints.

Most of them had been washed away with the rain and rising tide, but there was enough evidence to prove she had come through this way recently.

Opening a link with Aidan again, Kellen said *"I've found some more tracks at the beach. I have a feeling she's hiding out in one of the caves."*

"So, what are you going to do now?" Aidan asked. *"Are you going to search the caves?"*

"No, there's too many of them. Plus, she could easily move between them unseen while I'm searching inside one of them. So I'm just going to find somewhere to hide instead," Kellen told him. *"She has to come past this way at some point to get to her caravan."*

"Do you want me to join you?"

"No, stay where you are just in case I'm wrong," it wouldn't be the first time tonight he had been wrong, so it was better to have a back-up plan.

They knew she would return to her caravan at some point to collect her belongings. Kellen didn't think he was wrong though, but it didn't hurt to cover all bases, either way she was going to be caught.

"Okay, will do," Aidan said before closing the link.

Disappearing into the shadows, Kellen found himself

a hiding spot in one of the caves closest to the campsite. He checked that she wasn't hiding in the same one first. It wasn't a massive cave, so it didn't take him long.

Kellen sat on the floor near the entrance so he could see in both directions along the beach. He leaned back against the wall and settled in for the night, sheltered from the weather.

"How's the search going?" Connor asked a short while later.

"Well, I'm currently sat in a cave if that's any indication," Kellen told him.

"That good then," Connor said. *"Are you alone in your cave, or is Aidan with you?"*

"No, I left him at the female's caravan in case she returns," Kellen said.

"So why are you in a cave? Shouldn't you be out looking for her if Aidan is back at her place?" Connor asked.

"I have looked for her, which is why I'm now at the beach," Kellen told him. *"I found some of her tracks leading this way, so I'm keeping an eye out for when she returns to her caravan."*

"Why wait?" Connor asked. *"You could just search the caves if you think that's where she's hiding."*

"Have you seen how many caves there are along this stretch of beach? There's fucking loads of them, and that's not including all the other hiding places there are around here," Kellen told him. *"I'll happily let you take over the search if you want?"*

"What? And leave this nice warm bed?" Connor

asked in a shocked tone. *"Nah, I think I'll stay where I am, thanks."*

"Yeah, I didn't think so," Kellen said. *"Anyway, why are you talking to me if you're in bed with Anya? I assume she is with you."*

Connor chuckled. *"Yeah, Anya's with me, but she's fast asleep. Trust me, I wouldn't be talking to you if she wasn't. I'd have much better things to do."*

"Oh, I know you would," Kellen said as he laughed.

He would be the same if he were in Connor's position. Unfortunately, the only female in Kellen's life was his little sister. Don't get him wrong, he loved his sister dearly, but it was hard being her older brother while also taking on the responsibility of being both of her parents, especially when all he wanted to be was her brother.

"Anyway, if you need anything, just give me a shout," Connor said.

"If I need anything, I'll call Aidan," Kellen told him instead.

There was no way he was dragging Connor out of bed in the middle of the night and it had nothing to do with Connor himself. Kellen knew Anya would follow her mate anywhere, no matter what time of the day or night it was.

"Yeah, okay, I won't argue with you."

"I didn't think you would," Kellen said, smiling. *"Anyway, bugger off and get some sleep."*

"Will do," Connor said, yawning. *"See you in the morning,"*

"Yeah, see you in the morning," Kellen said and then closed the link.

Chapter Six

Nessa stretched out her limbs as she woke the next morning. The sun hadn't yet risen, but she knew it wouldn't be too long until it did. Before that happened, Nessa needed to get back to the caravan.

Slowly making her way to the entrance of the cave, Nessa peeked outside, checking that there was nobody around to see her as a panther. The sky looked a lot lighter than what it had done further back in the cave.

Hope I'm not too late.

The last thing she needed was to be stuck in this cave for the rest of the day. She was lucky that she didn't have a job to go to, she still had a little left in her saving before she had that to worry about, but it didn't mean she could hang around here all day.

After last night's activities, Nessa had no choice but

to move on. She couldn't risk staying at the campsite any longer; especially if the three men and the woman were working with the people she ran away from. So, it was time to collect her belongings and get going.

Nessa had no clue where she was going to go next. Admittedly, she hadn't thought that far ahead, but maybe that was something she needed to change. If she had been more prepared, then she might not be in the position she currently found herself in.

Filling her lungs with the fresh morning sea breeze, Nessa shook herself off before double checking that she was alone. When she was satisfied nobody else was around, she leapt down from the caves entrance, landing quietly in the soft sand.

With one last look up to the cave, Nessa raced across the sand for the campsite. She hadn't realized she'd wondered so far along the beach in her haste to find a safe place to bed down for the night.

She could have sworn it hadn't taken her as long to get to the cave as it was going to take her to get back to the campsite. But then, Nessa hadn't been paying much attention at the time. She had been more interested in getting as far away from those people as she could.

Nessa didn't make it far from the entrance to the cave when a sharp pain hit her right flank. She whipped her head around to see a dart embedded in her side.

As soon as it registered what had happened to her, the drugs contained within the dart started to take effect. Her vision became blurry around the edges as she lost balance.

Within seconds, Nessa was falling to her side in the sand as darkness overtook her, sending her straight to sleep.

***

"What the fuck?" Kellen wasn't sure he could believe what he was seeing.

One minute he was watching the feline Shifter racing across the beach, heading back to the campsite. Then she suddenly stopped and fell to her side, lying motionless in the sand.

From this distance Kellen could just about make out the rise and fall of her chest, so he knew there was nothing wrong with her. He also heard no sounds that would explain why she suddenly stopped and fell down.

"What is she doing?" he mumbled to himself. "She's going to be seen if she's not careful."

With that thought in mind, Kellen quickly scanned the area. He couldn't risk going over to her if there were any witnesses around. Thinking it was all clear, Kellen was just about to step out of the cave when he noticed movement at the top of the cliff.

After watching for a moment Kellen was in two minds on whether or not to try moving the Shifter before the Humans made it down from the cliff. It was best for both of their kinds if the Humans didn't find out about the Shifters.

After all, the Humans were a violent race, slaughtering anything that was different from them. The most recent to come under attack from them were the Witches. Admittedly, some Witches were evil, but there were also a lot of good ones among them. Not that the Humans cared which kind they murdered.

If it ever came to the Humans against the Shifters, the Humans would definitely lose. Kellen wasn't naive enough to think his kind would come off unscathed, but the Humans would take the most damage.

"Don't do it!" Connor shouted in his head.

"We can't just leave her," Kellen said.

Kellen wouldn't like to think about what might happen to the female if the Humans found out what she was. Even if it turned out she was working with the bad guy's, she didn't deserve whatever treatment the Humans dished out.

"We have no choice," Connor told him. *"There are more of them than just the two on the cliff."*

"How do you know?" Kellen asked, not seeing anyone other than the two on the cliff.

"Because I'm following them…" there was a short pause before he added *"…and they're bringing a cage with them."*

"Shit!" Kellen said as he ran a hand through his hair.

"My thoughts exactly,"

"It's even more reason to help her then," Kellen told him.

"You haven't got time," Connor admonished. *"They're just rounding the last caravan."*

At that moment Kellen spotted the Humans heading onto the beach, dragging a large cage behind them.

"Where are you?" Kellen asked him.

"We're not far behind them," Connor said. *"So, we'll be with you in a minute."*

"Is Anya with you?"

"Yes, and Aidan," Connor told him. *"We grabbed him on the way past."*

"Good idea," Kellen told him, *"There's no point in him staying there when she won't be returning anytime soon."*

"That's what we thought," Connor said. *"Anya wants to take her belongings back to the hotel with us."*

"Why?"

Not that Kellen had a problem with it, but the female might have something to say about it. If they wanted to get any information from her, then they needed her on their side. Moving her belongings without her permission might have the opposite effect. Instead of gaining her trust, they could give her a reason not to trust them.

"Aidan told her the female had packed up her belongings, so now she's worried the female might have just been packing to go home after a holiday, and that's why she packed her bags," Connor said.

"It's more likely she was running and that's why she packed her bags," Kellen told him.

"I know, and that's what I told her," Connor said, speaking aloud this time as he joined Kellen in the cave.

"Morning," Anya said as she followed closely behind her mate.

"Morning Anya," he replied. "Did you sleep well?"

Anya blushed. "Yes, thank you. I'm sorry you didn't

get any sleep."

"Good, I'm glad," he said with a smile. "Don't worry about me, I've gone without a night's sleep before, and I don't expect this to be the last time either."

Now that the female Shifter had been captured by Humans, none of them had any guarantee of getting any sleep tonight.

"Morning," Aidan said as he bounced in to the cave after them.

"Looks like someone else got a good night's sleep," Kellen said sarcastically. "So much for keeping an eye out for her returning."

"I knew you wouldn't be wrong about where she was, so I knew you would see her before I did," Aidan told him, unashamed by his actions.

Kellen didn't point out how many times he had been wrong in the last twenty-four hours. The last thing he wanted was them asking questions he didn't have an answer for.

"Couldn't they be more gentle with her?" Anya said, turning their attention back on to the female Shifter.

"It's just the way they are," Connor said, walking up behind her and wrapping his arms around her waist.

"But do they really need to drag her across the ground like that?" she asked, concern lacing her words.

"I don't think it's going to hurt her, it is only sand," Aidan pointed out.

Anya stared daggers at him. "It doesn't matter if it's only sand, they could still show a bit more respect."

"Hey, I didn't tell them to do it," Aidan said, holding

his hands up. "But it's not like I can go over there and tell them how to do it properly."

"Yeah, I know," Anya said. "I'm sorry."

"Don't be, I'm just as pissed with them as you are," Aidan told her.

Kellen had to agree, he was as pissed off as Anya and Aidan were, and no doubt so was Connor. Even if the female had just been a normal panther, they could have had a bit more respect in the way they were handling her as they moved her into the cage.

"What if she shifts back while she's unconscious?" Anya asked.

None of them knew the answer to that, so they stood in silence as they watched the Humans unceremoniously push the female fully into the cage before slamming the door closed.

Kellen crossed his fingers she didn't shift back because whether the Humans witnessed it or not, they would know something fishy was going on if they found a Human where they had left a panther.

"Right," Connor said as the Humans dragged the cage back across the sand. "Aidan, follow them and report back as soon as you know where they have taken her. Me and Anya will collect up all of her belongings from her caravan and take them back to the hotel."

"I thought you didn't think it was a good idea to move her stuff?" Kellen asked.

"Yes, I did, but my beautiful mate changed my mind," Connor admitted. "I couldn't refute her argument."

Anya smiled up at her mate. "You know I'm right."

"I just admitted that, didn't I?" he said, smiling back at her.

Kellen could see the love shining in their eyes, it was clear for all to see whenever they looked at each other. He wouldn't admit it aloud, but he envied Connor, and it wasn't because he wanted Anya to himself. No, that was far from it. Anya was more like a little sister to him.

What he envied was the love they had for each other, and the bond they shared. Kellen couldn't wait for the day when he finally finds his mate. He wanted someone to share his life with, not just his bed for the night.

He wasn't like Aidan; he didn't care for having a different female share his bed whenever he wanted. He wanted the same female to share his bed for the rest of his life, not some one-night stand.

"I'll go with Aidan," Kellen said.

"No, you can go get some sleep," Connor said.

"I'll be fine," he told Connor.

"There's nothing we can do to help her until we know where they are taking her," Connor said. "And even when we do, we can't rescue her until nightfall. There's no point in us getting caught trying to release a wild animal."

Kellen knew he was right, but that didn't mean he had to like it. The longer she was in the hands of the Humans, the more chance they had of finding out what she was.

"So, get some rest while you can because it looks like it's going to be a very long night again," Connor told him.

"For you, anyway," Aidan added.

Kellen gave Aidan a dirty look. "Yeah, thanks."

"Hey, it wasn't my fault," Aidan said adamantly. "You're the one that told me to stay in the caravan. We could have swapped places, you know."

"Yeah, I know," Kellen told him. "But you would have only fallen asleep in the cave instead."

"No I wouldn't have," Aidan said.

"Yes, you would," Kellen and Connor said in unison.

"Yeah, maybe," Aidan said with a cheesy grin on his face.

"Fine," Kellen said, turning back to Connor. "I'll get some sleep."

"Good," Connor said. "Because we'll need you with us later."

"Right, I'm off," Aidan said. "Catch you all later."

"Don't lose them," Kellen shouted after him.

"I won't," Aidan shouted back.

"Come on," Connor said, taking Anya's hand as he led her out of the cave. "There's no point hanging around here all day."

"Are we going to get her belongings now?" Anya asked Connor.

"Yes," Connor said. "Hopefully by the time we're back at the hotel with her stuff, Aidan will have some news for us."

"Well, wake me as soon as he does," Kellen told him.

"Don't worry, we'll wake you when it's time," Connor told him.

Kellen had a feeling Connor wasn't going to shout

him as soon as they knew anything. Normally that wouldn't bother him, but for some reason he wanted to be the first to know where she was being taken.

He wanted to be the one to rescue her, and that made absolutely no sense to him. He didn't even know the female, never even met her before. So why he felt the need to be her rescuer, he didn't know.

But he couldn't exactly say any of that to Connor or Anya, not without giving them some kind of explanation, which he didn't have.

"Fine," he said instead.

Chapter Seven

"The Humans have captured her," the mercenary said over the phone the next morning. "What would you like me to do?"

That was a lot quicker than he had expected. He thought it would have taken the Humans a couple of days to catch her, if they managed to full stop. So he hadn't been prepared for this call so soon. Still, he knew exactly what he wanted the mercenary to do next.

"Follow them," he said without hesitation. "Then tell me where they have taken her."

"Consider it done," the mercenary said before hanging up.

If all went as planned, the Humans would take her to the closest zoo. In which case, he would then be able to just snatch her out from under their noses before the wolf Shifters had a chance to.

Now he just needed to come up with a distraction for the wolves.

***

Nessa didn't know how long she had been asleep for, but when she did finally wake up, the first thing she noticed was the fact she was no longer at the beach. The cold hard ground gave it away before she even opened her eyes.

Peeking through half-closed eyes, Nessa could see that she was in a room, but other than that she couldn't make anything else out. When she didn't see any movement, or hear any sounds, she opened her eyes fully and looked around.

Fucking fantastic! she thought at the sight that greeted her.

The entire room was one large cage. From the cold concrete floor, to the thick metal bars along one wall, everything screamed out 'zoo'. Nessa didn't know what was worse, spending the rest of her life in a zoo, or being back in the hands of the madman that turned her into a panther in the first place.

On the upside, at least she hadn't shifted back into her Human form while she had been drugged. She would be in an even worse situation than she already was if she had shifted back.

Even if they hadn't witnessed it, they would know something wasn't right with her if they came in to find a Human in the cage instead of a panther. Without a doubt, the Humans would have experimented on her because they would want to know exactly how she managed to shift into an animal.

Nessa wasn't naive enough to think they would just let her go. They would want to replicate whatever it was that gave her the ability, and they wouldn't care what happened to her in the process.

It wasn't as if they could find out by asking her either. Even if they interrogated her, they wouldn't get any information because she honestly didn't have a clue how she was able to do it. Not that she was complaining, at least, not anymore.

At first, she had been scared of what she had become, thinking she was cursed to spend the rest of her life as an animal. But when she realized she could shift between a Human and a panther at will, and learned about all the other abilities that came along with it, she came to love her new life.

She soon came to realise how amazing it was being able to shift into a panther and take on all the abilities of the animal. The only downside was having to hide from everyone. She couldn't share her secret with anyone, not that she had anyone she could confide in anyway.

Well, that had been the only downside until now. Being locked in a cage like an animal far surpassed not being able to tell anyone.

There must be a way out of here.

After all, these places were designed to keep 'normal' animals locked up, and she was far from a normal animal. She was a Shifter, as the men from the campsite called her, which meant that she was also a Human. Not that she felt very Human at this moment in time.

Mentally shaking her head to clear the building worry and fear, she climbed to her feet and inspected her surrounding more closely.

There was a large shelf hanging from chains on one side of the room, thick metal bars created the wall opposite, part of it was a door. The door had the biggest lock Nessa had ever seen, which was understandable for the animals they kept locked up inside, but it didn't help much in her escape plans.

Straw was scattered across the floor, and there was a large pile of it underneath the shelf as well. Nessa assumed that was what passed for a bed in this place. It was acceptable for an animal, but definitely not something she wanted to sleep on, even for one night.

She could only see two ways out of the room. One was the door with the massive lock and the other was a square piece of metal that slid up when opened.

Nessa knew the square door would lead to an outdoor enclosure, so she definitely didn't want to go out that way. Knowing her luck, she wouldn't be the only panther in the enclosure.

Moving over to the door with the massive lock, Nessa inspected it more closely. If she could shift back into a Human, then she should be able to open it.

Nessa was about to shift when something out of the corner of her eye caught her attention.

Fuck!

A little black dome was sticking out from the ceiling with a flashing red light on it, letting her know that it was switched on and working. There was no way she could shift now, not with a camera aimed her way.

If it was only switched on in the day time then she might stand a chance at escaping, but Nessa wasn't stupid, she knew that wouldn't be the case. Why would they have security cameras if they weren't active, especially at the time they were most needed? They wouldn't.

Somewhere in the building Nessa heard a door open and close, followed by several pairs of footsteps heading her way. This would be a good time for her to know how a real panther would act, but unfortunately, she didn't. So, she was going to have to wing it and hope for the best.

On second thoughts, Nessa decided to lay back down where she had been when she woke up. It was definitely going to be easier to fake being asleep, than trying to pass herself off as a real panther.

Closing her eyes again, she evened out her breathing as best she could and then waited. It didn't take long before the footsteps stopped outside her cage.

"Shouldn't she be awake by now?" a male voice asked.

"Yes, she should be," another male said.

"Do you think there's something wrong with her?" the first man said.

"As far as we know, she has a clean bill of health," the second man said. "She was checked out by the vet and given the all clear."

"Maybe she just needs a little more time to come round from the tranquilizer," a woman spoke this time. "They gave her a strong dose, after all."

"Yeah, maybe," the second man said. "In any case, I want her watched closely until she wakes up. We need to know for sure that she's as healthy as she appears, which we'll only find out when she's awake."

Fucking fantastic!

The last thing Nessa needed was for someone to watch her closely. At least when she was with the bad guys they hadn't kept watch the entire time, and there hadn't been any cameras recording her every move either.

So much for thinking she was better off with the Humans than she was with the bad guys. If anything, she was in a worse situation.

"What do you want us to do?" the woman asked.

There was silence for a moment before the second man answered her. "Check on her every fifteen minutes, but if she's still not awake in an hour, call the vet to come and have another look at her. There could be something that the vet missed the first-time round."

"Okay," the woman said.

"She is a beautiful creature," the second man said. "It would be a shame if she doesn't survive. Visitors would flock to see her."

"Do you think so?" the first man asked.

"Of course," the second man said. "Just look at her. A beautiful black panther; and found on our own doorstep."

"I know a lot of people who would love to come and see her," the woman said.

"Anyway," the second man said. "I can't stand around looking at her all day. Keep me appraised on her condition."

Nessa listened as they walked away. She waited until the door closed behind them before cracking her eyes open slightly.

When she was certain nobody else was around, Nessa opened her eyes fully and sat up. She might as well start practicing if she was going to stand any chance in fooling them into thinking she was just your average panther.

At that moment in time, Nessa wished she had paid more attention to animal planet whenever it was on TV. She might have had an idea of how panthers naturally behaved if she had.

But no, she had been more interested in the cooking and home make-over programs instead. Neither of which were of much help to her.

Pacing they cage, Nessa tried to come up with a way out of here, but other than turning into a Human and risk being seen, she couldn't think of any. She might as well get herself comfy because it looked as if she was going to be there for some time.

Maybe she would have better luck going outside into the main enclosure after all. There was bound to be somewhere out there that wasn't being recorded on CCTV 24/7, somewhere she could at least shift back into a Human without being seen.

Nessa couldn't actually remember what the animal enclosures were like in a zoo. She had only ever been to one, and that was many years ago when she was in school. Like the nature programs on TV, it wasn't something she had been interested.

Hopefully when they come back to check on her and see she's awake, they'll open the door for her to go outside. Then at least she would know for definite if there was a way she could escape from out there.

All she could do was wing it and hope for the best.

Chapter Eight

Kellen hadn't managed to get much sleep, an hour max. Most of the time he'd been tossing and turning in bed, too concerned with the female Shifters welfare.

Aidan should have contacted them by now with news of where she had been taken, but they still hadn't heard anything from him. Kellen was starting to pace the hotel bedroom. He just wanted to get the rescue over and done with.

He kept telling himself that it was only because he was eager to carry on with the search, but deep down he knew that was bullshit. There was something about the mysterious female, something that pulled at him.

"Will you just sit the fuck down, already," Connor snapped. "You're going to wear a hole in the carpet if you carry on."

"Fine," Kellen snapped back as he took a seat by the window.

"What's wrong?" Anya asked him.

"Nothing," he lied. "Why?"

Anya pointed at his leg. "I've never seen you so agitated before."

Kellen looked down to see one of his legs was jiggling.

"Even when you've been mad at Kayla, I don't think you've been this wound up," she told him.

"That's because he hasn't been," Connor said. "I think miss kitty-cat has got under his skin."

That's exactly what was wrong with him, but no way in hell was he going to admit that to them.

"How the hell has she got under my skin?" Kellen asked instead. "I haven't even met the female."

"That means fuck all, my friend," Connor told him. "And you know it."

Yes, unfortunately he did. He had seen first-hand that when it came to mates, anything was possible.

Connor hadn't met, or even seen, Anya before the feelings for her began to appear. All it took was a dream, and he was hooked. He couldn't even see her clearly in the dream, all he knew was that she was in trouble and needed his help. That was all it took for him to want to send out a search party for her, but with so little to go on there was nothing they could do.

It wasn't until she appeared in the Shifter realm that they were able to put a face to the mysterious dream girl of his. Connor had thought that she was safe after she

68

arrived, but he hadn't expected her to run off, getting herself in deeper shit in the process.

Luckily enough, that was all in the past. Now they were happily mated, living together in the Shifter realm.

"That may have happened to you," Kellen told him. "But that's not what's wrong with me."

Connor looked at him sceptically. "Okay, if that's not it, then what's wrong with you?"

"I'm just getting pissed off with all this waiting around," he lied again. "If the stupid female hadn't run off in the first place, then we could be doing what we were sent here to do… search for the person responsible for turning Anya into one of us."

"You don't need to tell me why we're here," Connor said. "Trust me, I would much prefer to be hunting them down as well, but we can't just leave the female in the hands of the Humans."

"I wouldn't like to think what they would do to her if they found out what she is," Anya said.

"Hopefully we won't have to find out," Connor told her.

"I hope so too," she said.

"As soon as we know what we're dealing with, we'll make a plan of action," Kellen told her.

"Oh, I know you will," she told him. "I just… worry about her."

Kellen felt exactly the same way, but he wasn't willing to admit it out loud. It made it a little easier knowing he wasn't the only one worried about her though.

"Hey, sorry it's taken a while," Aidan said, opening a

link between all of them. *"But I wasn't sure if they were going to move her again or not."*

"That's fine," Connor told him. *"Where have they taken her?"*

"They've got her in the local zoo," Aidan told them.

It wasn't the best news, but at least she was somewhere they stood a chance of breaking her out without too much of a problem. It did mean that they still couldn't do anything about it until nightfall though.

"Have you been able to see her?" Connor asked.

"No, not yet," Aidan told them. *"I heard a couple of staff members talking about her still being asleep from the tranquilizer they used on her."*

"She should be awake by now," Kellen said, the concern for her growing with each new bit of information.

"That's what they said," Aidan told him.

Something must be wrong. Why hadn't she woken up yet? They shot her with the tranquilizer dart hours ago.

"Have you tried talking to her the way we're talking now?" Anya asked.

"Yes, but she's blocking me," Aidan told her.

Kellen had tried several times as well, with the same outcome. He didn't know how she was managing it, but it was like she had built up a wall surrounding her… an impenetrable wall.

"I've tried as well," Connor admitted.

"Why didn't you tell me?" Anya asked him.

"I didn't want to get your hopes up," Connor told her. *"Kellen, I take it you didn't have any luck last night either?"*

"Do you think we would be in this mess if I had?" Kellen snapped.

"What bee got all up in Kellen's bonnet?" Aidan asked.

"Well, ask a stupid question, get a stupid answer," Kellen told them.

"Oh, I see," Aidan said a moment later. *"Yeah, makes sense."*

"What do you see? What makes sense?" Kellen asked.

He was starting to get confused with the conversation. Unless…

"Stop fucking talking about me!" Kellen snapped.

Connor sat across the room with an amused look on his face, while Anya sported a guilty look on hers.

"Shit, sorry," Aidan said, laughing. *"I didn't realize you couldn't hear what Connor was saying."*

"What did he tell you?" Kellen asked Aidan, even though he had a good idea already.

"Nothing important," Aidan said.

"Yeah, alright," Kellen said sceptically. *"Why don't I believe you?"*

"Fine," Connor said. *"If you must know, I was telling Aidan that I think you've found your mate, and that's why you've been a snappy bitch."*

"So, is it true?" Aidan asked him. *"Is she your mate?"*

Even though Aidan couldn't see him, Kellen shook his head as he adamantly said: *"No, she's not."*

"It would explain a lot," Aidan said.

71

"Bullshit, it explains fuck all because she isn't my mate," Kellen told them all, hoping they would drop the subject.

"Fine, if that's not it, then why are you so fucking snappy at the moment?" Connor asked.

"It doesn't matter," Kellen told him. *"We have more pressing matters to deal with. Aidan, have you been able to see the female? Do you know where at the zoo she is being kept?"*

"No and yes," Aidan said. *"No, I haven't seen her yet. Yes, I know where they're keeping her."*

"Good," Kellen said as he stood. *"Stay where you are, I'm on my way."*

"Okay, see you soon," Aidan said before closing the link.

"Why are you going there now?" Connor asked. "There's nothing we can do for her until the zoo closes tonight."

"Yeah, I know," Kellen told him. "But someone needs to speak with her, let her know we're not going to hurt her. If she runs from us and gets herself caught again, then it's going to take us twice as long."

"Why can't we explain that we're there to help her tonight when we break her out?" Anya asked.

"Because it will take time that we won't have," Kellen explained. "The longer it takes us, the more chance we have of being caught ourselves."

"It would bring unwanted attention," Connor added.

"Exactly," Kellen nodded.

"Do you want us to go with you?" Anya asked.

It would probably go a lot more smoothly if Anya was there, but Kellen wanted to make sure the female wasn't a threat before letting Anya anywhere near her.

"No, it's okay," he told her instead. "It'll probably go a lot easier if there is only one of us there."

"But wouldn't it be easier if another female spoke with her?" Anya asked.

Kellen should have known Anya would have asked that, but luckily enough, he didn't have to come up with an excuse.

"It would be, but until we know if she's working with the bad guy, it's safer if you're not alone with her," Connor told her.

Anya smiled as she looked up at her mate. "Okay."

If he had known she would concede so easily he would have been honest with her from the start, but Kellen had expected her to argue about going anyway.

"Well, I'll let you know how it goes with her," he told them as he headed to the door.

"Just don't take as long as Aidan did to get in contact," Connor told him.

"I'll try not to," Kellen said before closing the door behind him.

It all depended on where they were holding her. If she was in one of the outdoor enclosures then it would be easier, he could just walk up to the fence to speak with her.

If they had her locked up inside somewhere then it was going to be a little more difficult to get to her, especially if they decided to put her in quarantine.

If that turned out to be the case, then they would have no choice but to wait and speak to her when they break her out. It would be too risky to break-in just to speak with her.

Kellen hoped they didn't have her in quarantine. He didn't want to wait until later; he wanted to see her now. He needed to make sure she was okay, that the Humans hadn't harmed her.

He told himself it was just because she was a Shifter, and even that she might have some information about the bad guy they're after. But the truth was, he wanted to finally meet the mysterious female.

Chapter Nine

So much for the staff at the zoo checking up on her every fifteen minutes like they were supposed to. It was blatant that the second man was the one in charge, the other one and the woman asked too many questions.

It was a good job she hadn't had a bad reaction to the tranquilizer dart, it took them hours to finally come back to check on her. It was the same woman from earlier, but she was with a different man this time.

They had the courtesy to bring her a meal. A meal fit for a wild panther, but not so much for a Human. Nessa liked her steak rare, but raw was a bit much.

The raw slab of meat sat in the middle of the floor where it landed when they threw it to her. Nessa didn't know if they expected her to catch it in the air, but they were sorely mistaken if they did.

"Wow, she's beautiful," the man said as he stared at her.

"Yes, she is beautiful," the woman agreed.

"Is she staying here?" he asked.

No, I'm not staying, Nessa thought.

"We're not sure yet," the woman told him. "I think it all depends on how she settles in."

"Well, I hope she does," the man said.

If Nessa had anything to do with it, then she would be out of here by the end of the day. There was no way in hell she was living in a cage for the rest of her life. She hadn't escaped the madman just to end up in a zoo.

Even if she wanted to, Nessa couldn't stay in this form permanently. She was lucky she hadn't shifted back already. Up until now, she had only been in this form for a couple of hours at a time.

"Go on," the woman said. "It tastes good, I promise."

I'd like to see you fucking eat it raw, Nessa bared her teeth as she hissed.

Not that they could understand her, but it made her feel a little better.

"Okay, okay," the woman said, holding her hands up as she back away from the cage. "I'll leave you to eat in peace."

Yep, that definitely wasn't what Nessa was convey-ing.

"Come on, let's leave her alone," the woman said, leading the man away.

"Okay," the man sighed as he followed.

Nessa thought they would have let her out into the

main enclosure when they returned, but no such luck.

Maybe they were waiting for her to eat something before letting her outside. Nessa hoped not; she really didn't want to eat raw meat. If she was starving then she might just give it a try.

She had to admit she was hungry, her stomach had been rumbling since they brought in her meal, but she wasn't hungry enough to eat raw meat.

When she heard the door close behind them again, Nessa crept over to the slab of meat.

It's worth a try, I suppose.

Leaning down, she sniffed at it before licking it with the tip of her tongue.

Yep, that's rank, she thought as the metallic taste lingered in her mouth.

What surprised Nessa the most, her mouth began to water and her stomach grumbled even more.

You can't be fucking serious?

In response, her stomach growled louder.

Fine, she thought.

Giving in to her animal side, she pinned the meat under one paw as she laid down next to it and began to alternate between licking and chewing it.

Before long, there was nothing but the bone left.

Nessa cleaned her paws and face, content now that she had a full stomach. She had been so engrossed in eating that she hadn't heard the woman return.

"See? I told you it would taste good," the woman said as she stood in front of the cage. "How about going outside for some fresh air and exercise? Sound good?"

She watched in silence as the woman walked over to the side of the cage and pulled a lever, sliding open the door behind Nessa.

"There you go," the woman said before leaving again. "Have fun exploring."

Yeah, sounds like loads of fun, Nessa thought sarcastically.

She still climbed to her feet and made her way outside. If she was going to find a way out, then she needed to fully explore her surroundings first. Especially since her every move had been caught on camera so far.

Nessa had a sneaky suspicion they were monitoring her through the camera aimed at her cage, and that's why they hadn't come back to check on her for ages. They knew without having to come back that she was awake and fine because they had seen her.

Sneaky fuckers!

Nessa hoped it wasn't the same outside. She only needed a small window where she wasn't being watched. Well, as long as it was close enough to an exit it only needed to be small.

As soon as she stepped outside her heart sunk. There was no easy way out. Nessa may be outside, but she was completely boxed in. A huge fence surrounded the enclosure, and there was even a net covering the top to prevent her from climbing out.

Fuck!

She knew it wasn't going to be easy, but she hadn't expected it to be impossible. It had been easier to escape from the bad guys and the prison they had her locked-up in.

They had been difficult enough, but she had still managed to find a way. It helped that she hadn't been on camera 24/7, if she had then it might have been a different matter.

Nessa couldn't deny that it was a nice enclosure the zoo had her in though. There were plenty of places for her to hide from the public, and there were lots of trees to climb.

A real panther might be content living here, a safe place to roam with food on tap, but Nessa wasn't a real panther. She would never be content living here even if she could stay in this form permanently.

Nessa spotted quite a few cameras as she wondered around the enclosure. They were mainly in the public areas, watching the visitors, but some were facing towards the enclosures.

She counted six different cameras pointing her way, and that was just the ones she could see. Nessa had a feeling there were plenty of hidden cameras as well.

It wasn't looking promising that she could escape on her own. It meant she could be here for some time since there was nobody she could turn to for help.

Nessa hated being so helpless. After she had escaped the bad guys, she swore she would never be in a situation where she felt helpless again, yet here she was. The only difference was, this time she really was fucked.

She needed to shift into Human form to open the cage, but there was no way of doing that without being caught on camera. Even if they weren't watching her every move, there was nothing she could do until the zoo closed.

Knowing her luck, if there was a blind spot with the cameras, it would probably be where she was centre stage for the visitors.

Nessa could feel them watching her as she wondered around, exploring the area. She ignored them as best she could, she tried to concentration on finding a way out.

Stupid people, she ranted. *Why don't you take a fucking picture, it'll last longer!*

Anyone would think they haven't seen a panther before. Surely if they've been to the zoo before they would have seen one?

Admittedly, Nessa hadn't seen one up close until she turned into one for the first time. She still knew what they looked like though, because she had seen them on TV... before turning the channel over.

Nessa stopped dead in her tracks as she caught a familiar scent on the wind. One of the people from the campsite was here.

Somehow, they managed to track her down at the zoo. She didn't have a clue how they found her, or even why they were looking for her, but she was certain nothing good could come of it.

Nessa looked towards the crowd and instantly froze as her eyes clashed with the tall man from the night before.

He stared at her for a moment before whispering just loud enough for only her to hear without being overheard by the Humans around him.

"I know you can hear me," he told her. "But it would go a lot easier if I could hear you as well."

Yeah, well, that's not going to happen, Nessa thought as she tilted her head to the side.

It wasn't as if he could understand her even if she did want to talk with him, which she didn't. As long as she was in this form, nobody could understand her.

How the hell did he even know it was her? Maybe he was just guessing.

"I know you saw me at the campsite," he continued. "I promise, I just want to talk."

Nessa hissed. *How the fuck does he know it's me?*

"Open a link to me and we can talk more privately," he told her.

A what? What the fuck is he talking about? A link? A link to what?

Now she was really confused. Was this man even sane? Nessa was leaning more and more towards not sane. Only a crazy person would think they could communicate with an animal. But what did that make her then? After all, she's the one that can turn into one.

Chapter Ten

Kellen couldn't take his eyes of her.

Her silky black fur glistened in the sun as she explored the enclosure. She gracefully strolled around as if she owned the place. She seemed completely oblivious to the Humans as they admired her beauty.

It had taken her longer than he expected to notice that he was watching her. He knew the exact moment when she realized he was there. The wind had changed direction, taking his scent straight to her.

Now she stared at him with a bewildered look on her face, as if she didn't understand a word he was saying. Which was utter bullshit; she could very well understand him. Unless…

"Do you know how to speak telepathically?" Kellen whispered so the Humans couldn't hear him.

Turning her head slightly from side to side, she told him no.

What the fuck?

There were only two reasons Kellen could think of for her not knowing how to communicate telepathically. Either she wasn't shown how to when she was growing up, or she had been a Human and turned into one of them.

If it was the latter and she had been a Human, then that meant the ones who turn Anya probably turned this female as well.

Nudging her mind softly with his, he asked her "Can you feel that?" When she tilted her head again, he added. "The slight push against your mind."

It took a moment before she nodded.

"That's me," he told her. "Now, imagine there is a door in your mind where you can feel me."

He wouldn't normally open a link that way, but it was the easiest and quickest way to explain how to do it.

Kellen watched as she closed her eyes to picture a door in her mind.

"Have you got it?" he asked after a moment. When she nodded, he told her "Now open it."

"This is stupid," he heard her mumble in his mind. *"It's never going to work, telepathy doesn't exist."*

"I think you'll find, it does," he said, smiling when he made her jump.

"Wow! That's so cool," she said in awe. *"I really didn't think that would work."*

"All Shifters can communicate telepathically," he

told her.

"Thanks for the info," she said. *"Don't think I'm ungrateful or anything, but who the fuck are you? And why are you following me?"*

"To answer your first question, my name is Kellen. The second question is a little more complicated," he told her.

"Well, since I'm a captive audience you might as well tell me," she said. *"After all, I have all the time in the world."*

"You won't be captive for very long, I can promise you that," he assured her.

"And how am I going to get out?" she asked.

"My friends and I will be breaking you out tonight," he told her.

"Why would you do that for me?" she asked. *"You don't even know me."*

"Because you are a Shifter and don't belong in a cage," he told her.

If Kellen had his way, they would be breaking her out right this minute. He hated seeing anyone in a cage, but especially her.

It didn't make any sense; he didn't even know her name, so why did he feel this way about her? Was it just because she was a Shifter? Or was there more to it?

Kellen didn't have a clue, and now wasn't the time to look in to it either.

"That still doesn't explain why you would be willing to risk getting arrested to rescue me, a complete stranger," she told him. *"And how do you know I'm a Shifter*

84

and not a normal panther?"

As she was talking, she began to sit down, still looking in his direction. He could hear a couple of people mumble about what she was doing, and that was the last thing they needed.

"Don't sit down," he told her. *"Keep moving around the enclosure, acting as if you are a real panther, otherwise you'll bring unwanted attention to both of us."*

She climbed to her feet, looking around at the gathering crowd as she did.

"So, why are you helping me?" she asked as she resumed exploring the enclosure.

"Why do you keep asking the same question?" he asked. *"I've already told you the answer."*

"No, you haven't," she said adamantly. *"At least, you haven't told me the whole reason."*

"You're right," he admitted. *"My friends and I are looking for someone, and we were hoping you might have some information about him."*

"Well, you're shit out of luck," she told him. *"I don't have any information about anyone."*

"How do you know? I haven't asked you anything yet," Kellen said.

"Trust me, I don't know anything," she said, looking back at him over her shoulder. *"So, does that mean you're not going to help me after all?"*

"Of course we are still going to help you," he told her. *"I hadn't lied, you are a Shifter and don't deserve to be locked up in a cage."*

"How did you know?" she asked.

"Know what?"

"How did you know I was a Shifter?" she asked. *"Are you one as well?*

"Yes, I'm a Shifter as well," he admitted.

"Is that how you knew?" she asked. *"Could you sense that I was the same as you?"*

Kellen lightly shook his head. *"No, I didn't know for definite until I found the caravan where you are staying. But it was highly likely that you were one of us because panthers are not native to this country."*

"Oh," she said. *"So, you can turn into a panther as well?"*

"No," Kellen said, smiling. *"I'm a wolf Shifter."*

"Really? You're a werewolf? That's so cool."

"No!" Kellen snapped. *"I'm not a fucking werewolf, I'm a wolf Shifter."*

"I'm sorry, I didn't know there was a difference," she apologized.

"No, I'm sorry, I shouldn't have snapped," he told her. *"But trust me, there is a big difference, so I wouldn't recommend calling any other wolf Shifters a werewolf."*

"Oh, I promise, I won't make that mistake again," she told him.

"What's your name?" Kellen asked when he realized he still didn't know.

"Nessa," she said.

"It's nice to meet you, Nessa," he said, bowing his head slightly.

"So, where are your friends?" she asked. *"The ones you were with last night."*

"Aidan, the male you saw me with, is here in the cafe," he told her.

"What about the other man and woman?" she asked.

Kellen hadn't thought she had seen Connor and Anya. He hadn't noticed her until after they had already headed back to the hotel, so he thought that was when she joined them, but he should have known better.

"They're at the hotel," he told her truthfully.

After all, there was no point in lying when she had already seen them and followed them to where they were staying.

"That was Connor, and his mate Anya," he told her.

"His mate?" she asked.

"Yes," he told her. *"Humans would say they're married."*

"Oh, I understand," she said. *"They're husband and wife."*

"Yes."

The more he conversed with Nessa, the more he came to realize she didn't know much about their kind. He didn't want to ask her outright, but he needed to know for sure.

"Didn't your parents teach you all about our kind when you were young?" he asked instead.

She was silent for a moment before she said. *"Both of my parents died when I was nine."*

Kellen could hear the sadness in her voice as she told him. He understood her sadness, even after years without them he still mourned his parents. What puzzled him though, was how much he wanted to comfort her.

"I'm sorry for your loss," he told her. *"I know how painful it is losing both parents."*

"Have your parents passed away as well?" she asked.

"Yes, a few years ago now," he told her.

"I'm sorry," she told him.

"Do you have any siblings?" he asked. *"Or any other family members around?"*

If the answer was no, then it was still possible that Nessa had been born a Shifter.

"No, I was an only child," she told him. *"And no other family either. I ended up in the foster system, bouncing around for a few years before I was old enough to move out on my own. How about you?"*

"I have a younger sister," he told her. *"We have other family around us as well."*

"So, you didn't end up in foster care?" she asked.

"No, I was old enough to take care of my sister," he told her.

"Your sister is lucky. I wish I'd had an older brother to look after me," she said.

He didn't want to tell her that even if he hadn't been old enough neither of them would have gone into foster care. Living with the pack as they did, someone would have taken them in until he was old enough.

Kellen had a feeling it would upset her if she knew, so he kept it to himself. It was likely she would find out eventually, but it wouldn't be from him.

"I wish my sister thought the same way," he said instead.

"I take it she's a handful," she said.

"Oh, yes," he said with a smile. *"She's fifteen."*

"Say no more," Nessa said with a laugh. *"I can well imagine what she's like."*

Kellen froze at the sound of her laugh. It was the most magical sound he had ever heard, and he wanted to hear it again.

"Are you okay?" she asked him.

"Yes, why?"

"You were quiet for a long time," she told him.

"Sorry, I was just thinking about all the trouble she could have gotten herself into while I've been away," he lied.

Not that he wasn't concerned about what Kayla had gotten up to in his absence. She was always doing something she shouldn't be doing, and he was always cleaning up her mess…or at least supervising while she cleaned up her own mess. But that wasn't why he went silent.

"How long have you been away from her?" she asked.

"Only for a week, but you wouldn't believe the trouble she can get herself into in that amount of time," he told her.

"Trust me, I do," she told him.

"So, I take it you were a trouble maker as well then," he said.

"Just a bit," she admitted.

"You'll probably get on well with Kayla then," he said.

"Is that your sister?" she asked.

"Yes."

"Your parents liked the letter K then," she said with a giggle. *"Kellen and Kayla. They are nice names though."*

"Thank you," he said, smiling at the compliment. *"Yes, they did like the letter K."*

"Have you managed to talk with her yet?" Aidan asked, making Kellen jump.

"Yes, I'm talking with her at the moment," Kellen said as he turned to look at him.

"Is that your friend Aidan?" Nessa asked.

"Yes."

Kellen expected her to be looking his way when he turned back around, but she wasn't. She continued to stroll around the enclosure as if she didn't have a care in the world.

"So, she's not going to cause any problems for us tonight then?" Aidan asked.

"No, I don't think she'll cause any problems," Kellen told him.

"You can tell him I want out of here, so I definitely won't cause any problems," she said, listening to their conversation like she had listened to him earlier.

"Why don't you tell him yourself," Kellen said.

"What?" Aidan asked, puzzled.

"I don't know how," she told him.

Without another word, Kellen brought Aidan into the link so she could speak with him.

"Aidan, this is Nessa," he said.

"It's nice to meet you," Aidan said.

Even from a distance Kellen could see Nessa jump when Aidan spoke. He couldn't help the smile from his face.

"Um…hello?" she said back.

"I'm sorry for the intrusion," Aidan apologized. *"But if we plan to break you out of here tonight, then we really must get going."*

"That's okay," Nessa said.

"We still have plenty of time before the zoo closes for the night," Kellen said.

"I think you'll find; it closes in an hour," Aidan corrected him.

"Really?" he asked.

Kellen knew closing time was coming up, but he hadn't thought it would be so soon.

"Don't worry, I understand," Nessa said.

There was a tinge of something in her voice that he couldn't put his finger on.

"I'll stay here," Kellen said out of the blue.

Aidan snapped his head in Kellen's direction. *"I don't think the zoo staff will let you."*

"Don't worry about me," Nessa told him. *"I'll be fine."*

"We'll be back soon," Aidan reminded him.

"I don't know…"

"Go," Nessa told him. *"I promise I'll be fine."*

Still unsure about leaving her, Kellen reluctantly agreed to go. *"Okay, we won't be long."*

"Kellen's right," Aidan said. *"We won't be too long."*

"It's okay," she told them. *"Take as long as you like."*

"If you need us before we're back, call us through a link," Kellen told her.

"I don't know how to do that," she said.

"It's easy," Kellen told her. *"Remember what I said earlier?"*

"About the door?"

"Yes, but next time imagine you're knocking on my door," he told her.

"Okay, I will do," she told him.

"Good," he said. *"We'll see you soon."*

"Kellen?" she asked.

"Yes?"

"Thank you," she said. *"For keeping me company."*

"You're welcome," he replied.

"Come on, let's go," Aidan said, heading towards the exit. "There's nothing we can do for her at the moment."

"Yeah, I know," Kellen agreed as he walked along side Aidan. "I still don't like the idea of leaving her here though."

"It's only for a couple of hours."

"You know as well as I that anything could happen in less time than that," Kellen said.

"What do you think is going to happen to her?" Aidan asked. "She's not going anywhere; she's locked up in a zoo."

He knew Aidan was right, but it didn't make him feel any better about leaving her.

Chapter Eleven

Nessa paced the enclosure as she contemplated the conversation she had with Kellen. She still wasn't sure she could believe a word he told her; he could be lying to her just to get her to cooperate. But why he would need her cooperation?

She didn't doubt he was going to help her escape. Whether it was because he truly wanted to help her, or because he had an ulterior motive, she didn't know. Nessa still hadn't ruled out the possibility that he was working with the bad guy. Until she did, there was no way she could put her complete trust in him.

Yes, he hadn't lied about being able to communicate telepathically, but that didn't mean he wasn't lying about everything else he told her.

She had to admit, speaking telepathically was a neat

trick and she could see it coming in handy, but she didn't think it was going to be something she used often. For that to happen, she needed to be around people that were like her.

Since she didn't know if she could trust the only people that she knew were anything like her, she didn't see that happening. Nessa knew Kellen was hiding something from her but she didn't know what.

He was asking her to trust him, but he wasn't giving her a reason to. Trust went both ways. If he wasn't willing to trust her with why he was here, then she certainly wasn't going to trust him.

If they had nothing to hide, then why hadn't the other two people from last night been with him today? Why had he come alone? If they wanted her to trust them, then why hadn't they sent the woman to speak with her instead of Kellen?

The only answer Nessa could come up with, was they were secretly working with the bad guy. In which case, as soon as they have broken her free, she needed to give them the slip.

She hoped they weren't working with him. It would be a shame if it turned out that Kellen was working with the bad guy. He was way too gorgeous to be associated with such evil.

Only time would tell though.

Nessa jumped when a loud voice blared out across the zoo.

"The zoo is now closed. Please make your way to the nearest exit." It informed the visitors.

There were a few grumbles, mainly from the children, as everyone slowly made their way home for the night.

Nessa wished she could go home as well, but that wasn't going to happen any time soon. Even when she was finally out of here, she still can't go home, not until the bad guy's had been caught and it was safe.

On the up side though, she shouldn't be locked up in here for much longer. Now that the zoo was closed, Kellen and his friends should be coming back for her soon.

It all depended on whether or not they were waiting for the staff to leave as well. She hoped not because she had a feeling there were staff here all night, in one form or another.

Not long after the last of the visitors left the zoo, Nessa could hear the staff calling to the other animals. One by one they were taken inside for the night.

Nessa didn't want to go back in that little cage, not when there was so much space for her to roam out here. She didn't think they would let her though, and she was right. It wasn't long before they were calling her inside as well.

Nessa shook her head at the name they had given her. Who in their right mind would call a black panther Smudge? A domestic cat maybe but not a panther.

Fucking Smudge! Whoever picks the animal names in this place should be sacked, she grumbled. *Next thing you know, they'll be naming one of the tigers Fluffy.*

Nessa knew it was for the children that they came up with these names, but seriously, they needed to come up with something more fitting than Smudge for a panther.

Huffing, Nessa reluctantly headed inside, if only to get them to shut up calling her Smudge.

As soon as the tip of her tail was through the door, they swiftly closed it behind her so she couldn't go back outside. Nessa jumped at the loud noise as it suddenly slammed into place, locking her in for the night.

"Here you go, Smudge," a new staff member said as he threw a slab of meat in the cage for her. "Here's your dinner."

Great! Just what I ordered, she moaned. *More raw meat.*

Nessa had a feeling she would be fed raw food three times a day if she stayed here, which was perfectly fine for an animal, but there was no way she could live like that. Once was bad enough, twice was pushing it.

Nessa was determined not to be here for a third.

***

Sasha paced the small cell, slowly scratching at the spell that was containing her magic.

She still didn't know who was behind her capture. She had met plenty of their minions, but they had stayed hidden from her. They must have something to do with the people who took Anya though, because the Demons were the same from the night she helped rescue her.

Whoever it was, they were going to regret ever knowing her. Most nights she spent dreaming of how she was going to make them pay.

When she wasn't dreaming of revenge, she was dreaming of her home realm. It had been so many years since she last stepped foot in her realm, but when she manages to escape this cage she still couldn't return there.

Sasha's heart ached with longing. She missed her home, her family. She missed her people.

Being around the Humans had kept her occupied most of the time, especially after she met Anya, but it wasn't the same. Even their realm was different. None of the realms Sasha had visited came anywhere close to being as beautiful as where she was from.

Shaking her head, Sasha put all thoughts of home back in the box she kept it in. There was no point wasting time thinking about a place she could never return to, not as long as the Queen sat upon the throne.

Plus, it wasn't going to help her find a way out of this cell. Turning her concentration back to the magic again, she continued to scratch at it.

She was close to making a hole in it. Albeit it was going to be small, but with a little more time she should be able to make it large enough for her to gain some of her magic back.

"Hello Sasha," a male voice came from behind her, making her jump in the process.

It was the first time anyone had spoken to her since she was thrown in the cage.

"Where did you come from?" she demanded.

Tilting his head to the side, he said "Does it really matter?"

"Yes," she told him.

"I thought you would be more interested in who I am," he said.

"You're a dead man walking, that's who you are," she told him. "It doesn't matter what your name is because as soon as I'm free, I'm going to kill you."

"Is that so?" he asked smugly. "Well, it's a good job you're not going to escape, isn't it?"

"If you think this cage is going to hold me forever, then you are sorely mistaken," she told him.

She wasn't about to let on that she was close to making a hole in the magic containing her, only a little bit more and she'll be through. So, it was only a matter of time before she was free.

"I don't plan on it holding you forever," he told her. "It just needs to contain you until your ride gets here."

"And when is that supposed to be?"

"Don't worry, it won't be too much longer now."

Sasha didn't like the gleam in his eyes. He looked entirely too smug for his own good, and that sent shivers up her spin.

"If you think moving me to a more secure cage is going to help, then you're wrong," she said, trying to garner more information without asking out right.

Instead of falling for her question, he said. "I'm surprised you haven't asked me about your friend."

Sasha's stomach dropped at the reminder of Anya. She still didn't know if her friend had been rescued or not. She hoped and prayed the wolf Shifters had managed to get to her in time and she was now living in their realm where she belonged.

"Trust me, if you've hurt her in any way, you will suffer for it," she told him.

He laughed at her. "Aggressive little thing, aren't you?"

"Open this cage and I'll show you how aggressive I can be," she said.

He tutted at her. "That's not going to happen."

"Ah, the big bad man is scared of lil ol' me," she taunted.

"I know what you're trying to do, and it's not going to work," he told her.

"What am I doing?"

"You're trying to piss me off so that I'll open the cage for you." Shaking his finger, he told her. "It's not going to happen, I'm not going to fight you."

"Why not," she pouted.

"Because, little fairy, you are worth more unharmed," he told her.

Well, that answered one of her questions. He knew what she was, which meant there was only one person that wanted her unharmed, and it wasn't because they cared about her wellbeing.

If he thought for one moment that she was going to let him hand her over to the Queen without a fight, then he had another thing coming. Sasha would rather die than be at the mercy of the Fae Queen, evil sadistic bitch that she was.

"I see the penny has finally dropped," he said, laughing evilly.

"I'm not scared of her," she said, lifting her chin.

"You look as if you've seen a ghost," he told her. "So, I would say you are."

"Think what you want," she said, turning her back to him.

"Well, as much as I've enjoyed our time together, I can't stand around all day," he said. "Other matters demand my attention."

"What other matters?" she asked.

"Wouldn't you like to know," he said.

"Well, duh, that's why I asked," she said sarcastically.

"You shouldn't have much longer to wait," he said instead of telling her anything.

"Oh, goody," she said, clapping her hands. "Something to look forward to because it's been boring as fuck here."

"I'm sure the Queen will keep you entertained when you are in her care," he said smugly.

"Yeah, loads of fun," she said, rolling her eyes.

"Goodbye, little fairy," he said before disappearing as quickly as he arrived.

"Goodbye, dickhead," she said, waving him away even though he'd already left.

There was no way in hell she was going to let him hand her over to the Queen. Once she was free, Sasha was going to look forward to killing the bastard for even contemplating the idea.

Turning her attention back on the spell containing her, she doubled her efforts to break it. Now more than ever, she needed her magic back…she needed to escape.

Chapter Twelve

"We're back," Aidan said as he let himself into Connor's room without knocking.

"About bloody time," Connor said.

"It's a good job they're not having sex," Kellen pointed out.

"I knew they weren't," Aidan said confidently. "I gave Connor a heads up when we were heading up the stairs."

"So, how did it go with the female?" Connor asked. "Did you learn much about her?"

"Do you think she's working with the bad buy?" Anya asked.

"Can I order some dinner before you all start with the questioning?" Kellen asked instead.

"Yes, sorry," Anya apologized. "I'm just eager to

know if she has anything to do with the bad guy, or if she knows anything about Sasha."

"That's okay," he told her. "Just let me order something to eat first, I'm starving."

"Me too," Aidan added.

While he was waiting for his meal to arrive, Kellen filled them in on the conversation he had with Nessa. By the time he was finished there was a knock on the door as room service was delivered.

Aidan took the trays from the porter when he opened the door and brought them over to the seating area by the window where Kellen was sitting. Connor tipped the man before closing the door again.

"So, do you think she's working with the guy we're after?" Connor asked when he re-joined them.

"I honestly don't know," Kellen told them. "With her parents dying at such a young age it's possible that she's always been one of us, but has never been taught our ways or about our kind."

"It's also possible that she hasn't been a Shifter for very long," Connor pointed out. "Without knowing more about her, we can't be certain that she isn't working with, or for, the person we're after."

"True," Kellen agreed.

"Hopefully we'll find out what we need when she's free from the zoo," Aidan said.

"I don't think it's going to be as easy as that," Kellen said.

"Why do you think that?" Connor asked.

"Just a vibe I got from her," Kellen admitted. "I don't

think she is going to be forthcoming with the information that we need. I think she's going to close up if we start interrogating her."

"We're not going to interrogate her, are we?" Anya asked.

"That was going to be the plan," Aidan told her.

"If that's the case, then I don't blame her," Anya said. "I would do the same thing in her position."

"What do you suggest we do then?" Connor asked Kellen.

"I don't know," he said, shaking his head.

"Why don't we take her back to the Shifter realm?" Anya asked. "Maybe if we show her we trust her, by taking her home with us, then maybe she will open up about who she is."

"That's not a very good idea," Aidan said.

"Why not?" Anya asked. "It's technically her home too, and if she sees there's more of her kind, then she might willingly open up."

"It's worth a try," Connor said.

"What did you do with her belongings?" Kellen asked.

He remembered they were going to collect them and bring them to the hotel, but Kellen hadn't seen any of her bags since he returned.

"Anya wanted to give the female her own room," Connor said.

"That female has a name, you know," Anya said angrily. "Kellen has already told you her name, so use it."

"I'm sorry, "I'll use it from now on, my love," Connor said, trying to placate her. "Anya thought it would be best if Nessa had her own room."

"I don't think that's a good idea," Aidan said.

Kellen agreed with Aidan, Nessa shouldn't be left alone, not while she was still a flight risk. Until they were certain she wasn't going to run off on them again, someone should be keeping a close eye on her and they can't do that from a different room.

"I think it's a very good idea," Anya countered. "If we're going to gain her trust, then we need to first show her that she can trust us."

As much as Kellen didn't like the idea, he couldn't dispute her argument.

"All her stuff is in her room then, I take it," Kellen said.

"Yeah," Connor said. "There was no point putting it in any of the other rooms. We don't want her to think we've been rummaging through it."

"I think she already knows," Kellen said. "She was watching us last night, from under the caravan behind hers, so I'm positive she saw me empty some of her bags onto the bed before searching through them."

"Well, there's nothing we can do about that now," Connor said.

"Hopefully she'll understand," Anya said.

"What about the things we're going to need tonight?" Aidan asked. "Have you had the chance to get it all together?"

"Yeah, everything we're going to need to break into the zoo is packed and ready over there," Connor said, pointing towards a pile of rucksacks.

"Good," Kellen said. "We'll be leaving soon."

"I think we need to wait a couple more hours yet," Connor said. "It'll probably be some time before the last of the zoo staff leaves the premises."

"It shouldn't be that long," Anya told him. "All they're doing is bringing the animals in for the night, and maybe give them some food as well, so it shouldn't take them long."

"Either way, we need to wait a little longer," Connor said. "Because there's no point in us getting caught breaking in, that'll bring too much unwanted attention our way."

Kellen didn't care if the staff were there, he was positive they could easily avoid them, but he didn't want to argue with Connor.

Kellen crossed his arms over his chest. "Fine, we'll wait for a bit."

"Good," Connor said.

"If anything, it gives me time to get changed," Anya said, grabbing some clothing from her bag. "I don't think it's a wise idea breaking in somewhere while wearing a dress and heels."

"You're staying here," Connor told her.

"I don't think so," she said, spinning around to stare at her mate. "We've already gone over this."

"Anya…" Connor started to say, but she interrupted him.

"No buts," she said sternly. "We've already been over this; I'm coming with you."

"It could be dangerous though," he said.

"It can't be that dangerous," she told him. "But even if it is, then it's more reason for me to go with you. You lot have made sure that I can now fight."

"Yes, my love, but we taught you that so you could defend yourself if you ever needed to," he told her. "We didn't teach you so you could run off into danger."

"Semantics," she said, waving her hand in the air. "The main thing is, I know how to fight now and I can help."

"I agree with Connor," Aidan said.

Anya pointed a finger at Aidan. "Stay out of this."

"Yes, ma'am," he said, holding his hands up. "Staying way out of this."

Turning her attention back to her mate, her hands on her hips as she scowled at him. "It'll be better if there's a female there when Nessa's free, she's less likely to do a runner from me. Not being funny, but if I didn't know you three, I would run from you as well."

Anya had a point, they stood more chance of getting Nessa on their side with Anya there. He could also see Connor's side. If they ran into trouble, then he wouldn't want her caught up in the middle of it.

Sighing, Connor said "You're not going to change your mind, are you?"

"No," Anya said, folding her arms across her chest.

"Fine," he gave in. "Get changed into something dark, and put on trainers."

Bouncing over to her mate with a massive smile on her face, Anya jumped onto his lap and gave him a kiss.

"You won't regret it," she said before getting back up and heading to the bathroom. "I promise."

"I hope not," Connor said after she closed the door.

Aidan laughed. "She's got you proper whipped."

"I heard that," Anya shouted from behind the closed door.

It was Kellen's turn to laugh as Aidan's face turned bright red.

"Wait until you find your mate, you'll be exactly the same," Connor whispered as he punched Aidan in the leg.

"I don't know why, but I keep forgetting she can hear just as well as us," Aidan whispered back.

Connor laughed. "Get used to it because your mate will be able to as well."

"Yeah, I know," Aidan sulked.

"For fuck sake, will you please sit down," Connor said after a while. "You're going to wear a hole in the carpet if you keep pacing."

Kellen hadn't realized he had stood up and started pacing until Connor pointed it out. He'd been so wrapped up in his thoughts that he hadn't been paying attention to what he was doing. By the look on Connor and Aidan's face though, he had been doing it for some time.

"What is wrong with you?" Connor asked.

"I'm just eager to get this over with," Kellen told him, which was technically true, but he didn't add that he was just as eager...if not more so...to see Nessa again.

"I'm ready," Anya said as she came back out of the

bathroom, dressed head to toe in black with her hair pulled up in a ponytail. "Is it time to go yet?"

"Nearly," Connor told her. "We'll give it another half hour before we leave."

"I still don't understand why we can't just go there now," Aidan said.

"Because the staff are there for a while after everyone else has left," Connor told him.

"I'm sure we can easily avoid them," Kellen said.

"Maybe," Connor agreed. "But it's not worth the risk. If we get caught breaking into the zoo, then we're not going to be much help for Nessa."

Kellen was with Aidan on this one, but then, he was ready to go just after he arrived back at the hotel.

"It's not long now though," Anya said. "I'm sure Nessa will be fine until we get there."

"Yeah, that's true," Aidan said.

"Are you sure you got everything we're going to need?" Kellen asked.

"For the thousandth time, yes," Connor told him. "You don't need to keep asking. I promise we have everything."

Anya and Connor shared a look. Kellen knew they were talking about him telepathically. He knew they thought Nessa was his mate and that was why he was impatient, but that wasn't it.

Kellen's only concern was about keeping their secret from the Humans. The longer Nessa was in their hands, the more chance they had of finding out what she really was. And that was the last thing any of them needed.

Without a doubt, if the Humans ever found out about their kind, they would be hunted to the ends of the earth. Not that the Humans would stand much chance against them, that's if they could find them in the first place.

"I can't stand this waiting," Kellen said as he jumped to his feet and started pacing again.

"Fine," Connor said on a sigh. "If it means that you stop fucking pacing, then we can go now."

"About time," Aidan said, throwing his hands up.

"Finally," Kellen said.

Grabbing one of the rucksacks, Kellen headed towards the door with the others hot on his tail.

"Let's get this show on the road," Aidan said enthusiastically.

"Is it wrong that I'm a little bit excited?" Anya asked. "I've never broken into a zoo before."

"Oh, hell, yeah," Aidan said. "I always get excited on a mission."

"It's okay to be excited," Connor told her. "Just remember to keep your mind on the task."

"I will do," she promised.

Kellen couldn't deny the fact that he was also excited, but it was for a whole different reason. And that reason was Nessa.

Chapter Thirteen

It took forever for the zoo staff to finally leave. Nessa wasn't stupid enough to think there were no security staff still on the grounds, but they would be few and far between, so should be easy to avoid.

The main problem was going to be the cameras all over the place. She didn't know what Kellen planned on doing about them, but he must know they were everywhere, he should have been able to spot them earlier. At least, she hoped he had seen them. If not, then what had been the point in his visit?

Time seemed to drag. There was absolutely nothing in the cage for Nessa to do while she waited. Why they couldn't leave the animals outside at night, she didn't know. It would be a hell of a lot nicer than being locked up in an empty room where there were only two options, either sleep or pace.

They couldn't expect all the animals to sleep through the night, especially since there were also nocturnal creatures here.

Nessa wondered if there was more inside the other cages to keep the animals entertained during the night. She hoped so otherwise it would be an incredibly boring existence for them.

Nessa thought about her time with Kellen again. Part of her wanted to believe he was a good guy and truly wanted to help her, out of the goodness of his heart. But the other part of her was still wary of him. Who was this person he was looking for? If they wanted her help, why hadn't he given her more information about the person they were after?

She was torn between wanting to get to know him, and wanting to get as far away from him as possible. Nessa had never felt so indecisive before. She had always known without a doubt what she wanted to do.

She had always followed her instincts, whether it was a good idea or not. But this time it was pulling her in opposite directions, and she didn't know which one to choose.

Nessa had been so caught up in her thoughts that she didn't hear anyone enter the building. It wasn't until they spoke that she realized she wasn't on her own anymore.

"Well, well, well…what do we have here?" a familiar voice said from behind her, sending shivers of dread down her spin.

Nessa spun around and came face to face with the monster responsible for turning her into a panther. He stood just out of reach on the other side of the cage bars, where the zoo staff had been earlier.

"Haven't you turned into a pretty kitty?" he said.

Nessa bared her teeth as she crouched down, ready to attack the moment he stepped foot in her cage.

"Now, now," he said, wiggling his finger at her. "There's no need for such aggression."

Step inside this cage and I'll show you aggression, she hissed.

"After all, I've come to offer you a proposition," he told her.

Nessa wasn't interested in anything he might be selling. She didn't want anything to do with such a despicable excuse of a man. So, she hissed her disgust at the thought of joining forces with him.

"You know I can't understand you in that form unless you open a link," he told her. "I saw you talking with the other Shifters earlier, so you can't tell me you don't know what I'm talking about. I know they would have shown you how to do it."

That may have been the case, but it didn't mean she wanted him, or anyone else, inside her head. Just being near the man made her feel dirty, like she would never be clean again. She dreaded to think what it would be like if she could feel him crawling around inside her mind as well.

Kellen was a whole different kettle of fish. He didn't send shivers down her spine. Well, he did, but for an entirely different reason, one that she wasn't going to look into at the moment.

She would look more closely into that when she wasn't locked up in a cage, face to face with the enemy.

"Ah, you're giving me the silent treatment, are you?" When he still didn't get a reply from her, he added "That's okay, I'm a patient man, I can wait for you to come around."

He could wait all he liked; she still wasn't going to change her mind. As far as she was concerned, there was no way in hell she would join him for anything, so he was just wasting his time if he thought she was going to change her mind.

"Well, I'll go for now," he said. "But I promise, we will see each other again real soon."

Not if Nessa had anything to do about it, they wouldn't.

Just as he turned around to leave, Kellen walked in. He stopped dead in his tracks when he caught sight of the man talking to Nessa.

"Nash?" he said, a frown appearing on his face.

With that one-word Nessa's stomach dropped to the floor as her world spun. She couldn't believe it; Kellen knew the man responsible for turning her into a panther. Even if he hadn't called the man by his name, she could see it all over his face, he knew this man.

Now she really was on her own.

Chapter Fourteen

Kellen couldn't believe his eyes. He never thought he would see Nash again, not after he left the Shifter realm with his banished father.

At least now he knew why it had been so easy to break in to the zoo. They weren't the first ones here.

"Long time no see," Nash said. "Where's…ah, there they are. You three were never far from each other growing up. I see nothing has changed there."

"What are you doing here, Nash?" Connor asked.

"Isn't it obvious?" Nash asked in return.

At that moment, Anya walked in. She gasped when she noticed who they were all talking to.

"No, it isn't," Aidan said, none the wiser to Anya's reaction.

"Well, let me enlighten you then," Nash said. "I'm

here to speak with miss kitty."

"That's him," Kellen heard Anya whisper to Connor.

Connor was about to lung for Nash when a dozen Imfera Demons suddenly appeared behind him, halting Connor in his tracks.

"I wouldn't do that if I were you," Nash said to Connor. "I'm not here to fight you, but I will fight if it comes to it, and you will lose."

"You think that a dozen Demons can stop us?" Connor growled.

"Who's to say there is only a dozen here?" Nash asked smugly.

Kellen could see Nessa out of the corner of his eye, and she didn't look happy at all. She was crouched down low, ready to attack at a moment's notice. Her eyes glued to her prey, glued to Nash as she watched his every move.

All she was waiting on; was for someone to open the cage door and she would be on him.

Kellen couldn't let that happen though, not with the Imfera Demons hanging around him. The nasty little bastards liked to set everything on fire, especially fur. They seemed to relish in the scent of singed fur, so it was always best to fight them in Human form.

"I'm going to kill you for what you did to Anya," Connor swore.

"Shouldn't you be thanking me?" Nash asked. "Because if it wasn't for what I did, then you two wouldn't be mated, would you?"

Kellen was surprised Nash knew about the mating. It

made him wonder what else he knew.

"Yes, of course I know about the mating," Nash said, reading the expression on everyone's face. "And I know a lot more than just that."

"Bullshit," Connor said. "You know fuck all."

"Really?" Nash said with one eyebrow raised.

"What else do you know then?" Aidan asked.

"I don't know," Nash said smugly. "I might know the whereabouts of a certain feisty female with long white hair."

"What have you done with her?" Anya demanded.

"Who's to say I have her?" he asked.

"What the fuck are you playing at?" Kellen demanded.

"I'm not playing a game, Kellen," Nash said.

"Then what the fuck are you doing?" Connor asked.

"Tut, tut," Nash said, waving his finger. "Now where would the fun be in that? No, you'll have to wait and see."

"You'll pay for what you've done," Connor said, but Nash had stopped listening to them.

He had turned his attention back to Nessa. He laughed when she hissed at him.

"Don't worry, my dear," he said sweetly. "We'll talk more later. I'll leave you in their capable hands for now."

Nessa hissed in reply, but there was no need. Nash had already vanished in to thin air along with the Demons.

"That's a new trick for a Shifter," Aidan pointed out.

"It was the Demons," Connor told him.

"Yeah, but I didn't see any of them touch him," Aidan said, baffled. "Did any of you?"

Now that Aidan had pointed it out, Kellen hadn't seen any of the Demons touch Nash. Unless the Demons have found a way to transport someone without having to make contact first, then Nash had learnt a new trick.

No, there must be another explanation, Kellen thought because it wasn't possible for a Shifter to teleport.

It was no surprise that the Imfera Demons were here with Nash. When they rescued Anya, they had to fight their way through a horde of Imfera Demons to get to her. But Kellen couldn't get over the fact that the bad guy they were after was Nash.

Kellen remembered Nash as being one of the nicest people he'd ever met. What happened to change Nash so drastically? And why was he turning Humans into Shifters?

There must be a reason he was doing it, but for the life of him, Kellen couldn't think what that might be.

"Hi Nessa," Connor said, breaking into Kellen's thoughts and reminding him why he was here in the first place. "My name is Connor, and this is my mate, Anya."

"Hi," Anya said.

"And you already met Kellen and Aidan earlier today," Connor continued. "We are going to get you out of this place, and then if you don't mind, we have some questions for you."

Kellen watched Nessa closely. She was still crouched at the back of the cage as if she was ready to attack them.

Connor read her body language as well, so he added: "I'll only let you out if you promise not to attack any of us."

It took her a moment, but Nessa eventually relaxed her posture.

"Good," Connor said, taking that as a sign she wasn't going to fight them. "Now, we've disabled the security cameras, so you can shift back into Human form any time you want."

Kellen could see her look towards the camera facing her cage. He knew she was looking for the little red flashing light to indicate that it was switched on, but Connor hadn't lied. They had made sure all the cameras in the zoo were switched off before entering.

He wasn't sure how Nash had gone unnoticed though, because they had been active before they arrived. But then, Kellen didn't know how long Nash had been here. He could have arrived after they turned the cameras off.

Nessa nodded her head and then shifted into her Human form.

"Thank you," she said, stretching her neck as she walked towards the bars of the cage. "You don't know how much I've wanted to change back."

Kellen was speechless. She was even more beautiful in Human form.

"You're welcome," Connor told her.

"Nice to finally see what you look like," Aidan said.

"Now, if you don't mind, I'd love to get out of this cage," she said.

"First, I need to know that you're not going to do another runner," Connor said.

"Fine," she said, huffing out a breath as she crossed her arms in front of her chest. "I won't run off. Now, let me out."

Connor nodded at Aidan to let her out. He had moved to the cage door while they had been speaking and held the lock in place.

Unlocking the door, Aidan held it open for her to walk through before closing and locking it again.

"Thank you," she said as she passed him.

"You're welcome," Aidan replied.

"So, you ready to leave this place?" Anya asked.

"More than ready," Nessa told her.

"The coast is clear," Kellen said, peering outside.

"Come on then," Anya said, hooking her arm with Nessa's. "Let's go."

Kellen led the way, Connor walked in the middle with the females, and Aidan took up position at the back as they made their way towards the exit.

Even though Nash had disappeared, it didn't mean he had left the zoo entirely. Nash could have just teleported to a different area of the zoo for all they knew. There were way too many places he could ambush them.

"Where are all the security guards?" Nessa asked as she followed them through the zoo.

"We don't know," Aidan said. "We haven't seen any since we arrived."

"That doesn't sound good," Nessa said. "Have you looked for them?"

"No," Kellen said bluntly.

"Why not?" she asked.

"Because we were too busy breaking you out," he told her. "Plus, we don't want them to know we have been here."

"But anything could have happened to them," she said.

"We can't risk being caught, Nessa, otherwise I'd get them to go and look for them," Anya told her.

"The Humans aren't our concern," Kellen told her. "Whatever has happened to them let their own kind sort it out."

"I was just asking," Nessa said to him. "No need to bit my head off."

"What?" he asked confused.

"You were a bit snappy there, Kellen," Anya told him.

"Well, I didn't mean to be, and I apologize if that's how it seemed," he said.

"Apology accepted," Nessa said, cheerfully.

Kellen shook his head. Nessa was going to be trouble with a capital T, he just knew it.

"How far is it to where we're going?" Nessa asked as they walked through the exit.

"Not far," Connor said.

"Are we walking the whole way?" Nessa asked.

"No, we've got a car just down the road," Anya told her. "We couldn't park any closer…"

"…just in case you were seen," Nessa interrupted. "Yeah, I get it. Just curious, that's all."

"I bet you're exhausted after the day you've had,"

Anya said. "I know I would be."

"Just a little bit," Nessa said.

"It's not too far, I promise," Anya said.

"Aidan, run ahead and get the car," Connor said.

"You don't need to do that on my account," Nessa said.

"It's all good," Aidan said, winking at her. "I don't mind."

Nessa smiled at Aidan. "Thanks."

Kellen didn't like the way Aidan was flirting with her. He knew Aidan was only doing it to get a reaction out of him, it would cement their belief that she was his mate, but it still didn't make it any easier to watch.

"Right, see you in a minute, sweetheart," Aidan said to Nessa before running off.

Kellen ground his teeth together to stop himself from saying anything.

"So," Nessa said after a moment. "When is the questioning going to start?"

"Let's get back to the hotel first," Connor said.

"Okay dokay then, hotel it is," Nessa said. "I hope you're not expecting much in the way of answers because I don't know anything."

"How do you know when we haven't asked you anything yet?" Kellen asked her.

"Touché," she said.

"Even the smallest detail could help us," Anya said. "So, any information is better than none."

Nessa looked at Anya for a moment before agreeing. "Okay, if I can help, I will do. After all, I owe you lot for coming to my rescue."

"We would have broken you out of there even if we didn't think you might be able to help," Connor said. "A zoo is no place for a Shifter."

"That's what Kellen said to me earlier," Nessa said.

"And I meant it," Kellen told her.

"Well, thanks for keeping to your word," Nessa said to him. "I don't think I could have handled another day on display like that."

"I would suggest not getting caught in your animal form again then," Connor said as a car came around the corner and stopped next to them.

"Did you miss me?" Aidan asked, leaning out the window.

"No, none of us missed you," Kellen told him. "In fact, we were enjoying the peace and quiet."

"Don't lie," Aidan said. "You love it when I'm around."

"Both of you are annoying," Connor added. "So just shut up and get in the car."

"Who turned you into a grumpy old man?" Kellen asked.

"That would be Anya's fault," Aidan said.

"Hey, don't start with me," Anya said sternly.

"Sorry, ma'am," Kellen and Aidan said in unison.

"Sorry, my love," Connor said at the same time.

"That's better," she said, putting her hands on her hips. "Now, you two get in the car, and you," she pointed at Aidan. "You know what you're doing, so just stop."

Kellen took the front seat next to Aidan, leaving

Connor in the back with Anya and Nessa.

"Are they always like this?" Kellen heard Nessa whisper to Anya.

"Pretty much, yeah," Anya whispered back. "They're like a bunch of children at times, but you get used to it."

"You do know we can hear you?" Connor asked.

"Of course, I do," Anya said, climbing in the back next to Connor. "And I'm sure Nessa does as well."

"Yep, I do," Nessa agreed, climbing in after her.

"But it still doesn't change my answer," Anya said.

"Wait until later," Connor said. "I'll show you how much I'm not a child."

"Too much info, man," Aidan said as he pulled away from the curb. "Way too much info."

Chapter Fifteen

Nessa was glad to finally be out of the zoo and back in her Human form. She was looking forward to a nice long soak in a hot bath, but she didn't think that was going to happen any time soon.

She didn't think Kellen and his friends were going to wait for her to have a bath before they interrogated her. Because that was exactly what they were going to do, Nessa was under no illusion it would be any other way.

"Are you hungry?" Anya asked as Nessa followed her into the hotel room. "Would you like me to order anything from room service?"

"Yes please, if you don't mind," Nessa said.

"What would you like to eat?" Anya asked.

"Anything, as long as it's cooked," Nessa has had more than enough raw food to last a lifetime.

"I'll order it," Aidan said, racing over to the phone.

"Only because you want something as well," Connor said.

"Is there a problem with that?" Aidan asked.

"Nope, no problem," Connor said. "You can order me some as well."

"Pizza's all-round okay?" he asked as he picked up the handset.

"Sounds good," Connor said.

"Everyone good with meat feast?" Aidan asked.

"Can I have cheese and pineapple please?" Nessa asked.

"Ewe, you've gotta be kidding?" Aidan asked. When she shook her head, he added "That's grim. But fine, if that's what you want, I'll get it for you."

"Thanks," she said with a smile.

Nessa had never liked anything else on her pizza. Aidan wasn't the first person to think her pizza topping was grim, but she didn't care.

"Don't listen to him," Anya told her. "If you want pineapple, you get pineapple."

"Don't worry, they're not the first to say it's disgusting, and they probably won't be the last," Nessa said.

"Once we've eaten, I'll show you to your room," Anya said. "We brought all of your belongings here and put them in your room for you."

"Umm...thank you?" Nessa said.

She wasn't sure if she should be thanking them for that. After all, her belongings had been fine at the caravan, she still had a few more days before she needed to be out.

Plus, the whole reason she hadn't booked into a hotel was because she couldn't afford it. Her finances were running on fumes these days, but she didn't expect it to be any other way.

Up to now, Nessa had survived on her savings, but they were drastically disappearing. She needed to find a job soon, or she was going to end up sleeping rough every night and begging on the streets every day.

It's a bit difficult getting and keeping a job while on the run though, which was why she didn't have one. Before all this started Nessa had a decent job.

She wouldn't say it was the best, but it paid the bills and gave her a little extra each month. Her employer even paid her last wage even though she left with no warning. But it wasn't as if Nessa could explain to her employer what had happened, at that point Nessa didn't even know the full extent of what had happened.

"You can sit down," Anya said, breaking into Nessa's thoughts.

"Oh…thanks," Nessa said.

"Are you okay?" Anya asked.

"Yes, why?" Nessa asked.

"Because you kind of spaced out for a couple of minutes," Aidan said.

Nessa looked around the room and realized they were all watching her.

"Sorry, just tired," she said, covering her mouth on a fake yawn.

"As Anya said, once you've had something to eat,

we'll show you to your room," Connor told her.

"I thought you wanted to talk to me?" Nessa asked, confused.

"We can talk while waiting for dinner," Connor said.

"Okay," Nessa said, taking a seat at the table.

She didn't trust herself not to fall asleep on the sofa. It wouldn't surprise her if she was out like a light as soon as her head hit the pillow tonight. After getting hardly any sleep last night because of being in a cave, and then spending the day in a zoo, Nessa was exhausted. Both physically and emotionally drained.

"Shoot," she said before she zoned out again. "What would you like to know?"

Sitting down opposite her, Connor started with the questioning. "How do you know Nash?"

"I don't, tonight was the first time I have seen him," she lied, not because she had anything to hid, but because she didn't trust these people.

"What did he say to you?" Anya asked.

"Nothing much, he was only there a couple of minutes before you arrived," which was true.

The trick to a great lie was to stick to the truth as much as possible. Well, that's what she's been told anyway. This was the first time she was putting it into practice, so she hoped it worked.

"We need a bit more information than 'nothing much'," Connor told her.

"Fine," Nessa said. "He wanted me to open a link with him so he could speak with me." *There, that's more information for you,* she thought sarcastically.

"Did you open a link with him?" Kellen asked.

"Oh, hell, no," she said.

"Why not?" Kellen asked.

"Because I didn't like the vibe he was giving off," she told him truthfully.

"A girl after my own heart," Aidan said, smiling.

Kellen growled at him and it sounded just like that of a dog. Nessa had never heard such a sound coming from a Human before, but she had to admit, she quite liked it.

"Did he tell you why he was there?" Connor asked.

"No, I swear, all he was going on about before you arrived, was opening a link with him so he could speak to me," Nessa said.

She didn't know if they were buying it or not, but they dropped the subject.

"Okay," Connor said. "Thank you for being honest with us."

"Sorry I can't be more help," she said.

"It's okay," Anya said.

"Is he the person you were looking for?" she asked.

"Yes," Connor said, shaking his head. "But we didn't know it was him until tonight."

"If you don't mind me asking, why were you looking for him?" she asked.

Nessa wondered if it had anything to do with what he did to her. She didn't know what she would do if it turned out to be the case. She still didn't trust them enough to tell them what happened to her.

"Because he kidnapped Anya," Connor said.

She had a feeling there was more to it than that, but it didn't look as if they were going to give her any more information. Which just cemented the fact she couldn't trust them with the truth either.

They seemed to think it was perfectly acceptable to ask her questions, but not so much the other way around. Well, two could play at that game.

"So, am I free to go now?" she asked.

"Yes, you're free to go whenever you like," Connor told her.

How was it then that she didn't feel like she was free to leave?

"But…" Kellen said.

"Ah, there it is," Nessa interrupted. "I knew there would be a 'but' somewhere. Go on then, why can't I leave yet?"

"We'd appreciate it if you could come back to the Shifter realm with us," Kellen said.

There's a Shifter realm? Nessa thought. *How cool is that?*

Nessa tried to conceal her excitement over the revelation that there were other realms out there.

"I don't know. Do I have a choice?" she asked.

"Of course," Anya said.

"Well, can I think about it?" she asked even though she was going to agree.

Nessa didn't want to appear too excited about it, she wanted them to think it was nothing new to her and that she had been there before. When in fact, she was like a kid that just got told they were going to Disney-land for a holiday.

"We'll be leaving tomorrow, so as long as you let us know by the morning, it'll be fine," Connor told her.

"Okay," she agreed. "I'll let you know first thing in the morning."

There was a knock on the door, followed by a man shouting. "Room service."

"One second," Aidan shouted back as he quickly jumped up off the bed where he had been lounging and raced over to the door.

"Five pizzas?" the man asked when Aidan opened the door.

"Yeah, thanks," Aidan said as he handed over a tip in exchange for the pizza boxes.

"Have a good evening," the man said before walking off.

Aidan shut the door and placed the boxes on the bed.

"Self-service from here on out guys," Aidan said, opening the boxes to find his own. "So, if you want your dinner, come and get it, otherwise I'm going to eat it. Except yours Nessa," he said when he came to her box. "You can keep yours."

"Why, thank you," she said.

"Trust me, nobody wants your pizza," he said adamantly.

"Why do you think I order it?" Nessa asked, winking at him.

"Ooh, you're crafty," he said.

Nessa couldn't help laughing, and she wasn't the only one. The look on Aidan's face was comical.

"He looks like you've stolen his favourite sweet or something," Anya said, laughing.

"I like her," Connor added.

"She's mean, that's what she is," Aidan pouted.

"But funny," Connor said.

Nessa was only joking about that being the reason she ordered a pineapple pizza, she really did prefer that type, but she had to admit it was funny the way Aidan had reacted to her comment. If she had the chance to do it again, she definitely would, even if just to hear Kellen laugh again.

Even though he hadn't said much, she was well aware he was nearby and watching her. She could feel his eyes on her the entire time they had been together.

It was the same earlier, when he visited her in the zoo. Without looking his way, she had known he was watching her.

Normally that would freak Nessa out, but for some reason, she enjoyed it when Kellen was watching her. She felt special, like she was the only thing in the world he wanted to look at.

Nessa knew it was stupid. He was only interested in her for what information she might be able to provide them, she would be naive to think any differently, and that was one thing she wasn't.

Maybe once long ago, but Nessa definitely was not naive anymore.

Chapter Sixteen

Kellen wasn't sure Nessa was being completely honest with them. There was something about the way she kept brushing off her encounter with Nash, as if there was nothing out of the ordinary about their meeting.

He still couldn't quite believe Nash was the bad guy they were looking for. When he had been living in the Shifter realm, he was completely different. He would have done anything for anyone, always going above and beyond to help a friend out. Which was why Kellen couldn't wrap his head around what he was like now.

Once upon a time, Nash had been inseparable with their alpha, Rush. He was one person Kellen was not looking forward to telling. He knew how close they had been growing up, and he had seen how much Rush mourned Nash when he left with his father.

Everyone thought Nash was going to stay in the Shifter realm after his father was banished, but he shocked everyone by choosing to go with him.

"I'll have to remember that trick," Anya said, breaking into Kellen's thoughts.

"I've wanted to do that to someone for ages," Nessa laughed. "It turned out better than I'd hoped, so I'll definitely be doing it again."

"You're both mean," Aidan pouted.

Kellen didn't see what his problem was, he had his own pizza for fuck's sake; he didn't need to eat everyone else's as well.

"Stop your bitching," Connor told him.

"You should know by now," Kellen said. "Aidan lives to bitch and moan."

"Do not," Aidan said.

"True," Connor agreed.

"Whatever," Aidan said. "At least I don't bitch as much as Kellen does about Kayla."

"Yeah, that's true," Connor laughed. "It's a daily occurrence for him."

"If she didn't give me so much to bitch about, then it wouldn't be a problem, would it," Kellen said.

"Kayla is Kellen's little sister," Anya said.

"Yes, I know," Nessa said. "Kellen told me when he came to visit me in the zoo."

"Ah, did he tell you how much of a handful she is?" Anya asked.

"He said she was a handful, but he didn't elaborate," Nessa said.

"Well, one of her many antics, was to cause a rock slide that covered the entrance to one of the dragon Shifters caves," Connor told her.

"Even with several people helping, it took days to completely clear the rocks away," Kellen told her.

He was still pissed with his sister for that.

"Dragon Shifters?" Nessa asked.

"Have you ever been to the Shifter realm before?" Anya asked her.

"No," Nessa said, shaking her head. "But it sounds an intriguing place."

"You'll love it," Anya told her. "You can roam free in your animal form without fear because everyone else there can turn into an animal in one shape or form."

"But dragons? Really?" Nessa asked, sceptically.

"Yes, I promise, there are real fire breathing dragons," Anya said. "But they are the nicest people you'll ever meet."

"Unless you piss them off," Kellen said.

"Yeah, you don't want to piss off a dragon," Connor said as Aidan nodded his agreement.

"I'll remember to stay on their good side then," Nessa said.

"Does that mean you're coming back with us?" Anya asked.

"Sure, why not," Nessa said, shrugging her shoulders. "I've got nothing else planned."

Anya clapped her hands in excitement. "I promise you won't regret it. You'll love the Shifter realm."

"You never know, you might have family there that

you don't know about," Kellen said, trying to find out if she knew more about Nash than she was letting on.

"That's true, I could have some long lost Uncle or something," Nessa said.

Kellen didn't believe her though. There was something in her eyes that made him doubt her words.

"It would be great if you found some family," Anya said.

Kellen felt a nudge in his mind as Connor and Aidan opened up a shared link.

"You've spent the most time with her, Kellen, do you believe she has family there?" Connor asked.

"No," Kellen replied.

"Why not?" Aidan asked. *"I think it's possible."*

"I think she's the same as Anya," Kellen said. *"I think she knows more about Nash than she's letting on, or at least seen him before tonight."*

"I had a feeling that might be the case," Connor agreed. *"There was something about the way she was earlier when we asked her about him."*

"See, I thought she was telling the truth," Aidan said.

Kellen looked over at Nessa. Anya was telling her all about the Shifter realm, not once giving away the fact she was once Human and knew nothing of the Shifters before a couple of months ago. Now she was an integral part of the pack.

Kellen wondered if Nessa would open up about what happened to her if they told her about what happened to Anya. It was Connor's idea to keep it a secret, and Kellen understood why, but it might be what was needed for her to trust them enough with the truth.

"Don't even think about it," Connor said.

"What?" Kellen asked.

"Don't even think about telling her what happened to Anya without first checking with Rush," Connor told him. *"You have to at least wait until he has had a chance to speak with her. You never know, she might open up about it on her own."*

"I wasn't going to say anything," Kellen swore.

"Don't lie," Connor said, slightly shaking his head so Nessa didn't notice. *"It's written all over your face. We still don't know if we can trust her. For all we know, this could all be an act."*

Kellen knew that, he wasn't stupid. Nessa was definitely hiding something, but he didn't think it was because she was working with Nash. Kellen thought it was because she had gone through the same as Anya but didn't want to admit it.

So, it all came down to who was going to be the first to trust the other.

"I'm going to show Nessa to her room," Anya said.

"Okay, I'll go with you," Connor said.

"You don't have to, either of you," Nessa said. "Just point me in the right direction and I'll find it myself."

"No, it's okay," Connor said. "I'd like to get a bit of fresh air before bed, anyway."

"Ooh, that sounds lovely," Anya said, gazing up at Connor as she slid under his arm.

"I thought you might like that," Connor said as he pulled her against him.

"Thank you for dinner," Nessa said. "And thank you for sticking to your word and breaking me out of the zoo."

"You're welcome on both accounts," Kellen said.

"Any time," Aidan said.

"We'll finish this conversation when I get back," Connor said.

"There's nothing more to say," Kellen told him.

Connor closed the link before Kellen could say more. "We won't be long," he said.

"See you in the morning Nessa," Kellen said.

"Sweet dreams," Aidan said.

"Night," Nessa said, waving as she walked out with Anya and Connor following closely behind her.

After a moment, Aidan turned to Kellen. "Connor's right, we don't know if she can be trusted with all the information. She could be working with Nash."

"I don't think she is," Kellen said.

"What makes you think that?" Aidan asked.

"It was her posture when Nash was there," Kellen said. "She looked ready to rip him to shreds."

"Yeah, I noticed that as well," Aidan said. "She seemed to relax as soon as he disappeared."

"If she was working with him, then why would she relax as soon as he left?" Kellen asked, not really talking to Aidan, more trying to figure it out in his head.

"I still can't believe that Nash is behind everything," Aidan said. "But if she was working with him, she wouldn't relax when he left, unless it was all an act."

"Yeah...that's a possibility," Kellen agreed. "But I

don't think she was acting."

"So, what do you want to do?" Aidan asked.

With that question came a flood of things he wanted to do, mostly to Nessa, none of which required her to be clothed. But that wasn't what Aidan meant.

Kellen mentally shook his head to clear his mind of the indecent images that came with the thoughts. "I think we should just tell her the truth."

Whether or not he got in shit with Rush for it, Kellen knew it was the right thing to do. Nessa needed to know that they weren't the bad guys here, and if that meant telling her everything that happened to Anya, then so be it.

"Tell her then," Aidan said. "To be honest, I don't think it matters whether or not we tell her, she's bound to know one way or another."

"Yeah, true," Kellen agreed.

After seeing Nash at the zoo with her, it was highly unlikely that she didn't know what was going on. They just needed to find out how much she already knew, and whether or not she is one of Nash's victims.

"Well, are you going to tell her?" Aidan asked after a moment.

"Yes," Kellen said, looking at the door.

"When?"

"In the morning," Kellen said, absently. "I'll tell her in the morning."

That way, he had time to plan out how he was going to bring up the subject again without it seeming like another interrogation.

For now, he would leave her to rest. It had been a long and eventful couple of days for Nessa, and tomorrow was going to be just as long and eventful, so she was going to need all the rest she could get.

Chapter Seventeen

Sasha was losing patience. She was so close to making a hole in the magic surrounding her, she could almost feel her own magic, which made it even more frustrating.

Screaming her frustration, she nearly leapt out of her skin when someone said "That's not going to help you" from behind her.

Spinning around, she came face to face with her captor again.

"I take it you haven't come back because you've changed your mind about handing me over to the queen," she said.

"No, I haven't come back to release you," he said. "Nice try though."

"So, what do I owe this pleasure then?" she asked,

placing her hand on her hip.

"I thought you might like to know I've just seen your friend, Anya," he said.

"Ah, that's a shame," she said.

"What?" he asked, confused. "What's a shame?"

Sasha sighed dramatically. "I had high hopes she would kill you next time she saw you."

A booming laugh erupted from him.

"You think a little too highly of a newly turn wolf Shifter," he told her once he finished laughing.

"She's had plenty of time to learn, and no doubt the other wolf Shifters would have taught her everything she needs to know," Sasha said.

Outwardly, Sasha tried to convey confidence in her words, but internally she didn't have a clue if what she said was correct. It was possible Anya was still being held captive somewhere, but Sasha hoped not.

She hoped the Shifters had been successful in rescuing Anya, and that she was now living happily in their realm with the rest of their kind. That's where she belonged now.

As much as Sasha was going to miss her in the Human realm, seeing her every day at work, she knew Anya would be a hell of a lot happier living there.

"Her mate certainly wanted to try, but then thought better off it when he realized I wasn't alone," he said.

Sasha's heart leapt at the news. Not only was Anya safe, she had found herself a mate.

Yes! You go girl, Sasha mentally fist pumped while keeping a stoic appearance on the outside so he couldn't see how happy the news made her.

"But, alas, several Imfera Demons were with me at the time," he continued, none the wiser to her excitement. "As we were there, hoping to recruit another candidate."

Wait…what? Sasha thought she must have heard wrong, so she asked "Who were you hoping to recruit?"

She knew it was a long shot, but she wanted to see if he would give her more information if she carried on the conversation like it was normal between them.

Why the fuck is he recruiting people? And what does he want them for?

Shaking his head, he seemed to clear his thoughts and remember who he was speaking with.

"It's none of your concern," he said, sternly.

"Hey," she said, holding her hands up. "You brought it up, not me."

"That doesn't mean I'm going to tell you anymore," he said.

"Fine," she said. "I couldn't care less, anyway."

"Somehow, I don't quite believe you," he said, smirking.

"Anyway, I thought you said I'd be leaving soon, and that you wouldn't see me again before I left," she said. "So, what's happened? How come I'm still here?"

"There has been a slight delay," he told her. "But don't worry, you won't be here much longer."

"What's the delay?" she asked. "I know for a fact the queen is eager to get her claws into me, so what's the hold up?"

"Nothing for you to concern yourself with, my dear," he told her.

Clearly something had gone wrong, or at least not gone to plan. Sasha had a feeling the problem was his end because if the queen knew where Sasha was, then she would be here within seconds.

"Has the negotiation not gone as planned?" she tormented, trying to get the truth out of him that way.

"Nothing of the sort," he assured her. "Everything is fine, just a slight delay, that's all."

Sasha didn't believe a word coming out of his mouth.

"Anyway, I haven't come here to discuss this with you," he said.

"What have you come here for then?" she asked, cocking her head to the side with one brow raised.

"I…I don't know," he said with a sigh.

It was then that Sasha took a really good look at him. She didn't know him, had only met him twice now, but there was something in his eyes. He looked…sad.

What the fuck? Sasha thought. *Why is he sad?*

Sasha was well and truly confused. Earlier he had seemed so confident and in control, now he seemed sad and lost. What had changed in the time between?

"What's your name?" she asked him out of the blue.

"You might as well know, everybody else does," he said, shrugging his shoulders. "My name is Nash."

Yep, something has definitely happened.

And not for the better as far as Nash was concerned obviously. The question was, could she use it to her advantage?

Sasha wasn't above trying. If it meant she could get out of here before the queen arrived for her, then she would use anything in her arsenal.

There was a faint buzzing noise coming from Nash. She assumed it was a phone, but he didn't answer it. He just stood staring into thin air, deep in thought for a moment before finally snapping out of whatever it was he was thinking about.

"I've got to go," he blurted out.

"Okay," she said, but he didn't hear her because he had already vanished.

Sasha was even more confused about Nash than she had been after his last visit. There was no doubt in her mind that Nash was the bad guy, case in point with her being locked away and him refusing to release her, but there was definitely more to him than meets the eye.

As soon as she was out of here, Sasha planned to find out as much as she can about him. After all, the best way to defeat the enemy, was to first get to know the enemy.

Chapter Eighteen

Stepping into a hot bath filled to the brim with water and overflowing with bubbles, Nessa released a contented sigh as the heat surrounded her.

As much as she had enjoyed her stay in the caravan, there wasn't a bath, only a shower. Don't get her wrong, Nessa loved to have a shower in the morning, there was no better way to wake up, but nothing could beat relaxing in a hot bath after a long day.

Since today had been an exceptionally long day, a bath was definitely called for. So, she was grateful Anya had insisted on getting Nessa a room at the hotel they were staying in.

It was even better having all of her belongings here as well. Once she was finished washing, she could pull on a clean pair of her own pyjamas before climbing into bed.

Nessa had enjoyed spending the evening with them, she was extremely grateful that they helped her get out of the zoo, but she needed to be alone for a little while now.

Lying to them had been harder work than Nessa thought it would be, especially to Anya. Nessa could see them becoming close friends if the circumstances were different.

Unfortunately, they weren't, so Nessa had to keep some distance between them. Everything could change in the space of a minute. Just because they seemed to be on her side now, it didn't mean they would still be on her side once they knew what happened to her.

There was one person in particular that Nessa wanted to get better acquainted with, and that was Kellen. She wouldn't mind getting to know him a lot better.

She wanted to know what was hidden under the pristine white shirt and perfectly pressed trousers. Nessa had a feeling it would be as perfectly sculpted as the outer appearance.

It had been extremely difficult to keep her eyes from wandering to his direction while she was talking with Anya earlier. It didn't help that he caught her looking his way a couple of times.

Nessa had felt her cheeks heating a few times because she'd been caught, and not just by him either. All three of the others noticed at one point or another, but none more so than Anya.

Luckily enough, Anya didn't comment on it at all.

No matter how much she wanted to get to know any of them, she couldn't, especially not Kellen.

She didn't want him to know she wasn't a real Shifter like he was. Nessa knew it was stupid because what was she if not a real Shifter? But she hadn't been born one like he probably was. She didn't know if he'd hold it against her, but she'd rather not find out.

Nessa let the scent of the lavender incense and essential oils sooth and relax her as she laid back with her eyes closed. She recalled everything that had happened over the last few weeks.

It was amazing how tense she had been without even realizing it. Her neck and shoulders ached from where she'd been so tense. It hadn't helped that she's spent most of the day in her animal form.

Hands down, that was the longest she'd spent in her animal form so far. Usually she only shifted for an hour or two. Nessa had always been too worried about being spotted as a panther, but now that she already has been she wasn't so worried anymore.

If the worst the Humans would do with her was throw her in a zoo, then she could live with that if she had to, as long as she could stay in animal form that is. It was a walk in the park compared to being in Nash's care.

Nessa still couldn't get over the fact that Kellen and his friends knew who Nash was. She wondered if they knew what he had been up to. If so, did they plan on stopping him? Was that why they were looking for him? If he really was the person they were after, that is.

Nessa didn't know, and she certainly wasn't going to

find the answers out by lounging in the bath.

Climbing to her feet, she quickly washed her hair and body, rinsing off all the bubbles under the shower when she was done.

Wrapping a towel around her body, she stepped out of the bath and made her way into the bedroom.

Tastefully decorated in cream and brown, the room was larger than any hotel room Nessa had ever been in. Not that she's been in that many.

There was a seating area and dressing table over by the window. The door was on the opposite wall with plenty of storage space for all of her belongings and more. A large double sled bed was on the wall opposite the bathroom.

All of her belongings were in bags covering the bed. Since they were moving on in the morning, Nessa didn't bother unpacking everything. She pulled out what she needed for tonight and a clean set of clothes for tomorrow, then left everything else packed away.

Nessa slid her pyjamas on before clearing the bed. She placed her clean set of clothes on one chairs and piled up the bags on the floor next to it. She grabbed her toothbrush and toothpaste from her wash-bag and quickly brushed her teeth before switching off the lights and climbing into bed.

Pulling the blanket over her, Nessa sighed as she relaxed into the soft mattress.

It didn't take long for Nessa to drift off to sleep, that didn't surprise her because she was exhausted. What surprised her though, was the fact she wasn't alone in her dreams.

Kellen stood waiting for her in front of the hotel room door…completely naked. There was not a stitch of clothing on him, and Nessa took full advantage of the fact it was just a dream.

She eyed him up like a piece of man candy and liked what she could see. Liked what she saw so much that her mouth watered for a taste. He was just as stunning as she thought he would be, if not more so.

Kellen didn't need to tense his muscles for her to see them, they were clearly defined even from the other side of the room. She itched to run her hands over his body, she wanted to feel the dips and valleys under her fingertips.

A small trail of golden-brown hair led her eyes south to his growing manhood.

She knew it was only a dream, but…*damn, he's big!*

Nessa's mouth dropped open at the size and thickness of him. If he kept growing, then she was going to have serious issues accommodating him, not that she wasn't willing to give it a try no matter how large he grew.

After all, it would be a really shit dream if she imagined him too big to fit. And since it was only a dream, she could let herself enjoy the moment.

With that thought in mind, Nessa boldly stepped forward. "I've been waiting for you," she said in her most sultry voice.

No point in wasting a perfectly good dream standing around admiring the view when I could go for the ride of a lifetime, she thought.

Even though it was a dream, Nessa wasn't going to waste this time by being her usual timid and shy self. She was going to be confident and unabashed. She was going to enjoy him.

Chapter Nineteen

Kellen knew as soon as he walked into the hotel room that he was in a dream. The first thing that gave it away was the fact it wasn't his bedroom, it was Nessa's. Not to mention that a very naked Nessa was standing in the doorway to the en suite.

Frozen in place, Kellen waited to see what she would do. He knew this wasn't an ordinary dream; they were dream sharing and would both remember everything the next day.

Kellen found out about dream sharing through Connor, he'd dream shared with Anya. It wasn't quite the same as Connor's experience because he started dreaming about Anya long before they met.

In Connor's case, he had been trying to save Anya in all the dreams, but he described how real the dreams felt. Then when he met Anya, not only did the dream change, but he found out she'd been having the same one as him.

Kellen wondered if Nessa realized she wasn't in an ordinary dream.

Obviously not, he thought a moment later.

"I've been waiting for you," she said in a sultry voice.

Kellen couldn't deny the fact he found her incredibly sexy, the evidence was standing right front and centre for all to see, and growing under her watchful gaze as he stood just as naked as she was.

Yep, definitely a dream, he thought. *But I bet it's not quite the one she was expecting.*

If Kellen was honest, then it was definitely the dream he was expecting, especially after spending some time with her.

"Really?" he asked, one eyebrow raised as he took in the sight of her. "I hope I haven't kept you waiting long."

"No," she said, gently shaking her head. "Not long at all."

"I've been waiting for you too," he told her honestly.

There was no doubt in his mind now that she was his mate, which meant that he'd been waiting for her for a very long time. If he was right about her, that she's only been a Shifter for a short time, then it meant he's waited for her for more years than she's been alive.

Luckily enough, one of the main benefits of being a Shifter was they stopped aging when they reached twenty-five. So, even though they get older as each year passed, they still looked the same as what they did on their twenty fifth birthday.

"I hope you haven't waited long," she said.

"Baby, I've been waiting my entire life for you," he said huskily as he walked towards her. "And I don't want to wait a moment longer."

Stopping just in front of her, Kellen lifted his hand to brush a strand of hair off her face.

"Sorry I made you wait so long," she said, gazing up at him.

"Don't worry," he said softly. "You were worth the wait."

Leaning down, Kellen took possession of her mouth in a fiery kiss that had them both panting for breath when they finally came up for air.

Nessa moaned when he broke the kiss, then gasped as he picked her up without preamble. She instantly wrapped her legs around his waist, pressing her moist pussy against his fully erect cock.

Kellen bit his lip as he fought the desire to adjust his position and slide balls deep inside her. When he had some semblance of control over his body again, Kellen carried her over to the bed.

Following her down as he gently placed her on the bed, Kellen found her mouth with his for another fiery kiss. Her hands roamed over his back as she started rubbing herself against him.

Nessa groaned when Kellen pulled back from the kiss again.

Placing a gently kiss on the tip of her nose, he said

"Impatient little thing, aren't you?"

Instead of answering him, she tried to pull him back to her mouth.

"Don't worry, you'll get more," he assured her. "But first, I need to taste you before I go insane."

Her scent was slowly driving him insane. Even without being able to smell her juices, he could feel how wet she was for him and he was dying for a taste.

Before she could say anything, Kellen moved down the bed, keeping eye contact with her the whole time to make sure she was okay with where this was leading. As much as it would kill him to do so, he would put a stop on what they were doing if Nessa indicated that this wasn't what she wanted.

Nessa showed him that she wanted this as much as he did by bending her knees and spreading her legs, giving him easy access to the most vulnerable part of her.

Breaking eye contact, Kellen took in the sight before him. Her swollen lips glistened with moister, tempting him to lean in for a taste, so he did exactly that.

"Mm…" he moaned as he flicked out his tongue, tasting her. "So sweet."

She was like the finest ambrosia, made just for him, and he was instantly addicted. He wanted… needed… more of her.

With one last look at Nessa, to make sure she was still okay with what he was about to do. Her eyes were swimming in desire, letting him know that she wanted this as much as he did.

Leaning in, Kellen let go of all restraints, losing

himself totally in pleasuring her. He licked, sucked, and nibbled on the bundle of nerves until she was squirming underneath him.

Kellen placed one arm over her waist, pinning her to the bed so she couldn't buck with his next move.

Now that she wasn't going to wriggle away from him, Kellen slide his tongue inside of her. If he hadn't of been holding her, she would have bucked violently against him.

Panting, Nessa moaned "More!"

"Your wish is my command," he said and then repeated the movement.

He fucked her slowly with his tongue, when she still asked for more, he added a finger. Pushing it in as far as it would go, wiggling it inside her before pulling out until just the tip remained inside her.

Kellen repeated the motion, moving a little faster this time. Only, when he pulled out this time, he lifted his finger to his mouth a sucked off the juice. Nessa watched him the entire time, silently begging him for more.

When he returned his finger, he circled her entrance before pushing back in with two fingers this time. Nessa was so wet he could easily slide his fingers in and out.

Starting slowly, Kellen soon built up speed. Nessa tried to lift her hips to take his fingers deeper, but he still had her pinned.

Leaning in, Kellen added a third finger at the same time as he began to flick his tongue on the bundle of nerves. It wasn't long before Nessa's head was thrashing from side to side as she begged for more.

Nessa moaned when he removed his fingers again. Licking them clean, Kellen ignored her complaints. He took his sweet time crawling back up the bed.

Posed above her, the tip of his cock lined up with her dripping wet pussy, he asked. "Do you want this?"

Kellen didn't know where he was going to find the strength to pull away, but if that's what she wanted, then that's what he would do. Luckily enough, Nessa didn't want him to pull away.

Taking hold of his cock in one hand, Nessa began to stroke the length of him. Her movements rubbed the tip of his cock in her juices, driving him insane.

Not wanting her to stop, but needing to be inside her, Kellen pushed the tip of his cock inside her pussy. It took all his strength not to push all the way in since she was still stoking up and down his length, but it was becoming increasingly difficult.

Nessa gasped as he breached her entrance, momentarily stopping her hand.

Leaning all of his weight on one hand, Kellen moved his other hand to where they were joined. Using the pad of his thumb, he wet it with her juices then circled the bundle of nerves, making her squirm under him.

It didn't take long for Nessa to release his cock. Sliding her hands around to his arse, she tried to pull him into her, but he hadn't finished tormenting her just yet, so he held firm in place.

"Please," she begged.

"What do you want, kitten?" he asked huskily.

"I…I need…" she stuttered.

"What do you need?" he asked. "You need to tell me."

"I need more," she moaned.

"More what? More of this?" he asked, pressing against the nerves with his thumb.

"No," she said, shaking her head from side to side on the bed.

"Tell me what you need," he encouraged her.

"This," she said, trying to pull him down to her at the same time as lifting her hips off the bed.

"Ah, you want this," he said, pushing his cock in a little more.

"Yes!"

"All you had to do was say," he told her huskily as he pushed in further. "Any time you want my cock buried deep inside your pussy; all you have to do is say."

Nessa lifted her legs up so he could go deeper. When he was buried to the hilt, Kellen held still inside her so she could adjust to his size.

She was so tight he could barely move; it didn't help that she tensed up the further he was inside her. If she hadn't been dripping wet, he would have struggled to fit.

"Fuck me, you're so tight," he told her as he held still. "It's a good job you're dripping wet for me."

Nessa moaned as her walls squeezed him tighter.

"Fuck!" he said. "I can't stay still much longer."

"Don't…" she said, pushing against him.

"Fuck! I've gotta move," Kellen said, locking eyes with her.

Slowly pulling out to the tip, he adjusted position, then pushed back in. His movement slow at first but he soon picked up speed until he was almost slamming into her.

Nessa met him thrust for thrust, panting as her breast bounced tantalizingly close to his mouth. Leaning down, he sucked the tip of one nipple into his mouth. Nessa gasped as she lifted her breast up for more.

Spinning them round suddenly, so Nessa was now riding him. Kellen pulled her down so he could continue playing with her breast while she rode him.

So neither breast felt left out, while he was sucking and nipping one nipple with his mouth and teeth, he was massaging and tweaking her other nipple with his hands and fingers, alternating between the two.

When Nessa began to slow, he sat up with her still on his lap. Holding her chest close with one arm around her back, he continued sucking on her nipples. The other hand he held against her perfect little arse, helping her grind against him.

Nessa held onto his shoulders with both hands as she rode him as hard and fast as she could.

Kellen was so close to coming, but so was Nessa. There was no way he was going to come before her. Spinning them around again, this time he put Nessa on her hands and knees on the bed.

Kellen didn't wait for her to orient herself, he slammed into her hard and fast, nearly knocking her flat on her chest.

Moving a little slower, Kellen reached round her to

massage her breasts while he built up the pace again. When he could feel her nearing the edge, he slid one hand to where they were joined. He gently pinched her bundle of nerves, sending her over the edge.

A moment later, Kellen joined her. Pumping into her as hard and fast as he could, dragging out both of their climax's for as long as possible.

Finally spent, they both collapsed to the bed. Still buried to the hilt, he pulled Nessa against his chest, holding her tightly against him as she drifted off in his arms.

Chapter Twenty

The next morning Nessa had a massive smile on her face as she was getting ready to join the others. She knew it was stupid to be so happy about having dream sex with Kellen.

She knew it wasn't real, but that didn't stop the butterflies in her stomach as the memories floated around in her mind, reminding her of what they had done.

She was just packing up her night clothes when something on the TV caught her attention. Turning it up so she could hear them, Nessa caught some of what the news presenters were saying and it sent shivers down her spine.

*(...several ambulance's leaving the scene. So far
there has been no word from the zoo, but it appears*

that several members of their security staff have
been murdered during the night. Police have cordoned
off the road leading up to the zoo with no sign of them
letting anybody near anytime soon. We will keep you

Nessa couldn't believe what she was hearing. Those poor people didn't deserve to die, they were only doing their job.

Was that why they didn't want to check on the staff last night? Were Kellen and his friends responsible for their deaths? Nessa didn't want to believe they had anything to do with it, but she couldn't be certain.

After all, how much did she actually know about them other than they could shift into an animal like her?

Nessa jumped when someone knocked at her door. She knew it was going to be them, wanting to know if she was ready to leave yet. After what she just heard on the news, Nessa wasn't so sure she should go with them, but she couldn't think of a good enough excuse for why she's changed her mind.

When they knocked again, Nessa reluctantly shouted "Just a sec."

Switching the TV off, Nessa stuffed her pyjamas in her bag, then zipped it up and put it with her other bags by the door.

"Morning," Anya said as Nessa opened the door. "Are you ready to go?"

"Um…yes," Nessa said.

Without having a decent excuse, Nessa couldn't see another option. She had agreed to go with them last night when she knew she should have waited and let them know in the morning.

Now she was stuck, traveling to some unknown place, with potentially a group of killers.

Yep, it's just my luck that they turn out to be a group of murderers, she thought as one by one they entered the hotel room.

"Did you sleep okay?" Anya asked.

Nessa couldn't stop her eyes from snapping to Kellen. She could feel her cheeks flush at the images that question evoked.

"Yes," she said, quickly looking away when he turned to her. "Thank you."

Grabbing one of her bags before the men could take them all. When Nessa turned to Anya again, she had a massive grin on her face as if she knew about the dirty dream she'd had last night.

Nessa knew she was being paranoid, but from the way everyone except Kellen was looking at her, she could have sworn they knew about her dream. Which was stupid, how could they know what she dreamed about?

"Did you sleep well?" Nessa asked, trying to get the attention away from her.

"Oh, I slept like a baby," Anya said, all dreamy eyed as she looked at Connor. "I always do when Connor's holding me."

If it was anything like falling asleep in Kellen's arms in the dream, then Nessa knew exactly what she meant. It was the first time she'd ever fallen asleep like that, but she had to admit, she could get used to it very quickly.

Connor winked at Anya as he asked "Ready to go?"

"Yep," Anya said, bouncing over to the door.

Nessa tried being the last to leave the room but Kellen wasn't having any of it.

"After you," Kellen said, holding the door open for her.

"It's okay," she said. "You've got your hands full; I'll close the door for you."

"We can stand here all day," he told her. "But I'm not leaving the room before you."

"Worried I'll do another runner on you?" she asked jokingly.

By the look on his face, she probably shouldn't have joked about it.

"I don't think you'll get very far," he told her. "But you're welcome to try."

Kellen didn't have to say the words, she knew he would chase after her, that didn't surprise her. What did surprised her though, was at how turned on she was by the thought of Kellen chasing her.

Images flashed in her mind of what he might do to her once he finally caught her.

Kellen took in a deep breath and grinned.

Shit! Nessa thought as she remembered his sense of smell was just as good… if not better… than hers.

Her cheeks were on fire with embarrassment as she quickly walked out the room and raced after the others. Connor and Aidan were halfway down the corridor, carrying her bags as they followed Anya, by the time she caught up to them.

Nessa didn't even stop to see if they noticed. She bypassed them and headed straight for Anya.

Anya didn't have to say a word; it was written all over her face.

"Don't," Nessa said, shaking her head. "Being around other Shifters will take some getting used to."

"Yeah," Anya agreed. "It's not easy to hide how you feel about someone when everyone around you can pick up minute changes in your scent."

"It's not a problem with the Humans," Nessa said. "They can barely smell anything."

"Yeah, I know," Anya laughed. "It's both a curse and a blessing."

Nessa laughed. She knew what Anya meant. Sometimes it was fantastic having an enhanced sense of smell, other times not so much.

"Oh, god," Nessa said after a moment.

"What's the matter?" Anya asked, concerned.

"Don't tell me I've got to sit in a car with all of them now."

Anya giggled.

"So not funny," Nessa said.

"Don't worry," Anya told her. "You get a choice."

"Really?" Nessa asked, hopeful.

"Yeah, it's not much of a choice though," Anya said, pulling a face. "You can either travel with Connor and me in our car, or you can go with Kellen and Aidan in their car."

Not much of a choice, but "I'll go with you."

"I probably would have picked the same in your position," Anya said. "I take it Kellen is to blame?"

Nessa spun around to look at Anya. "How did you guess?"

"I could tell by the way you kept looking at him last night," Anya pointed out.

Nessa quickly looked over her shoulder to see if the men were in hearing distance.

"Don't worry about them," Anya told her. "I told Connor to hang back with the others so we could talk without them hearing us."

"Good thinking," Nessa said. "That's another thing that's going to take some getting used to."

"It's not too bad," Anya said. "Just remember, if you want a completely private conversation with anyone, just open a mental link. That way, nobody can overhear you unless you want them to."

"Thanks for the advice," Nessa said. "I'll try to remember in the future."

"Any time," Anya said.

Kellen and the others quickly caught up with them again when they left the hotel.

"Did you leave a tip?" Anya asked as Connor joined them.

"Yes, my love, I remembered this time," he told her.

"Good," she said. "Nessa's going to travel with us."

"No problem," Connor said, unlocking the car as they walked up to it. "We might need to put her bags in their car though. Someone's taken up the entire boot."

"I haven't brought that much stuff," Anya said,

punching Connor playfully in the arm.

"Ow," he said, rubbing the same spot on the opposite arm as he pretended to be hurt. "You're mean."

Anya laughed at his antics as she shook her head.

Nessa smiled as she watched them. It would be lovely to have someone in her life she could be that playful with. It would be nice just to have someone in her life.

Nessa sobered at the reminder she was all alone in the world. It wasn't often she was bothered by that, but seeing the way Anya was with Connor made her heart ache for the same.

She made the mistake of looking up at Kellen as those thoughts drifted around her mind. She didn't know how long he had been watching her, but she could see concern in his eyes.

"Ready?" Anya asked, snapping Nessa's attention back to her.

"Yes," she said as she quickly looked away from Kellen's concerned stare.

Climbing in the back of Anya and Connor's car, Nessa tried her hardest not to notice that Kellen was still watching her.

"It should only take a couple of hours to get to there, depending on traffic," Anya said, peering over her shoulder at Nessa.

"Okay," Nessa said.

Plenty of time for her to spend with her thoughts, just what she needed.

Chapter Twenty-One

Something was troubling Nessa. Since they left the hotel, she'd been a lot quieter. He didn't think it had anything to do with their time together in the dream, but something was on her mind.

Kellen didn't have to ask if she remembered the dream, he could tell by the look on her face every time she looked his way. Her cheeks would turn a nice rosy shade of pink as she quickly diverted her eyes somewhere else.

But there was definitely something troubling her. She had barely spoken a word as they walked to the portal from the cars. Other than the odd question, or a short answer when asked something, she'd been silent the whole time.

Kellen had asked Anya if Nessa said anything in the

car about what was troubling her, but she told him Nessa had barely spoken a word since they left the hotel. It was like one step forward, three steps back.

"You might not like this next bit," Anya told Nessa when they reached the portal.

"It can't be worse than lugging these bags all the way up that fucking mountain," Nessa said. "You could have pre-warned me that we would be hiking. I would have put trainers on instead of these boots."

"Sorry about that," Connor said. "I guess we all kind of forgot about it."

"You could have left some of your bags," Aidan told her. "We would have gone back for them."

"Don't worry about it," Nessa said. "I don't mind carrying my own shit. But honestly, there isn't much further to go, is there? I don't have to hike up another mountain, do I?"

Kellen would have happily gone back for her belongings, he would have even taken her with him if that's what she had wanted. But she'd insisted on carrying her bags, saying something about not wanting her stuff to get stolen.

How anyone could steal her belongings from a locked car in a locked garage, he didn't know. But hey, she wouldn't be swayed.

"No," Aidan said, laughing. "We'll be hiking down a mountain this time instead."

Nessa spun round in the small space to glare at Aidan. "So not funny," she told him.

"Just ignore him," Connor said. "Yes, we'll be heading down the side of a mountain, but I promise it's not as far up as we climbed a minute ago."

"Wonderful," Nessa said, turning back around. "So, is that the bit I'm not going to like?"

"No," Anya said. "If you like spiders then it's not a problem."

"What?" Nessa said, looking around her quickly for the eight legged creepy crawlies.

Kellen couldn't help smiling. It always amused him how people could fear the little things. They were more scared of people than the other way around.

"I take that as you don't like spiders then," Connor said, smiling as well.

"No, I can't stand the things," she said adamantly.

Kellen heard Anya try to conceal a giggle from Nessa, but she didn't succeed.

"I'm sorry," Anya said when Nessa glared at her. "I promise it's not spiders. It just feels like you're walking through their web when you go through the portal."

"Ewe, that's even worse," Nessa said, pulling a disgusted face.

This time Anya burst out laughing.

Kellen took pity on her.

"It's not a real spider web," he said, smiling gently. "It just feels like you're walking through one."

"I'm sorry," Anya said, still giggling. "But the face you pulled was so funny."

"Fine," Nessa said. "But if I see a spider, I will scream, so just be warned."

Kellen grinned at her. "Fair play. We won't stop you."

"Might join in just for the fun of it," Aidan said, smiling.

"Don't expect me to be going first," Nessa said.

Anya couldn't stop smiling. "I'll go first with Connor. You can go next with Kellen, and Aidan can go last."

Nessa looked at Kellen over her shoulder, but said nothing, she just nodded.

"Right, we're here," Anya said a few minutes later.

"I swear, you best not be lying about the spiders," Nessa said.

"I'm not," Anya assured her. "I'll see you on the other side."

Kellen stepped up next to Nessa as she watched Connor and Anya disappear through the portal.

"It'll be fine," he assured her.

Nessa took a deep breath. "I'm ready."

"Let's go then," he said, holding his hand out for her to go first.

Just as they were about to hit the invisible web, Nessa grabbed his hand and squeezed tightly.

In a matter of seconds, they were on the other side. Anya stood waiting for them with Connor next to her.

She had a smile on her face as she said "See? It's not that bad."

Nessa shook herself off. "Fine, there weren't any spiders, but that doesn't mean it's not that bad." She shivered before adding; "It was bloody awful."

"You won't have to go through it again unless you want to go back to the Human realm," Anya said.

"Yeah, I know," Nessa said.

"I didn't hear any screaming as I followed you through," Aidan said as he walked out of the portal. "So, I take it you didn't see any spiders."

"Nope," Nessa said, smirking as she shook her head.

"Did Kellen have to stop you from running off," Aidan said, looking at their still joint hands.

Looking down, Nessa blushed as she quickly let go of his hand.

"Sorry," she said. "I didn't realize I squeezed your hand."

"Don't worry about it," he told her. "You can grab my hand any time you need to."

"And other things, ay Kellen," Aidan said, wiggling his eyebrows.

"Grow up," Connor said as Kellen sighed.

Anya just rolled her eyes as she said "Come on Nessa, it's this way out."

Nessa didn't reply to Aidan comment, but Kellen noticed the slight blush to her cheeks as she followed Anya out the cave.

When she was out of sight, Kellen punched Aidan in the arm.

"Ow," he said, rubbing his arm. "What was that for?"

"Do you have to be so crude?" Kellen asked.

"What did I do?" Aidan asked.

Kellen shook his head as he walked away. One of these days, Aidan was going to meet his mate, hopefully by then he would have grown up.

Nessa and Anya didn't hang around waiting for them, they were already heading down the mountain by the time Kellen and Connor caught up with them. Aidan dragged along behind them all, sulking.

"Which way now?" Nessa asked as they reached the bottom.

"Rush wants to speak with us," Connor said.

"Who's Rush?" Nessa asked.

"He's our alpha," Kellen told her.

"He's the wolf Shifter's alpha," Anya clarified.

"Ah, I see," Nessa said. "I take it he wants to speak with me as well."

"Yes," Connor said. "He just wants to ask you a couple of questions."

"And he wants to meet you," Anya said, elbowing Connor in the side.

Looking down at Anya, Connor added "Yes, he would like to meet you as well."

"Okay," Nessa said. "Lead on."

"We're going to make a quick pit stop at our house," Anya said. "So, you can leave your bags there if you want, saves dragging them to Rush's with us."

"Thanks," Nessa said. "That'll be great."

"You two can dump your stuff there as well if you want," Connor said. "Just don't forget to pick it back up because I don't want your dirty clothes cluttering up my house."

"What? You don't want to do my washing for me?" Aidan asked.

"You don't need me to do your washing," Connor said. "You keep telling us that's why you still live at home."

"I live at home because I can," Aidan said. "I'll move out when my parents no longer want me there."

"They already don't want you there," Kellen told him. "They're just too polite to tell you to fuck off and get your own place."

"How old are you?" Nessa asked.

"I'll be seventy-six in a couple of weeks," Aidan told her.

Nessa's jaw dropped at Aidan's reply.

"You're…you're…how old?" she asked again.

"Nearly seventy-six," Aidan said slower this time.

"Fuck, you don't look that old," she told him. Turning to the rest of them, she asked "Are you all that old?"

"All except me," Anya told her.

"Are you older or younger?" Nessa asked.

"Much younger," Anya said. "I'm twenty-nine."

"Fuck me, that's a big age gap," Nessa said.

"It is, and it isn't," Anya said. "How old are you?"

"I'm twenty-five," Nessa said.

"So, you're at the age where Shifters stop aging," Anya said.

"Does that mean we're immortal?" Nessa asked, excitedly.

"Kind of," Kellen said. "We can still die, just like any other species, but generally we live a very long life."

"Cool," Nessa said.

"Didn't you get taught all of this by your parents?" Aidan asked.

Kellen knew what Aidan was up to, had even tried something similar himself. He was trying to figure out if she was turned into a Shifter like Anya had been, but without asking her straight out.

"No," Nessa said, shaking her head. "I don't remember them telling me any of this."

"If you don't mind me asking, how old were you when they passed away?" Anya asked.

"I take it Kellen told you," Nessa said, looking at Kellen.

There was no point in denying it, they wouldn't have known if it hadn't been for him. Luckily enough, Nessa didn't seem bothered about him telling them.

"Yes, I hope you don't mind," Anya said.

"No, it's okay," Nessa assured her. "I was eight when they died. After that I was in foster care."

If anyone could relate to growing up in foster care, it would be Anya.

"I grew up in foster care as well," Anya told her. "But it was because I was abandoned as a baby."

"I'm sorry," Nessa said.

"Don't be," Anya told her as she smiled warmly. "Now I have the best family I could have ever asked for. I even have two sisters."

"You make it sound as if having sisters is the best part," Connor said.

"No, my love," she said looking up at him with love shining in her eyes. "You are the best part."

"Soppy bastards," Aidan said.

"You're only jealous," Connor told him.

"Well, I have always said Anya picked the wrong man," Aidan said.

174

Connor growled at Aidan as Kellen laughed.

"Trust me, I made the right choice," Anya told Aidan.

"She didn't pick you because you still live with your parents," Kellen said.

"Na, that's not it," Aidan said. "Everyone loves my parents."

"They do, but it doesn't mean everyone wants to live with them," Connor said.

"Yay," Anya said excitedly. "We're home."

"Not for long though," Connor said with sigh. "Rush wants to know what's taking us so long."

"We've only just arrived," Anya said.

"Yeah, I know," Connor said. "But he wants a de-brief."

"Okay," Anya said. "We'll have to give you the tour later."

"That's okay," Nessa said. "I understand."

"Here," Kellen said to Nessa. "Pass me your bags and I'll run them in for you."

Connor was already heading inside with his and Anya's bags.

"Thank you," she said, passing them over to him.

"Do you want mine too?" Aidan asked.

"Do I fuck," Kellen said. "You can carry your own shit in."

"See what I have to put up with?" Aidan said to Nessa.

"He's right," Nessa said to Aidan. "You should offer to help him with my bags, not adding yours to the pile."

"Fine," Aidan said. "Pass them over."

"Here," Kellen said, throwing over two bags as they

headed inside.

"Just put them in the dining room," Anya shouted as they walked away.

"Will do," Kellen shouted back.

"Well, she seems to be okay now," Aidan said about Nessa.

"Yeah," Kellen agreed as they joined Connor in the kitchen. "But I still want to know what was bothering her."

"Bothering who?" Connor asked.

"Nessa," Aidan told him, tossing his bag on the floor next to Connor's and placing Nessa's on the table. "Kellen thinks there was something bothering Nessa today."

"What gives you that impression?" Connor asked.

"I don't know," Kellen admitted, placing his and the rest of Nessa's bags on the table. "She's just been really quiet, like she's distancing herself from us."

"Us, or you?" Connor asked.

"Us," Kellen said. "I asked Anya if Nessa has said anything to her, but even she said Nessa seemed off today."

"What can I say," Connor said. "Sometimes females are just like that, she might just be taking everything in. Anya's the same sometimes as well."

"Yeah, it's a lot to take in if you've been thrown in at the deep end," Aidan said.

"You remember what it was like for Anya," Connor said. "If Nessa was turned like you think she was, then this is all new to her. And even if she wasn't, this is still new to her because her parents died when she was so young, they wouldn't have had the chance to tell her."

"Yeah, maybe," Kellen said.

"Give it time," Connor said. "If I've learnt anything from Anya, it's that she'll open up when she's ready. Until then, you just have to have patience."

Kellen knew Connor was probably right, but that didn't make it any easier. He was trying to get closer to Nessa, wanting to get to know her better, but she seemed intent on keeping him at arms' length.

He thought he was getting somewhere after last night's dream share, but maybe he was wrong. Either way, Kellen wasn't about to give up.

"Come on," Connor said. "Let's go before they wonder what's taking us so long."

Chapter Twenty-Two

Nessa was already falling in love with the Shifter realm and she'd only just arrived.

Taking a deep breath of fresh air, nothing but the scent of nature surrounded her. All she could see was trees and mountains. Not a single high rise building in sight. It was much like the Highlands of Scotland where the entrance to the portal was located.

If they hadn't shown her the way, Nessa would never have thought to look in the cave for a portal to a different realm.

She couldn't help wondering how many other realms there were that she didn't know about... that Humans didn't know about. Surely if there was one, then there must be more.

"So, what do you think of the Shifter realm?" Anya

asked when they were finally alone.

"It's stunning here," Nessa said. "I can see why you like it so much, and your house… wow… it's beautiful."

"Connor built it for me," Anya said proudly. "Well, technically he built it before we met, but he built it for his mate…"

"Which turned out to be you," Nessa finished for her.

"Yes," she said, smiling fondly. "So he did it for me."

"You're very lucky to find someone who dotes on you like Connor does," Nessa said.

"You'll find a male that's the same with you," Anya said.

"Yeah, maybe one day in the distant future," Nessa said, not really believing that she would.

"Maybe sooner than you think," Anya said.

There was a gleam in Anya's eye as she spoke, as if she knew something about Nessa's love life that she didn't.

At least she doesn't know about the perverted dream you had about Kellen last night, Nessa told herself. *That definitely would have made the trip here more awkward.*

As it was, Nessa had a hard time not imagining the dream while sat in the back of the car. Over and over the imagines played out in her mind, at the most inopportune times as well.

"I'll give you a tour of the house when we've finished at Rush's," Anya said, breaking into Nessa's thoughts.

"Yes, please," Nessa said. "I would love to see what the inside is like."

"I can promise, you won't be disappointed," Anya said.

It dawned on Nessa then, that she didn't know where she was meant to be staying tonight. Did they even have hotels or B&B's in the Shifter realm? She hoped so otherwise she didn't know what she was going to do.

As much as she liked Anya, she didn't want to ask if she could camp out in their spare room if they have one. She definitely didn't want to stay at Aidan's with him and his parents.

And Kellen? After that dream, even if he didn't have his sister living with him, she wouldn't feel comfortable staying with him. What if she had another dream like last night? She would be mortified if she made noises in her sleep because of a dream and Kellen or his sister overheard her.

It would be just her luck that they would think she was having a nightmare and come rushing to wake her. So no, she certainly didn't want to stay at Kellen's house.

Before she could bring up the subject with Anya, Kellen and the others came around the corner of the house.

I'm sure I'll find out soon enough, she thought.

"You two ready to go?" Connor asked as he wrapped an arm around Anya.

"Yep," Anya said. "We're ready."

Nessa wasn't so sure she was ready to meet their alpha, but she didn't see that she had much choice in the matter. So, she nodded anyway.

"Come on then," Connor said. "Let's get this over

with."

"Yeah," Kellen said. "Then I can find out what trouble Kayla has got into while we've been away."

"She might surprise you," Anya said. "She might have behaved herself while you've been away."

"Hmm…I don't think that's likely," Kellen said. "It's more likely that she caused nothing but trouble since the moment I left the Shifter realm."

"I'm with Kellen on this one," Aidan said. "But I can't wait to find out what she's done this time."

"Do you have to be so excited about it?" Kellen said.

"Well, yeah, I'm not the one that has to deal with her, so of course I find it funny watching her," Aidan laughed. "It's amazing the amount of shit she gets herself into."

"I can't wait until you have kids," Kellen said. "I hope they turn out just like you."

"What? Intelligent and handsome?" Aidan asked.

"No," Kellen said. "A little shit that never moves out."

"Hey, I'll have you know, I'm not a little shit," Aidan said. "And my parents love having me there."

"Who are you kidding?" Kellen asked. "Don't forget, I know the shit you got up to growing up."

"Yep, the stories we could tell," Connor said, laughing.

"That's because you two were right there, getting into trouble with me," Aidan said.

"Yeah, but some of us grew up," Connor said.

"Some of us had to," Kellen added.

Silence enveloped them at Kellen's words. They all knew why he had to grow up.

Nessa knew how hard it was dealing with the loss of both parents, but then to have to take on full responsibility of a sibling as well? No, Nessa didn't think she would have been able to cope with that on top of her own grief.

It might have been because she was so young when they passed away, but she didn't think she would have handled their deaths any better as an adult either.

Being so close to both of her parents, it was like her heart was ripped from her chest, never to be whole again. She still mourned their loss, and probably always would.

"You'll like Kayla," Anya said, breaking the silence as they walked. "She isn't as bad as this lot make out."

"I'd like to meet her," Nessa said honestly.

She sounded like a very interesting young lady by what Nessa had heard about her so far. She was intrigued to find out for herself what she was like, and she definitely wanted to hear more about the antics she has got up to in the past.

"Not far now," Aidan said as they came to a clearing.

Several buildings stood on the opposite side of the clearing, the largest of them looked like a large warehouse with lots of windows. A few houses were dotted around the clearing, most backed onto the woodland behind.

The building they were heading towards was set aside from the rest. It wasn't a large or flashy building, nothing that screamed 'the alpha lives here'. Nessa wouldn't have had a clue that someone important lived there if she hadn't been told who they were going to see.

"Aren't you going to knock on the front door?" Nessa asked as she followed them around the back of the house.

"No," Kellen told her. "Rush doesn't like it when people knock."

"His door is always open for pack members," Anya elaborated.

"But I'm not a pack member," Nessa pointed out.

She was sure Rush wouldn't want a stranger walking around his house, even if she was with members of his pack.

"He's expecting you," Connor said. "If he wasn't, then it might be a different matter."

Not that it made it any better, but Nessa said "I understand."

"About fucking time you got here!" a male voice shouted from inside.

"That's Rush shouting," Anya said.

"We got here as quickly as we could," Connor said as he walked in the kitchen.

Leaning against the counter, the man Nessa assumed was Rush, watched as one by one they filed in.

"Help yourself to the coffee," he said, pointing to the full pot. "It's freshly made."

Nessa held back while everyone else made a beeline for the coffeepot. She didn't feel comfortable helping herself to anything in a stranger's house. It felt rude even though he said to help themselves. He probably wasn't talking to her, anyway.

Nessa stepped aside when Kellen walked back over to her.

"Would you like a coffee?" he asked.

"Yes please," Nessa said.

Expecting him to say 'help yourself then', she was surprise when he held out his cup for her.

"White, two sugars," he said.

"Um…yes, thank you," she said, taking the cup.

"You're welcome," he said, smiling gently.

Sipping the coffee, Nessa watched as Kellen returned to fill a cup for himself. She could feel her cheeks heat every time she looked at him, images of his naked body kept flashing in her mind.

Rush caught her eye as she looked away from Kellen. He'd been watching her closely as she'd watched Kellen.

It was embarrassing to realize she'd been caught eying up Kellen as if he was a piece of man candy by his alpha.

What a way to set a good first impression, she thought.

Luckily enough, he didn't comment on it, just continued to watch her closely. Nessa was feeling like a goldfish in a bowl being watched by the hungry cat, and she didn't like it one bit.

Everyone, except her and Rush, took a seat around the dining table. Chatting amongst themselves, they were oblivious to Nessa and Rush having a staring match.

Nessa refused to look away first. Rush wasn't her alpha, so she wasn't going to back down to his authority. Because that's exactly what he was doing, he was trying to show dominance over her by staring her down.

Well, he's met his match because I'm not looking away first.

Nessa didn't care how childish that sounded. She was going to stand her ground.

"Rush?" Kellen asked.

"Yep," he said, finally breaking eye contact.

"Everything okay?" Connor asked.

"Yep, everything is good," Rush said. "How did your trip go? Was it eventful?"

"Yes and no," Connor said. "There was no sign of him at the campsite, but we did find Nessa there."

Connor nodded in her direction as he said her name, which brought Rush's attention back on her again.

"It's nice to meet you, Nessa," Rush said as he strolled over holding out his hand for her.

Not wanting to seem rude, Nessa shook his hand even though she really didn't want to. Not after the staring contest a minute ago.

"Hi," she said.

"I hear they had to rescue you from a Human zoo," he said.

"Yes."

"I bet that wasn't the best experience, was it?" he asked.

"No," she agreed. "It's definitely not something I want to do again."

"I bet," he said, raising his eyebrows.

"That's where the eventful part came in to play," Kellen said.

Turning to look at Kellen, Rush said "What? Rescuing a damsel in distress wasn't eventful enough?"

"Nope," Connor said, shaking his head.

"You'll never believe who we bumped into while we were there," Aidan said.

"Who?" Rush asked.

With one word, Rush's outwardly calm and relaxed demeanour changed instantly.

"Nash," Kellen told him.

The hairs on the back of Nessa's neck stood on up. She could almost cut the atmosphere with a knife; the tension had risen so drastically.

"What?" Rush finally said after a long-drawn-out silence.

"Nash was already at the zoo when we went to rescue Nessa," Aidan told him.

"Anya said he's the one responsible for kidnapping her," Connor added.

"He was," Anya said.

Spinning on her, Rush demanded "How do you know him?"

"I...I don't know him," she told him truthfully.

"What was he doing at the zoo then?" he asked.

"I wish I knew," she lied. "If I knew I would tell you."

Rush didn't look as if he believed her, but he didn't question her further. Nessa released the breath she hadn't known she was holding when Rush turned back

186

to the others.

"What did he say?" Rush asked.

"Not much really," Kellen told him. "He said he was there to speak with Nessa, but he didn't say what about."

Turning back to her, Rush said "Do you know what he wanted to speak to you about?"

"No, sorry," she said. "Kellen walked in before he could tell me."

Which was technically true, Kellen and the others had arrived moments after Nash. But even if she knew what he wanted to talk to her about, there was no way she was going to tell Rush. Especially with the mood he was in now.

If he'd picked that moment to have a staring contest with her, Nessa definitely would have been the first person to turn away.

Chapter Twenty-Three

"He wasn't alone either," Aidan said. "He was with a group of Imfera Demons."

"Like when we rescued Anya?" Rush asked.

"Not as many, but yes," Connor said.

Rush didn't say a word as he walked over to the window. He stood silently, staring outside before turning back around.

"Okay," he said calmly. "Anything else?"

"He knew about me and Anya," Connor told him. "He knew we had mated."

"We haven't kept it secret though, have we," Anya said.

"Did he say anything else?" Rush asked.

"Apparently he knows a lot more than that, but he didn't tell us what," Kellen said.

"I can't see what he might know," Rush said. "At least, not anything he could use against us."

Neither could Kellen, but why else would Nash say he knew more about them if he didn't? He must have something to use against them, otherwise there was no point in mentioning it.

"Well, whatever it is, we're not going to find out today," Rush said. "So, you might as well head home."

"What about Nessa?" Anya asked.

Rush turned to look at Nessa. "Oh, yes, we can't forget about you."

"Is there a hotel or B&B here?" Nessa asked.

"Nope, sorry," Rush said, shaking his head. "You're going to have to stay with someone."

"Oh," Nessa said, looking uncomfortable.

"Don't worry, you'll be in safe hands," Rush said, with a wicked grin on his face. "Kellen will take great care of you."

Kellen's head snapped to Connor and Aidan. He knew those two had something to do with Rush's decision. They must have told him that they think Nessa is Kellen's mate.

"I forgot to tell you," Anya said with a cheesy smile of her own. "I've told Kayla that she can have a sleepover when we got back."

"Funny how this is the first I've heard of it," Kellen said. "There's been no mention of Kayla having a sleeping over."

"Well," Rush said, clapping his hands together. "That's decided then. You'll be staying with Kellen."

Nessa was blushing when Kellen turned back to her and Rush.

"That okay with you?" he asked her.

"Yes," she said, softly nodding.

"Okay then," Kellen said. "We'll grab our stuff from Connor's first and then head to mine."

"Okay," she said quietly.

"Good," Rush said. "Now that's sorted, in the nicest possible way, fuck off."

Aidan laughed. "I thought you loved it when we visited."

"Yeah, like a hole in the head," Rush said, rolling his eyes.

"Fine," Connor said as he stood up and held out his arm to Anya. "We know when we're not wanted. Come on, my love, let's go home."

Jumping up from her seat, Anya hooked her arm with Connor's. "Let's go home," she said, a massive smile on her face as she looked up at him.

Nessa waited for Kellen before following Anya and Connor outside. She didn't say a word to him on the walk; she barely even looked in his direction. Every time she did, he could see a slight blush appear on her cheeks.

Kellen wasn't concerned that she wasn't speaking with him though. At the moment she was quite happy chatting with Anya, wanting to know more about the realm. He overheard her asking if there were more of her kind here, more panthers and not just wolves and dragons.

"You don't mind if I show Nessa around the house before you go, do you?" Anya asked when they arrived.

"Yeah, that's fine by me," Kellen said.

"See?" she said to Nessa. "I didn't think he would mind."

"Thank you," Nessa said to him before following Anya inside the house.

"I'm gonna grab my bag and go," Aidan said, racing in after them.

"Are you sure you don't mind Kayla staying with you?" Kellen asked Connor when they were alone.

"Na," Connor said. "It'll be fun."

"If you say so," Kellen told him.

"She always behaves for Anya," Connor said. "So, I'll just make sure Anya deals with her if she causes any trouble. After all, it was her idea."

"I knew it," Kellen said. "She's trying to play match-maker, isn't she?"

"Something like that," Connor said, smiling.

"It's not going to work," Kellen told him. "Nessa doesn't seem interested in me, at least, not when she's awake anyway."

"What do you mean?" Connor asked.

Kellen sighed as he ran a hand through his hair.

"Last night we dream shared," he admitted quietly so Nessa wouldn't hear if she walked out at that moment.

"Really?"

"Yeah, but today she can't even look at me," Kellen said.

"Oh, trust me, she can," Connor assured him. "I've

caught her a few times, and so have Anya and Aidan. You should have seen how she was watching you at Rush's house. She couldn't take her eyes off you."

"Yeah, alright," Kellen said.

He knew she'd looked in his direction a couple of times, but not taking her eyes off him? No, that was bullshit.

"No, seriously," Connor said. "After you gave her a coffee, she watched you like a hawk while you got your own."

"She was staring at Rush when I turned around," Kellen said. "They seemed to be having a staring match."

"Yeah, but that was after she was watching you," Connor said.

"What are you two talking about?" Aidan asked as he came back out carrying his bag.

"Kellen doesn't believe that Nessa hasn't been able to take her eyes off him," Connor told him.

"Connor's right," Aidan said without preamble. "Every time she's near you, she struggles to keep her eyes off you. I'm surprised you haven't noticed it."

"I've noticed her avoiding me like the plague," Kellen said. "But no, I've not noticed her constantly looking at me."

"Of course not," Connor said. "Haven't you noticed how she blushes every time you catch her looking at you?"

"I just thought she blushed a lot," Kellen said.

"Nope," Aidan said. "That's all been for you."

"So, you must have made a good impression in the

dream you shared last night," Connor said.

"You what?" Aidan asked.

"Yeah, looks like Kellen here shared a dirty dream with Nessa," Connor said.

"I said nothing about it being dirty," Kellen said.

"You didn't have to," Connor said with a grin. "Nessa told us loud and clear with all the blushing she's been doing today."

"You dirty dog," Aidan said, laughing.

"Shut up," Kellen growled. "Nessa doesn't know it was a dream share, she thinks I don't know about the dream."

"Ah, that's why she's been avoiding making eye contact with you," Connor said. "She thinks she just had a dirty dream about you, not with you."

"Yep," Kellen said.

"Wow, how are you going to break it to her that you were there as well?" Aidan asked.

"I'm not," Kellen said.

"You've got to tell her," Connor said.

"Why?"

"Because she has a right to know," Connor said. "Trust me, it's best to be honest with your mate."

"I don't even know if she is my mate," Kellen said.

"Of course, she is," Connor said. "Otherwise you wouldn't have dream shared."

Before Kellen could say anymore, Anya and Nessa emerged from the house.

It didn't take them long to reach him and Connor. Nessa had her hands full with her bags, while Anya carried his for him.

"I would have come in for them, and given you a hand with your bags, Nessa," he told them.

"That's okay," she told him. "I can just about carry mine, but I didn't have space to grab yours, so Anya grabbed it for me."

"Thank you," Kellen said as he took his bags from Anya.

"You're welcome," Anya said.

"I'll take these for you," he said, taking the heaviest of Nessa's bags.

"I can carry them," she assured him.

"I don't doubt that you can," he said. "But why struggle when I'm happy to help?"

"Okay," she gave in. "Thank you."

"You're welcome," he told her.

Nessa turned back to Anya and Connor. "Thank you for helping me, and for showing me around your beautiful home."

"Any time," Connor said.

"You're more than welcome," Anya said. "Maybe you could come over for dinner sometime soon."

"That would be nice, thank you," she said.

"Right," Kellen said. "Are you ready to go?"

"Yep, ready when you are," she said, cheerfully.

"Come on then, it's this way," he said, nodding towards the woodland. "See you two later."

"Have fun," Connor said.

"Don't forget to send Kayla over when you get back," Anya shouted after them.

"Will do," he shouted back.

Within moments Connor and Anya, along with their house, disappeared from view as they headed deeper into the woodlands.

"Is it far to your house?" Nessa asked after a couple of minutes of walking in silence.

"No, it's not too far," he told her. "I can carry some more if you're struggling."

"No, I'm good," she said. "I was just wondering, that's all."

"If we keep this pace, we should be there in about ten minutes," he told her.

He hoped the house was still standing when they finally got there.

Kayla was supposed to be staying with friends while he was away, but there was nothing stopping her from returning. Even if he'd locked up before he left, Kayla could still get in. It wouldn't be the first time she'd broken in somewhere.

Luckily enough, the Shifter realm wasn't like that of the Human. They could leave their homes unlocked without fear of being stolen from.

Humans used to be able to do that many years ago, but so much has changed in their realm. It wasn't safe to leave the doors unlocked while they were home, let alone while they were out.

"I bet you can't wait to get back to your sister," Nessa said.

"I just hope she's behaved herself while I've been away," he said.

"Don't you think she has?" she asked.

Kellen shook his head. "No, it's more likely that she's got herself into some form of trouble."

"So little faith in me, big brother," Kayla said from behind them.

Spinning around, he asked "What are you doing here?"

"I missed you," she said sweetly.

"What have you done?" he asked suspiciously.

"Nothing," she said laughing. "Honestly, I've missed you."

"I've missed you too," he said honestly.

She may be a pain in the ass at times, but he loved his little sister dearly.

"Are you going to introduce me to your new friend?" Kayla asked, looking over his shoulder at Nessa.

"Sorry, where's my manners," he apologized. "Nessa, this is my little sister Kayla. Kayla, this is Nessa. She's a panther Shifter."

"Ah, cool," Kayla said. "It's nice to meet you."

"You too," Nessa said. "I've heard a lot about you."

"Really?" Kayla asked with a raised brow. "I hope it's all good."

"It's all truthful," Kellen answered for her.

"So, not all good then," Kayla said with a smile. "Don't believe everything Kellen tells you, he likes to exaggerate."

"I do not," Kellen said.

"You do," Kayla said. "Has he told you about me and the cat Shifters?"

"No," Nessa said.

"Well, I promise," Kayla said. "When he does, don't listen to half of it. I didn't terrorize the cats."

"I take it, you mean Shifters like me," Nessa said.

"Yes," Kellen said. "Kayla thought it would be funny to chase some of them up trees."

Kayla laughed. "He makes it sound so much worse than it was. I was just playing with some of the younger cats."

"I was called away from work to deal with you," he said, pointing a finger at her. "So, yes, it was worse than you think."

"Anyway," Kayla said. "Anya said I'm staying at their house tonight, is that true?"

"Yes, it's true," he said. "You're staying with them for tonight."

"I got the impression it was for longer," Kayla said.

"Nope, just for tonight," he said.

Kellen knew what they were up to. Connor and Anya would have offered to have Kayla for as long as it took for him and Nessa to get together.

He appreciated what they were doing, but it wasn't necessary. He was more than capable of wooing Nessa without their help.

Chapter Twenty-Four

Nessa didn't know what she was expecting when she met Kellen's sister, but it certainly wasn't the polite, well mannered, young lady that stood before her.

She could definitely tell that they were related though. They both had the same eyes. They both had deep blue eyes full of warmth, and thick light brown hair. Nessa could easily lose herself in his eyes.

"Ah…but I was looking forward to staying with Anya for a couple of days," Kayla whined.

"And there was me thinking that you missed me," Kellen said. "I'm sure that's what you said a minute ago?"

"I have missed you," Kayla said. "But I really want to stay at Anya's."

"Fine," Kellen said. "You can stay there for two

nights."

"But…"

"No buts," Kellen said. "Behave yourself and we'll see about longer."

"Okay," Kayla said excitedly.

She kissed Kellen on the cheek before running off.

Kayla shouted back over her shoulder. "I'll see you at home."

Shaking his head, Kellen continued walking.

"She seems nice," Nessa said as she followed him.

"She can be when she's not misbehaving," Kellen said. "In all honesty, she isn't so bad. Considering she was so young when our parents died, she could be a hell of a lot worse than what she is."

"How old was she when they died?" Nessa asked.

"Kayla was five," Kellen told her. "Since I was sixty-five when they died, it was my responsibility to look after her until she's old enough to live on her own."

"Wow, there's a massive age gap between you," Nessa said.

Kellen was old enough to be her grandfather, not her brother. Not that she was going to tell Kellen that. There was no way an age gap like that would be possible if they had been Human.

"My parents tried for many years to conceive after having me," Kellen told her. "They were about to give up when they found out they were expecting Kayla. They were so happy when they found out."

Nessa could see from the look on Kellen's face that he had been just as happy for them.

"I just wish they could see her grow up," Kellen said sadly. "As much as she's a pain in the ass, they would be so proud of the person she's growing up into."

"They would be proud of you as well," Nessa said. "The way you've taken care of your sister for all these years."

Kellen looked down at her with warmth in his eyes.

"From what I can tell, you've done a wonderful job," Nessa said honestly. "I know I've only just meet Kayla, but she seems like a really nice girl."

"Thank you," he said. "It's not been easy, but I try."

"I think that's all anyone can do," Nessa said.

"It must have been hard for you, as well," he said. "Growing up with no family at all couldn't have been easy."

"I'm not going to lie, it wasn't easy," Nessa said. "But it wasn't always hard either. Some of the foster homes they placed me in were really nice, the carers really made me feel welcome."

"I bet it was difficult hiding your true self growing up," he said. "It can't have been easy living among Humans, not being able to shift whenever you want."

"You kind of get used to it," she lied.

"Still, it must have been difficult," he persisted.

It didn't matter how much he asked; she wasn't going to give away that she wasn't a Shifter as a child.

Nessa was grateful when a stunning house came into view. It gave her a great excuse to change the subject.

"Oh, wow!" Nessa said. "That's breath-taking."

"Thank you," Kellen said.

Peeling her eyes away from the beautiful building, Nessa turn to Kellen and asked "This is your house?"

"Yes, my father built it for my mother," Kellen said proudly.

"It's beautiful," Nessa said honestly.

Blood red roses climbed up the corners of the house, spreading their limbs out to reach each other. Pure white roses created an arch over the front door, welcoming visitors with their wonderful scent.

Beautiful flower beds surrounded the house. Nessa recognized most of them, but there were a few she'd never seen before. Admittedly, there were a lot of plants and flowers back in the Human realm she hadn't seen before, but she didn't think that was the case here.

"My mother thought so," Kellen said. "She used to say that it was one of the reasons she mated with my father."

"It's about time you two got here," Kayla shouted from the front door. "Are you just going to stand there all day?"

Nessa hadn't realized she'd stopped walking until Kayla commented.

"Sorry," Nessa said, embarrassed.

"Don't worry about it," Kellen said. "I'm glad you like it."

"Oh, I definitely like it," Nessa said.

Standing to one side, Kellen waited for her to enter the house first.

Who said chivalry was dead?

"You can put your bags over there," Kellen said,

pointing towards the stairs. "I'll carry them up for you once I've shown you around."

"Okay," Nessa said.

As soon as Nessa placed her bags down, she stood up and looked around the large entrance hall.

Wow! This place is amazing!

It wasn't a massive entrance hall, but it was decorated in such a way that it appeared larger while still having the homely feel, a theme that ran throughout the house.

Nessa followed Kellen as he showed her around, not really paying any attention to what he was saying, she was more interested in the little trinkets. Not to mention the artwork hanging on the wall.

"Wow! These paintings are fantastic," she finally said when she found her voice again.

"Thank you," Kellen said proudly.

Peeling her eyes away from one of the paintings...a small wolf playing in a field with two older wolves... she turned to look at him. The love she saw shining in his eyes was just as beautiful as the painting.

"Did you paint these?" she asked.

"Yes," he said. "This one is of Kayla playing with our parents before they died."

"They're stunning," she told him.

"I would love to paint you," he blurted.

Speechless, Nessa just stared at him. The scene of Jack painting Rose from the movie Titanic popped into her head. Heat crept up her cheeks at the thought of posing naked for Kellen to paint her portrait.

"That's if you don't mind me painting you in panther form," Kellen said when he noticed her shocked expression.

"Oh…um…that would be nice," she said.

She could have kicked herself for her wayward thoughts. Likely enough, Kellen couldn't see inside her mind, at least she hoped not. She hadn't been able to see in his mind when they had spoken telepathically, only hear his voice inside her head, but that didn't mean he couldn't.

There was so much about being a Shifter that Nessa still didn't know. She didn't want to ask any questions thought, just in case they became suspicious of her. She wasn't ready to tell them what happened to her just yet.

"Kellen's a fantastic artist," Kayla said, making Nessa jump.

She hadn't heard Kayla walking up behind them.

"You'll fall in love with the painting of you he does," Kayla continued. "He's been asked to do portraits of people in Human form, but Kellen won't. He says he can't paint people's faces. I think that's just an excuse."

"I don't know why," Kellen said. "But I can never get Human face right, they always turn out wrong."

"No, they don't," Kayla said. "You just don't have faith in your abilities."

"I would love a painting of my animal form," Nessa said, interrupting them.

"You won't regret it," Kayla said.

Butterflies took off in her stomach when Kellen smiled at her. Nessa could easily look at Kellen's smile all day long.

"Where will I be staying tonight?" she asked, changing the subject.

He'd shown her around the rest of the house, but he hadn't shown her to the room she'll be sleeping in tonight.

Kayla opened her mouth to answer, but Kellen beat her too it. Nessa was positive she saw Kellen nudge Kayla at the same time.

"You'll be sleeping in the guest room," he said, turning and heading for the stairs. "Follow me."

Grabbing most of her bags on his way past, Kellen climbed the stairs two at a time. Nessa didn't waste any time. Quickly grabbing the last of her bags, she followed him up the stairs.

"I'm off to Anya's now," Kayla shouted up after them.

"Okay," Kellen said. "Behave yourself there."

"I will," Kayla told him.

"This is my room," Kellen pointed as he walked past. "Kayla's is opposite."

"Okay," Nessa said.

"The family bathroom is opposite your room," he said.

Stopping outside a room, Kellen held the door open for her.

"This is your room," he said. "I hope you like it."

"Thank you," Nessa said as she passed him.

"You're welcome," he said.

The room was just as stunning as the rest of the house. A large four poster bed stood in the middle of the room, perfectly made ready for the next guest to stay.

A dressing table and chair were in front of the window, along with a freestanding wardrobe and chest of drawers. There was also a love seat at the foot of the bed.

Kellen's paintings adorned the walls. Nessa couldn't help but admire them because he really was a fantastic artist.

"Are you hungry?" he asked, placing her bags on the love seat.

"Um…a little," she admitted.

"Okay, I'll make some dinner while you settle in," he said.

"Thank you," she said.

"When you're ready, just head down to the kitchen," he said, pulling the door closed behind him.

"Will do, thank you," she said before he closed it completely.

Alone at least, Nessa breathed a deep sigh of relief. She didn't know how much longer she could go on making out that she was truly one of them. The only thing holding her back was the thought of how Kellen was going to take the news.

The last thing she wanted was for him to not want anything to do with her after he finds out the truth about her, especially since it wasn't her fault that she wasn't born one of them.

She hoped that wasn't the case; she hoped he didn't look at her differently after he found out the truth. She could handle it from anyone else, but not Kellen.

Which she knew was stupid, she barely even knew

the man, but she didn't want to see hatred or disgust in his beautiful eyes. She'd seen that in enough people's eyes that she once cared about, and she didn't want it to happen with him.

Nessa dumped all her bags on the floor in front of the wardrobe. She didn't see the point in unpacking everything yet because she didn't know if she was going to be staying here long.

So, for the time being, she was going to live out of her bags. It wasn't the first time she's lived like that, and it probably wasn't going to be the last either.

Chapter Twenty-Five

Kellen didn't have a clue what he was going to cook for her. He'd been away for a couple of weeks, so he didn't know what food he had in.

He hoped Kayla hadn't cleaned him out while he'd been away. He should have asked her before she left, but Kellen only thought about it after she'd already left.

Searching the cupboards, Kellen managed to find just enough ingredients to throw something together that was at least edible. He just hoped Nessa wasn't a picky eater and liked scrambled eggs on toast because that's all there was, unless she wanted tinned soup.

"I thought you might need some food," Anya said as she let herself in through the back door.

"You're a life saver," Kellen said. "Kayla hasn't left much in the way of food."

"I didn't think she would," Anya said, smiling.

"No, I didn't think she would either," he agreed. "We were gone longer than I thought, so I'm lucky she left me anything at all."

"That's teenagers for you," Anya said.

"You don't have to tell me," Kellen said. "I live with one."

Anya smiled before smoothly changing the subject to Nessa.

"Were you about to cook scrambled eggs for you and Nessa?" she asked.

"Yep," he said. "That was, until you came to my rescue."

"Where is she?" Anya asked.

"Upstairs," he said. "I've just showed her where she's staying, so she's getting settled in."

"That's good," she said. "Well, I'll leave you two in peace."

"You don't have to go," he told her, unsure if he was ready to be left alone with Nessa.

"I do," she said. "I've left Connor alone with Kayla."

Kellen burst out laughing.

"I bet he loved you doing that," he said.

"Yeah, he did look a little scared as I walked out the door," she said, laughing with him.

"I bet," he said.

"It'll give him good practice," she said. "He's going to need it someday."

"Don't worry about him too much," Kellen said. "He'll be a fantastic father when the time comes."

"I know he will," she said, smiling fondly. "Anyway, I best go rescue him now."

"Thanks again, Anya," he said as she was on her way out the door.

"Any time," she said.

Then she was gone again, leaving him alone with Nessa.

Rummaging around in the bags Anya brought over, he pulled out a mix of vegetables, potatoes and two large steaks.

"Perfect," he said. "This'll definitely be better than scrambled eggs."

"I quite like scrambled eggs," Nessa said from the doorway. "They go lovely with tomatoes and toast."

Kellen looked up at her. "Which would you prefer, scrambled eggs or steak?"

"What would you say if I choose the eggs?" she asked with one brow raised.

Kellen couldn't help himself, he looked longingly at the steak, but if she didn't want it, then he wouldn't cook it.

Before he could answer her, she burst out laughing.

"Don't worry," she managed to say through the laughing. "I'm not going to make you give up the steak."

"So, you're choosing steak then?" he asked just to be certain.

"Yep, I'm choosing steak."

"I promise you've made a good choice," he said. "Especially with my culinary skills."

"Ah, so you're a chef," she said.

"If you mean 'chef' as in I can cook, then yes," he said. "But if you mean professionally, then no. I haven't poisoned Kayla yet, so you should be okay."

"That's good to know," she said, walking over to him. "Do you want some help?"

Looking at the food laid out on the counter, Kellen nodded "Yeah, I could do with help."

"What would you like me to do?" she asked as she rolled up her sleeves.

"Can you wash and prepare the vegetables while I peel the potatoes?"

"Yep, no problem," she said.

Before starting on the potatoes, Kellen showed Nessa where everything was kept.

"I'll probably still forget where anything is," she said as she stood at the sink washing the vegetables.

"If you can't find what you're looking for, then just ask," he said. "I don't mind showing you again."

"Don't worry," she said. "I'll probably just search through the cupboards until I find what I want."

"Everyone else does," Kellen said, smiling. "So you might as well. I don't have anything to hide."

Nessa didn't say anything else while they prepared dinner. Kellen had a feeling he said something that upset her, but for the life of him, he couldn't think what he might have said.

She seemed deep in thought every time he looked her way, so he left her in peace.

Before they knew it, dinner was on the table, and that's when the silence became too much.

Sitting opposite her, Kellen blurted out "I'll show you around some of the realm after dinner, if you would like."

"That would be lovely," she said, smiling up at him. "Would it be possible to explore in animal form?"

"Of course," he said. "We won't be the only ones out in animal form."

Even if it wasn't the norm, Kellen would still take her out in animal form, simply because of the smile she gave him. She lit up the room, making Kellen want to see her smile more often.

"Really?" she said.

"Yes, really," he said, smiling.

He could see that Nessa wanted to say something, but she held back. So, Kellen decided he would be the one to start.

"If you love nature, you'll love it here," he said.

"Oh, I do," she said. "I can't wait to go exploring."

"Well, as soon as we finish dinner, we can get going," he said.

"I know there are wolf, panther, and… dragons?" she said, questioning if she was right about the dragons.

"Yep, all three," he agreed.

"Are there any other types of Shifters?"

"Yes," he said.

"How many?"

"Too many to list," he said honestly. "It's best if you just assume any living creature here is a Shifter until you get to know the difference."

"Okay," she said.

"You don't have to worry about the livestock though," he said. "Cattle, chickens, and sheep, they're all just animal."

"That's good to know," she said. "Note to self…don't chase the wildlife."

Kellen couldn't help himself, he burst out laughing. He knew it wasn't a laughing matter, but the way Nessa put it and the face she pulled at the same time made him find it funny.

Plus, Nessa wouldn't be the first person to chase the wildlife here. His sister did it on nearly a daily basis.

"I wouldn't," he said. "Trust me, they really don't appreciate it."

"I bet they don't," she said. "I wouldn't either."

"Try telling Kayla that," he said. "I can't seem to stop her from chasing the felines."

It was Nessa's turn to laugh this time.

"If she's not doing that, she's harassing the dragons," he said, shaking his head. "She's an absolute nightmare at times."

"She didn't seem so bad," Nessa said.

"Trust me, once you get to know her, you'll think differently," he told her.

Kellen watched as Nessa played with what was left of her food.

"Aren't you going to eat that?" he asked as she pushed her plate away.

"No, I've had enough," she said. "Thank you, though, it was lovely."

"That's okay, I'm glad you liked it," he said. "Just

give me a couple of minutes and then we can go."

"Don't rush on my account," she told him.

Even still, he finished eating as quickly as he could. He had to admit; he was just as eager to get going as she was. He wanted to be the one to show her around. And knowing his luck, if they didn't leave soon then they wouldn't be going alone.

As much as Kellen liked his friends, he wanted… needed…to be alone with Nessa for a while. He wanted to get to know her, and that wasn't easy when they were surrounded by others.

Once his plate was clear, Kellen picked up both and took them to the sink, scrapping the leftovers in the bin on his way past.

"Right," he said, turning back to Nessa. "Are you ready to go?"

Smiling, Nessa nodded as she stood. "I'm more than ready."

"Good," he said, smiling back. "Let's go."

Heading over to the back door, Kellen held it open for Nessa to go first. Only then did he realize she'd already shifted into her panther.

A streak of black raced past him and out the door.

"That's cheating," he told her, wagging his finger at her.

Nessa tilted her head in reply before rolling around in the grass like a kitten.

"You'll regret that later," he said sternly as he pointed a finger at her.

Not showing any remorse, Nessa looked up at him

with big golden eyes.

Wasting no more time, Kellen quickly closed the door behind him, and then shifted into his wolf. Before she had a chance to react, he pounced on her.

Instead of fighting to get free, Nessa rubbed her body against his. Shocked, Kellen froze just long enough for her to slip free. By the time he realized what she'd done, she had disappeared up the closest tree.

Kellen tried finding her, but she was in her element, blending seamlessly into the canopy.

Nudging her mind with his, she opened a link with him straight away.

"Where are you?" he asked.

"Can't you see me?" she taunted. *"I can see you."*

"All I can see is trees and leaves," he said honestly.

"Here I am," she said, pouncing on him as she leapt out of a tree behind him.

Unprepared, Nessa managed to knock him off his feet momentarily. He couldn't be cross though, not with her giggling in his mind.

Spinning around, Kellen playfully nipped at her hind leg.

"Hey, no biting," she said.

"No cheating then," he counted.

Nessa blew a raspberry sound in his mind. He couldn't help but smile at her. She kind of reminded him of Kayla, of how playful she could be when she wanted to be, which was more often than not.

Bounding off into the dense shrubs, Nessa soon vanished from sight again.

"Come and find me if you can," she taunted.

Kellen was up to the challenge. *"Ready or not, here I come."*

Smiling as he raced after Nessa, her giggle ringing in his ears. He felt like a young pup again, and he loved it.

Chapter Twenty-Six

Nessa was so excited to see more of the shifter realm. She had nearly jumped on Kellen when he offered to show her around after dinner. It was only the fact that they were sat at the table eating at the time that she hadn't leapt on him.

There was no table in the way now though. So, she took the first opportunity she could, spurred on by the fact he pounced on her as soon as he shifted.

Nessa hadn't expected him to be as playful as he was. She'd thought he would be more about showing her around, but he had surprised her once again.

Who would have thought playing a simple game of hide-and-seek would be such fun. Nessa couldn't re-member ever having this much fun playing the game as a child. She had a feeling it wouldn't be the same if she was playing it with anyone other than Kellen.

It was easier than she thought it would be to hide from Kellen, even with his many years of experience. As long as she stayed up wind from him, as well as blending in with the canopy of the trees, she was able to hide from him. At least, until the wind suddenly changed direction.

Nessa lost track of how long they were outside playing. Before she knew it, darkness had fallen. She expected Kellen would want to start heading home soon, but she wasn't ready yet. She wanted to explore some more.

"Do we have to go back yet?" she asked, hopeful the answer was no.

"Do you want to go back yet?" he asked instead.

"No, I want to see more," Nessa said, eagerly.

"Do you want to continue playing this game?" he asked.

"No," she said.

"Good," he said. *"In that case, follow me."*

"Where are we going?" she asked, intrigued to know where he was taking her.

"You'll see," was his reply. "*But trust me, you'll like it.*"

"Is it far?" she asked.

Not that it would be a problem. She would quite happily explore all night long if she could.

"No, it's only a couple of minutes' walk," he said.
"Okay."

"I promise you won't regret it," he said, turning to

look at her as she walked alongside him. *"Do you trust me?"*

That was the question, wasn't it? Did she trust him? She wanted to. She wanted to so badly it hurt, but she still wasn't sure if she could, not completely.

Nessa didn't think he meant it the same way she did, but that didn't stop the question from ringing out loud and clear in her mind.

Kellen was looking at her expectantly, so she nodded her head. She didn't trust her voice not to give away how indecisive she was. Luckily, he seemed okay with her non-verbal answer.

One of the main downsides to being in animal form, was she couldn't read his facial expressions, but it was also one of the benefits as well because he couldn't read hers either. Like a double-edged sword, there were both pros and cons to being in animal form.

Unless she was going to ask him to shift so she could read his face, she had no choice but to go with it and hope he believed her.

From what she could tell, they were heading towards water. She could hear the sound of it crashing as they got closer to it. And sure enough, within minutes, they were at the base of a waterfall.

"Wow!" she breathed as they walked into a clearing in the woods. *"That's stunning."*

Surrounded by trees and plants on one side, and a small cliff with the waterfall on the other side. It felt as if they were cocooned from the world around them, an intimate place just for the two of them.

Moonlight glistening off the water as it pooled at the bottom of the falls. Gentle waves gave it a rippling effect before it flowed down in a stream that snaked through the woods. Beautiful white flowers echoed that of the moon, the scent absolutely intoxicating.

The place had such a magical vibe about it that she never wanted to leave.

"I'm glad you like it," he said.

"I don't like it," she said, turning to him. *"I love it. Thank you for bring me here."*

"You're more than welcome, Nessa," Kellen said.

Shifting back into Human form, Kellen walked over to the water's edge.

"I love coming here," he said, gazing up at the water-fall. "It's so peaceful."

Shifting as well, Nessa walked up and stopped next to him.

"I can see why," she said. "It stunning here."

"Yes, it is," he agreed.

They stood in silence for a few minutes, both enjoying the peaceful surroundings.

Nessa could stay here forever. Not just at the water-fall, but in this realm. Nature definitely ruled this realm, and it was all the better for it.

Since she arrived, she hadn't seen a single piece of litter anywhere. The air was cleaner, she hadn't picked up any bad scents at all and everything smelled as it should because there wasn't any pollution clogging up the air.

Kneeling down, Kellen ran his hand through the

water.

"It's a perfect temperature if you want to go for a swim," he said, gazing at her over his shoulder.

Nessa thought about it for a moment before saying "But I don't have anything to wear."

It was a lame excuse, but it was true. She didn't own a swimming costume, hadn't done since she was a child.

"Neither do I," he said. "But I'm still going in."

Nessa had always wanted to swim in a natural pool, but never had the chance. She had seen a couple over the years, but she never had the courage to actually go swimming in one. Most of them were tourist attractions in the Human realm, with no swimming signs all around them.

"Okay," Nessa agreed.

Thinking they would just go in their underwear instead, Nessa followed Kellen's lead as he started to strip, but he didn't stop at his underwear. Nope, those came off as well.

My god! She thought, getting her first good look at his naked body as he turned around to place his clothes away from the water's edge. *That dream had been mighty accurate.*

Nessa quickly checked herself to make sure she didn't have her mouth wide open as she drooled.

Mouth open? Check. Drooling? Nope, we're good, she thought. *Thank god! How embarrassing would that have been?*

Very embarrassing was the answer.

Kellen may be comfortable going commando, but

Nessa drew the line at skinny dipping.

Folding her clothes neatly, she heard the water splash as Kellen jumped in. Nessa turned around in time to see him emerge through the falls.

Nessa was eager to join Kellen as she watched him swimming. She wanted to see what it was like on the other side of the curtain of water.

Quickly making her way over to the edge, she wasted no time waddling into the deeper parts so she could swim over to Kellen, who was still under the falls.

"Aren't you taking off your underwear?" he asked.

"Nope," she said. "It's like a bikini, so it's easy to wear swimming."

"Okay," he said. "If it makes you feel more comfortable, go for it. I prefer to wear nothing when swimming, it's easier to move around."

Treading water, Nessa nodded her head towards the curtain behind him.

"What's back there?" she asked.

"It's a small cave," he said. "Would you like to see?"

"Yes, please," she said eagerly.

"Here," he said, holding out his hand. "Take my hand and I'll show you through."

Nessa didn't hesitate; she grabbed his hand as quickly as she could. Instantly she was dragged through the water until she was inches away from him.

In one second, he let go of her hand and wrapped his arm around her waist, pulling her closer to him. Before she knew it, she was pressed up tight against him.

Gasping at the sudden movement, Nessa automatically wrapped her arms around his head to steady herself and keep afloat.

Kellen had a wicked grin on his face. "It's a tight squeeze in there."

"You could have warned me you were going to do that," she said.

"Would you have come this close willingly?" he asked.

Nessa wasn't sure what to say. In all honesty, if she'd known, she probably would have said no. But it was only because she didn't trust herself being so close to a very naked Kellen.

"See?" he said, reading her silence as an answer. "That's why I didn't tell you. Then you would have missed out on something beautiful."

His words said one thing, his voice said a completely different thing. As innocent as the words were, the way he spoke made them sound seductive.

His voice wasn't the only thing that changed either. Where she was pressed tightly to his body, she could feel his manhood growing against her.

Before she could protest, he spun them around so she was going backwards, and took them both under the waterfall. A second later they broke through to the other side.

The smallest amount of moonlight filtered through the curtain of water, and only just. As they moved further into the cave, they were quickly enveloped in darkness.

Kellen was right though, there wasn't much space to squeeze through the entrance to the cave, but they could have gone in one at a time. Not that she was complaining, she was enjoying the feel of Kellen's body pressed against hers.

Luckily enough though, the cave widened the further back they went, until it opened up into a cavern. Nessa could barely see inside the cavern. If it wasn't for Kellen holding on to her, showing her the way, she would never have found the ledge sticking out at the back of the cave.

Without saying a word, Kellen effortlessly lifted her out of the water and sat her on the ledge.

"Hold there a moment," he told her. "I'll sort out some light in here."

"Okay," she said.

Nessa heard Kellen climb out the water and then his footsteps as he walked away from her. A moment later, the cavern was gently lit and she got her first good look around the place.

It was larger than she thought it was. Over half of the surface area in the cave was dry rock, but as far as she could see, it was only accessible by coming through the waterfall.

"What do you think?" Kellen asked.

"It's larger than I thought it would be," she said, then instantly blushed as it occurred to her what she said. "I mean… the cave… it's more… um… spacious…" she tried to explain, but it came out as more of a jumbled mess.

Nessa looked everywhere except towards Kellen. She didn't want him to see how red her cheeks had turned. It was embarrassing enough as it was.

I should just quit while I'm ahead, she thought. *But no, I just keep digging that hole deeper.*

She would have smacked her palm against her head to knock some sense into herself, but it would just make her look even more of an idiot than she already did.

"Yes, it is rather spacious in here," Kellen agreed.

Even without looking at him, Nessa could tell Kellen was amused, the tone of his voice gave it away.

"It's warmer as well," Nessa said when she finally trusted herself to speak again.

She had noticed straight away that it wasn't as cold in here as she thought it would be, especially for the time of night it was.

"That's because of the hot spring," he said, pointing to a rock formation at the other side of the cave. "It's why the water outside is warmer as well."

"Oh, wow," Nessa said.

Climbing to her feet, she joined Kellen by the hot spring. It reminded Nessa of a Jacuzzi; the large oval basin was big enough to fit at least six people comfortably. There was even a couple of ledges dotted around the inside that were large enough to slouch on.

"Climb in," Kellen said. "It's lovely and hot in there."

"Really?" she asked, finally looking Kellen in the eyes. "I can get in?"

Bathing in a hot spring was definitely on her wish list, but it was something she never thought would actually happen.

"Yes, really," he said, smiling down at her. "If you

want, I'll get in first."

"Nope," she said, already climbing over the side. "No need."

Within seconds, Nessa was enveloped by the hot steaming water.

"Ahh…" she let out a contented breath as she took a seat and leaned back against the wall with her eyes closed.

"Good, isn't it?" Kellen asked as he joined her.

"Fucking amazing," she said.

When she next opened her eyes, Kellen was opposite her in the water. Slouching against the wall, he seemed totally relaxed and at home. But that wasn't what caught her attention.

The way Kellen sat, with his legs wide open, gave her a fantastic view of his full erect manhood. She tried concentrating on his face, but it kept twitching, dragging her attention right back to it.

Nessa couldn't stop her tongue from sneaking out and licking her lips. She wouldn't be surprised if she was definitely drooling at that moment in time. And honestly? She really didn't give a shit if she was.

After her night of passion with dream Kellen, she wanted a taste of the real thing. And she was going to get it, she was going to take the leap and go for what she wanted for once.

Decision made, keeping her eyes on Kellen, Nessa slowly sat forward. Reaching behind her, Nessa unclasped her bra and seductively slid it off her shoulders.

Once free, she dropped the bra over the side of the

hot spring and then repeated the action a moment later with her knickers. Kellen's eyes were glued to her, watching her every movement. His cock twitched when she licked her lips.

Encouraged by his reaction, Nessa pushed away from her perch. Slowly gliding through the water, she didn't stop until she was nestled between his spread legs.

Nessa gently ran her hands up the sides of his legs before wrapping both hands around his shaft.

Kellen groaned when she took hold of him, but he didn't look away from her. His eyes holding her prisoner as she slowly began to work up and down his shaft.

Even surrounded by water, Nessa could feel herself getting wetter for him. She wanted him buried deep inside her, but she wanted to taste him in her mouth first.

After a couple of minutes, Nessa released his manhood. When he went to take over, she nodded towards the edge of the hot spring.

Understanding dawned on Kellen's face a second later and he instantly took the position she wanted.

"You don't have to tell me twice," he told her.

With only his feet and ankles in the water, Kellen perched on the edge of the hot spring so she could easily take him in her mouth without drowning.

Nessa had never been so bold in all her life, but something about Kellen that made her feel bolder. He made her feel safe, made her feel as if she could do whatever she wanted to do, and she wanted to do him.

So, taking hold of him once again, she lowered her head and guided him to her salivating mouth.

226

Chapter Twenty-Seven

Kellen had spent many a night relaxing in the hot spring, especially if he'd had a long day cleaning up after Kayla's mess. It was one of the best ways to wind down before turning in for the night.

When Kellen first decided to show Nessa the waterfall, it hadn't been with the intention of seducing her. He truly thought she would enjoy the beauty of the place as much as he did. He wasn't even going to show her the cave and hot spring, at least, not yet.

Kellen was going to save that for another day. Maybe even take a picnic and spend a few hours here during the day. However, after seeing her reaction to the falls, he couldn't resist showing her one of his favourite places.

Now, perched on the edge of the hot spring, Kellen watched as Nessa's head bobbed up and down on his cock, taking him deeper and deeper with every stroke. As much as he was enjoying having her sweet mouth wrapped around his cock, he couldn't let her carry on for much longer. It was difficult enough staying still, but if she continued, he wasn't going to be able to stop himself from coming.

Gently pushing her away, Kellen lifted her out of the water and swapped places with her. Guiding her hands behind her, he leaned her back so she was supporting her weight on her hands before lifting her legs out of the water.

Kneeling between her legs, he hooked her ankles over his shoulders, the entire time Kellen had kept his eyes glued to hers. Once he was sure she was comfortable, he slid his hands round her thighs and held them open slightly.

"God, you're beautiful," he said, making her blush.

Breaking eye contact, Kellen finally looked at all of her. His cock throbbed at the sight before him. Legs spread, Nessa was completely open to him.

Not able to resist the temptation, Kellen leaned in for a taste.

"Mm…" he moaned, taking his first lick. "You taste fucking amazing. Like the sweetest nectar."

Kellen was addicted from the second it touched his tongue, he could happily spend the rest of his life feasting on her and her alone.

Nessa blushed at his words, but he could see the desire swimming in her eyes. She wanted this as much as he did.

Not wasting any more time, Kellen leaned in for another taste. He intended to take his time and savour the moment, but within minutes he was devouring her. Like a starving man, he couldn't get enough of her.

Releasing one of her legs, he gently traced his fingers across her skin until he was at the apex of her legs. Circling her entrance with his finger, Kellen coated it in her juices before slowly pushing it inside her as far as it would go.

Nessa gasped, but instead of moving away, she pushed against his hand, making him go deeper. When he couldn't go any further, he twirled his finger inside her before pulling it back out to repeat the process.

He began slowly at first, but soon built up speed, pumping his finger in and out of her. Nessa rocked with the motion of his hand. He could feel her arms begin to shake, so he added a second and then a third finger.

Kellen waited until all three fingers were sliding in and out of her with ease before finally pulling away altogether.

Nessa groaned with the loss of his hands and mouth, but it soon changed as he stood and entered her in one swift move. Nessa gasped at the sudden invasion, so Kellen held still until she adjusted to his size. He was a lot thicker and longer than his fingers, so he knew it would take her a moment.

Kellen couldn't stop the moan from escaping his mouth. Her slick walls squeezed his cock to perfection, it took all of his willpower not to move.

She was so wet, that even though it was a tight fit, he

could easily slide in. With her legs still over his shoulders, she was in a perfect position to take all of him.

Unable to resist, Kellen placed his thumb on the bundle of nerves just above were their bodies joined together, and began to gently rub. Instantly Nessa's muscles relaxed and she released her vice like grip on his cock.

"Are you ready?" he asked.

"Yes," she said breathlessly.

"Good because I can't stay still any longer," he said, pulling out of her at the same time and eliciting a moan from her.

Leaving just the tip inside her, he grabbed hold of her hips with both hands before sliding back inside her more slowly this time.

"Fuck me!" he said. "You're so fucking hot and wet, and it's all for me."

Nessa moaned in answer.

She was enjoying herself, that was clear by the desire swimming in her eyes and the moister between her legs, but she was struggling to keep herself in that position. Kellen could tell that her arms were about to give way on her.

So instead of pulling out again, he slid her legs off his shoulders and wrapped them around his waist. While she was impaled on his cock, Kellen lifted her up and spun them around.

Submerging them under the water again, Kellen sat on the ledge where he'd been to begin with so that Nessa was now sat on his lap. In this position Nessa's breasts were right in front of his face.

Taking full advantage, with one hand behind her back to hold her close, Kellen sucked one peeked nipple into his mouth while he massaged the other with his free hand.

Nessa arched her back, pressing her chest even closer to him and making his cock twitch inside her.

Bringing his other hand round to her chest as well, Kellen massaged both breasts while alternating between her nipples with his mouth. Even when she began squirming on his lap, Kellen held still inside her as he continued playing with her breast. Only when she was grinding against him did he finally relinquish her breasts.

Pulling her mouth to his for a fiery kiss, he used his other hand to help her grind against him. Kellen wanted to stay like that forever, and if he didn't need air, then he would. They were both breathless when Kellen broke the kiss.

"You're so fucking gorgeous," he said.

Lips swollen from the kiss, strands of wet hair sticking to her flushed face, and the desire he saw reflected in her eyes. Nothing was more beautiful than Nessa at this moment in time. He would die a happy wolf if he died right now.

Unwrapping Nessa's legs from his waist so she could straddle his waist, he held onto her hips with both hands. Kellen lifted her up so only the tip was inside her before lowering her back down again.

After a couple of times, Nessa brushed his hands

away and took over. Her breasts bounced teasingly in front of his face as she rode him, building up speed until she was riding him as hard and fast as she could.

Bringing his hands up to her chest, he cupped her breasts and began playing with her nipples with his fingers, rolling the tips before gently pinching them. Nessa groaned as he did, encouraging him to continue.

Each time he pinched them he used a bit more pressure and held them like that for a little bit longer.

Still, she pushed her chest out for more, so he gave her more. Pulling on them before letting go, he could feel her getting wetter and wetter as her walls tightened around his cock. Much more of it and Kellen was going to come.

Luckily, it wasn't long before Nessa began to slow down, so Kellen shifted their position again. This time he pulled all the way out of her and lifted her off his lap.

Turning them around, he placed Nessa's hands back where they were when he feasted on her, only this time her arms were out in front of her.

Bending her forward and spreading her legs as wide as possible, Kellen lined his cock up with her welcoming entrance and slammed home.

"Yes!" Nessa groaned as she pushed back against him.

Keeping still, Kellen asked "You want it hard and fast baby?"

"Yes!" she said, wiggling her ass at the same time.

Kellen couldn't help himself. He slapped her ass cheek and then massaged it.

Nessa gasped as his hand made contact, not because she didn't like it, but because she did. She soaked his cock even more, letting him know how much she'd enjoyed it. So, he slapped her other cheek and was rewarded as her walls squeezed him.

"Like that, do you?" he asked.

"Yes," she said breathlessly.

"I thought you might," he said, slapping her again on either cheek before grabbing her hips. Leaning down over her back, Kellen whispered "If you're a good girl, I'll do it again later."

Moaning, Nessa ground against him in response.

Standing up straight, Kellen held on tight to her as he pulled out, slamming back in a second later. This time there was no going slow, not now that he knew she liked it hard and fast. So that's what he gave her. Nessa met him thrust for thrust, relishing every second.

Water splashed all around them, but Kellen didn't care. He was too far gone to care about anything other than bringing them both closer to the edge of bliss.

Nessa's hot, wet pussy pulsed around his swollen cock, letting him know that she was close. But so was he.

Sliding one hand around to grab her breast, Kellen pinched her nipple hard between his thumb and forefinger. At the same time, he slid his other hand to her pussy and did the same with the bundle of nerves there.

Within seconds Nessa was screaming as she tipped over the edge. Soaking his cock as her pussy squeezed him, Kellen soon followed her over the edge, pounding into her as he did so until she had every last drop.

Before he collapsed on top of her, still buried to the hilt, he gently lifted her up and turned so she could lean back against him as she sat on his lap.

"Fuck me," she said when she finally stopped panting and got her breath back.

"If that's an offer," he said, twitching his still hard cock inside her. "Then I'm game if you are."

"Really?" she asked, looking at him over her shoulder. "Don't you need a rest?"

Spreading her legs open wide with his as he leaned them back further, he pulled out slightly before pushing back in.

"I'm sure I could go again," he said, smugly.

"Mm…" she moaned. "Sounds like a good idea to me."

Using one hand, Kellen tilted her face so he could claim her mouth as he slid the other to the bundle of nerves between her legs.

Gently pressing and rubbing against it until she was panting once again.

"Round two, it is then," he agreed, just as breathless when he broke the kiss. "I hope you know, it's going to be a long night," he told her, dragging out the word long.

"I look forward to it," she said huskily.

He was going to make sure she was fully satisfied before the night was over, even if it killed him.

Chapter Twenty-Eight

Nessa stretched under the blankets. She was deliciously sore in the best of places, letting her know that last night definitely hadn't been a dream.

She still couldn't believe how brazen she'd been at the hot spring. It was unlike her to make the first move. The only other time she'd made the first move was in the dream she had of Kellen.

There was definitely something about Kellen that gave her the confidence to go for what she wanted, and she wanted him. Even now, she wanted him just as much as she did before last night.

Nessa still couldn't believe how much she'd enjoyed being slapped on the ass. She'd never in a million years thought she would not only like it, but be incredibly turned on by it. Kellen certainly brought out a side of her that she never knew even existed.

It hadn't been a one-hit-wonder either. After they left the cave, Kellen brought her back to his house so they could carry on. He was like the energizer bunny, ready to go again within minutes of finishing.

Exhausted, Nessa had all but passed out after the last round. Curled up in Kellen's arms, Nessa had slept soundlessly through the night. She couldn't remember the last time she had such a peaceful night's sleep. It certainly hadn't been since she was kidnapped.

Ever since then she'd had nothing but nightmares, constantly waking her up covered in sweat as her heart raced as she relived it in her dreams. Twice now Kellen had helped to keep the nightmares away.

Wondering where he was, Nessa climbed out of bed. Wrapping a sheet around her body, she made her way into the bathroom to clean up. She didn't want to walk around in only a sheet in case he had guests. Just because she couldn't hear anyone, didn't mean he was alone.

As she dressed, Nessa couldn't help going over everything that has happened over the last few days. After all Kellen had done for her, not to mention what they had done last night, she felt guilty for not being honest with him.

Since he'd met her, Kellen had done everything in his power to make her feel safe and welcome, trusting her enough to stay in his home and has shown her more pleasure in one night than she'd had in her entire life.

In return, she'd kept her guard up. Trusting him

enough to pleasure her body, but not enough to tell him the truth about what happened to her.

She kept telling herself it was because of what she'd seen on the news about the zoo staff, but after spending time with them, she knew they weren't the ones responsible for killing all those innocent people. No, Nash was the one responsible, she knew that.

If she was honest, it was because a small part of her was scared to tell him. She didn't know what his reaction was going to be at finding out she wasn't always Shifter. Was he going to hate her because she was born a Human? Would he think less of her because she was turned into a panther?

Nessa didn't know if she was ready to find out the answers, but the thought of those other people that she left behind kept playing in her mind.

Alone, she didn't stand a chance of breaking them free. But with the help of Kellen and his friends, Nessa was certain it could be done. She just needed to pluck up the courage to tell Kellen everything.

Thinking it would be best if she told him sooner rather than later, Nessa decided there was no better time than the present.

Taking a deep breath, Nessa made her way downstairs. Kellen was sat at the table with a cup between his hands.

He smiled as soon as he spotted her.

"There's fresh coffee in the pot if you want some," he said.

"Yes, please," she said. "Where do you keep the cups

again?"

Kellen laughed. "Take a seat and I'll get it for you."

"It's okay, I can grab it myself," she said. "Just point me in the right direction."

But he was already up by the time she finished speaking.

"Sit," he said pointing to the chair opposite his.

"Okay," she relented.

"Did you sleep okay?" he asked as he pulled a cup out of the cupboard above the pot.

Nessa could have kicked herself. Why hadn't she just looked there in the first place? Maybe because she didn't want to be wrong and end up looking through all the cupboards. Knowing her luck, if she'd looked for herself, it would have been in the very last cupboard she checked.

"I slept very well, thank you," she said, remembering how nice it had been to fall asleep in his arms.

It was the first time in her life she had ever felt safe in someone's arms as she drifted off to sleep. Nessa had to admit, she could easily get used to sleeping that way, especially if it was with Kellen.

"Good, I'm glad," he said, winking as he set the cup down in front of her. "Because I slept extremely well."

Nessa smiled. "Thank you."

Lifting the cup to her lips, she blew on the top before taking a sip. Kellen watched her like a hawk as he sat opposite her.

"Mm…" she said. "This coffee is perfect, thank you."

"You're welcome," he said.

238

After a moment…and half a cup of coffee…Nessa finally plucked up the courage to say something.

She blurted out "I'm not a Shifter."

"What?" Kellen asked, visibly taken aback.

Trying again, Nessa said slower this time "I wasn't born a Shifter, I was turned into one."

"I had a feeling that might be the case," he said out of the blue.

It was the last thing Nessa expected him to say, so she was stunned into silence for a minute, unsure what to say next. Luckily Kellen saved her from trying to think up a reply.

"When did it happen?" he asked.

"Just over six weeks ago," she said.

"Was Nash involved?"

"The man from the zoo?" she asked. When Kellen nodded, she added: "Yes, he was responsible."

Nessa couldn't read Kellen. As soon as she mentioned that she wasn't born a Shifter, Kellen had closed himself off from her. He gave nothing away about how he felt about the news.

Feeling uncomfortable, Nessa wished she hadn't said anything, but she reminded herself why she was telling him in the first place. The other prisoners didn't deserve to stay there all because she was too scared to tell Kellen.

Even if it ruined any form of future she might have with Kellen, it was worth giving it all up if it meant those people would be safe.

"So, you knew who he was all along?" Kellen asked,

turning back to her.

"No, not like you might think," Nessa said. "I don't know who he is, only that he's the one responsible for doing this to me."

"Was he the only one?" he asked.

"What do you mean?"

"Was he the only one involved with turning you into a Shifter?" he asked.

"No," she said, shaking her head. "Those other things were there as well."

"Imfera Demons," he said.

"Is that what they're called?" she asked.

"Yes," he said. "They like to play with fire."

"I couldn't tell you how many of them there were because they all look the same to me," she said honestly.

"Yeah, ugly bastards," he said, lifting his lip in disgust.

"What made you think I wasn't born a Shifter?" she asked. "Are there more like me?"

"Only one," he said.

"Oh, so it's not common?" she asked, surprised.

"No, it's definitely not common," he said. "The only other Shifter that we know who has been turned so far, is Anya."

"Really?" Nessa knew something had happened to Anya, but she hadn't known it was that.

"Yes, she was turned a few months ago," he said. "That's why we were searching in the Human realm. We were looking for the person responsible."

"So, you didn't know it was Nash until you saw him

talking to me at the zoo?" she asked.

"Yes," he agreed. "Unfortunately, Anya couldn't give us much of a description of him, or the other person he was working with. She couldn't even give us a name because he gave her a false name."

She never would have guessed that Anya was once a Human. She seemed to be right at home here, like she had always belonged. Nessa definitely wouldn't have thought she'd only been a Shifter for a few months.

"Do you know who the other person is?" he asked.

"No, the only other people I saw were the Demons," she said. "If you can even call them people."

"You're right," Kellen said. "They're not people, they're Demons, and one of the worst types as well."

"There's more than one type?" she asked.

"Yes, there's hundreds of different species of Demon," he said.

"Fuck me," she said, shocked at the news. "I thought it was bad enough with one type."

"Not all of them are as evil as the Imfera," he said. "Some of them are peaceful creatures, especially if you don't piss them off."

"Don't worry, I don't ever plan on pissing off a Demon on purpose," she told him.

"You'll be okay then," he said, smiling at her.

Taking a deep breath, Nessa got to the reason she was telling him in the first place…the other prisoners.

"There's more I need to tell you," she said.

Kellen looked at her suspiciously. "Go on then."

"I wasn't the only person being held captive," she

said.

"What?" he asked.

"There were at least a dozen other people there as well," she told him. "I couldn't break them out at the same time, I would have been caught if I'd tried. So, I had to leave them behind."

"Why didn't you tell me this earlier?" he asked angrily. "Anything could have happened to them since you left."

"They had already been moved," she said. "The police checked out the building just after I escaped, they didn't find anything there."

"The Human police can't see shit," he said. "If there's magic involved, which we know there is, then they could have been hidden from sight."

"I didn't know, I'm sorry," she said.

Kellen stood and began pacing. Nessa wasn't sure what to do. Did she feel guilty about not saying anything sooner? Yes, but it wasn't as if she hadn't tried to help them. How was she supposed to know they could have been hidden from view?

Up until she was captured by them, she hadn't even known that Demons were real, and she didn't know about Shifters until she turned into one. So how the hell was she supposed to know there was also magic in the world?

Was she meant to assume every creature imaginable was real? If so, that was a hell of a lot to take in.

"You're pissed off with me, aren't you?" Nessa asked, unable to bear the silence any longer.

"Of course, I'm pissed, Nessa," Kellen told her. "What did you expect? You've kept this a secret while knowing all along that lives were at stake. Anything could have happened to those people since you left, and we could have prevented at least some of it if we'd known about them sooner."

"I'm sorry," Nessa said.

"Sorry doesn't change what's happened to them," he said angrily.

"I know," Nessa said quietly as she looked down at her hands.

"Come on, let's go," he said after a moment.

"Where are we going?" she asked, worriedly.

"Rush needs to know this," he said. "So that's where we're going."

"Okay," she said, following him outside.

"Be warned, he's going to ask you a lot of questions," Kellen said.

"I know," she said, barely keeping up with him.

She didn't want to ask him to slow down. Kellen was already pissed off with her, she didn't want to give him even more reason to be. So, she kept up with him as best as she could.

Chapter Twenty-Nine

Of course Kellen was pissed off with Nessa. Did she really think he wouldn't be? After all the time they had spent together, she could have told him long before now. She had plenty of opportunities to tell him in the Human or Shifter realm. So, yes, he was pissed it had taken her until now to finally say something to him.

He couldn't help thinking about the people she left behind. He knew she wouldn't have been able to help them on her own, he wasn't angry that she didn't try rescuing them by herself.

What he was pissed about, was the fact she's waited until now to say something, when she could have said something sooner. They could have been rescued days ago if she'd told him when they first met.

He just hoped it wasn't too late. Mostly so she didn't

feel the guilt of not helping them. Which was one of the reasons he was racing over to Rush's house.

He'd already given Rush the rundown over a tele-pathic link. Hopefully by the time he arrived at Rush's house with Nessa, everyone else would be there ready and waiting to go. If they stood any chance in rescuing those people, they had to move quickly.

"Not far now," he told Nessa.

"Okay," she puffed as she all but ran alongside him.

Kellen could see that she was struggling to keep up. If they weren't in such a hurry, then he would have slowed down for her. As it was, they were on a time limit, and not by their choosing.

A couple of minutes later, they were walking through Rush's back door into the kitchen.

As he hoped, the place was packed with hunters. He wasn't surprised none of the other Shifter species were here. Kellen didn't know if it was a decision Rush made, or if they just didn't think it had anything to do with them.

It wouldn't be the first time something that involved all of the species was left for the wolves to clean up. The other species do generally join in after a while, but they have to be shown hard evidence that whatever is going on effects them as well.

Kellen understood why they were like that, he would be the same if he were in their boots, but it did make life a hell of a lot more complicated when it was just left to the wolves to deal with. Sometimes…not often, but sometimes…they needed a little help from the others.

Not that Rush would ever admit it, but even he some-times needed their help as well.

"About time you got here," Rush said as a greeting.

"We got here as quickly as we could," Kellen assured him.

"Right," Rush said, grabbing everyone's attention. "Now that we are all here, and everyone has been briefed on what has been going on, we can get a move on. These people aren't going to be waiting around for long. Especially if they know we are on to them, they'll have the prisoners moved in no time."

"Are we all going?" Kellen asked.

"No," Rush said. "I've already split us into groups. The same as last time, some people will stay behind and look after everyone here, the rest will come with us."

"Are there more people going this time?" Kellen asked.

It wasn't that they didn't have enough people on their side last time, but from what Nessa has told him, they were going to need a lot more people, even if it's just to help the prisoners.

He couldn't imagine they would be in much of a state to be traveling far on their own, especially if they've been locked up for weeks on end.

When they had rescued Anya after she was taken, they had ended up having to fight their way through a horde of Imfera Demons to get to her. None of their people had been injured in the fight, but Anya's friend had disappeared at the end.

Nobody had seen or heard from her since then. There

was a lot of speculation as to what happened to her, but no-one knew for sure what really happened to her.

Anya was convinced Sasha was in trouble, and she wasn't going to stop looking until she found her. Connor tried telling her that Sasha had probably gone back home, but she wasn't having any of it. Kellen knew Connor didn't believe it either, he was just trying to reassure her.

"Don't worry," Rush said. "There'll be plenty of hunters going with us."

"Good," he said.

"Are you sure you can show us the way?" Rush asked Nessa.

"Yes," she said quietly. "I know the way. Just take me back to the Human realm and I'll show you."

"Good," Rush said, nodding at her.

It was no surprise that Connor and Aidan were here. Kellen didn't think Anya would have been though. He bet Connor wasn't happy about her being here, but knowing Anya, she wouldn't have had it any other way.

Kellen had to admit, if they didn't need Nessa's help in finding the place, he wouldn't want her here either.

From the look on her face, Nessa didn't want to be here to begin with, so he couldn't see her putting up much of a fight if he told her to stay behind. She would probably stay willingly if she could.

He didn't blame her for not wanting to go with them. If she'd been treated anything like Anya had, then he completely understood.

"Are you sure you're okay with this?" he asked her.

"Yes," she said, barely looking him in the eye.

Kellen knew he'd upset her this morning, and knew he needed to make it up to her, but this wasn't the time or place. He would have to wait until they returned.

"Don't worry," Anya said, walking over to them. "We'll make sure you'll be safe."

"It's okay," Nessa said, smiling weakly. "You don't have to. I'll be fine."

"Anya's right," Connor said. "We'll all be there; we'll all look out for you."

"Stick with us, sweetheart," Aidan said, nudging his shoulder against hers. "We'll make sure you're good."

"Honestly," she said to all of them. "It's okay, you don't need to look out for me. I can take care of myself; I always have done."

Her words said one thing but her body language said something completely different. As much as she tried to hide it, it wasn't hard to see her hands shaking. She was scared, but she was trying not to show it.

Kellen wanted to shake her and tell her she'll never have to fight alone again, that he would always be by her side, but he didn't think she would appreciate him doing that in a room full of strangers.

He may know every single person in the room, but he had to remember she only knew a couple of people. All of which were stood around her, showing her that she wasn't alone anymore.

She had friends here, she had family here. All she had to do was look around her. Not a single person in this room, whether she knows them or not, wouldn't lay down their lives to protect hers.

Before he could tell her any of that, Rush shouted. "Let's go."

Kellen stuck close to Nessa as everyone began to file out of Rush's house. Some people broke off from the group, they were the ones staying behind, but the vast majority headed towards the portal to the Human realm.

Rush was right, with the amount going with them, they should have more than enough of their people to cover all basis.

Kellen had a feeling Nash was just as prepared as they were. Since they didn't know who else was working with Nash, they had to assume it wasn't going to be just him and the Imfera Demons. Not that they weren't enough to deal with, but still, it was possible there would be others there as well.

They still didn't know what happened to the Witch Nash was previously working with. As far as they knew, she could still be hanging around somewhere. Kellen hoped not, it was bad enough with the Imfera Demons and their fireballs, without having magic thrown into the mix.

"No matter what happens," Kellen said to Nessa. "Don't wonder off on your own."

"Don't worry, I won't," she said.

"There's safety in numbers," Anya said, backing Kellen up.

"Yeah, I know," Nessa said. "But seriously, you don't have to worry, I'm not going anywhere. I promised I'd show you where to go so we can finally break those people out, and I don't break my promises."

That's not what Kellen meant, but he didn't bother correcting her. Even though he didn't know her all that well yet, Kellen knew she wasn't the type of person to break a promise, or run away when she could be of help.

"We might find Sasha there," Anya said, hope filling her voice.

Kellen was glad she changed the subject. He couldn't think of what to say to Nessa. Whatever he said at the moment, Nessa seemed to take the wrong way, or miss understand.

"Don't get your hopes up, my love," Connor said gently. "She might not be there."

"Yeah, I know," Anya said.

"We will find her, my love, I promise," Connor said. "It just might not be today."

Anya gazed up at Connor, with love shining in her eyes.

"I know we will," Anya said.

"Will you two get a room already," Aidan said. "Giving each other gooey eyes every two minutes, it's enough to make a man sick."

Connor punched Aidan in the arm. "You're just jealous."

"Wait until you find your mate," Anya said. "I bet you'll be just as gooey eyed as we are."

"Yeah, whatever," Aidan said. "Haven't you heard? I'm going to stay single for the rest of my life. Less hassle that way."

Kellen and Connor laughed. They knew Aidan wanted to find his mate; he just didn't want to admit he was the biggest softy out of all three of them.

There was only him left now, to find his mate. Connor had Anya, and now Kellen had Nessa. If she would have him, that is. After this morning, Kellen wasn't so sure she would want to be his mate.

When they returned to the Shifter realm again, they had a lot to discuss... and he had a lot to make up for. Maybe if he'd told her what happened to Anya instead of keeping it a secret from her, then maybe she would have opened up to him sooner about what happened to her. Kellen knew he was as much to blame for those people still being held prisoner as she was.

Now, it was time to remedy the situation with the prisoners, and then salvage what he could of his relationship with Nessa.

Chapter Thirty

Just a little more, Sasha mentally encouraged herself. *You can do it.*

She was so close now. Only a little bit more coaxing and she'll be free at last. And when she was finally free, those responsible for imprisoning her were going to regret ever laying eyes on her. She was going to make sure of it.

All hell was going to break loose along with her.

Sasha absently thought about teleporting to the Shifters realm first, to see if they wanted in on the action, but she soon crossed off the idea. She wasn't opposed to sharing the fun, but she didn't want to risk losing track of her target.

It wouldn't take much effort for them to pack up shop and move somewhere else. Sasha couldn't let that happen. These people needed to learn a lesson, and she was going to be the one to teach them.

Don't play with fire if you don't want to get burned, she thought.

Yes, she knew that comment was stupid. Imfera Demons loved playing with fire, especially if it meant throwing fireballs at people, but it didn't change the fact that they made a huge mistake in making an enemy out of her.

Think of the idiots, and they appear, she thought just as one entered the room she was being held in.

He was carrying a tray. "Here's your dinner."

Sliding it through a gap at the bottom of the door, he sneered at her, then turned and left again.

"Such manners," she said out loud.

Even though he'd left the room, she knew he heard her. Dumb? Yes. Deaf? No, they had better hearing than she did and she would have been able to hear what she said without a problem, so he definitely heard her.

Sasha didn't know what the slop was that they kept bringing her to eat. Obviously, none of them knew how to cook, but seriously? Oatmeal would be better than this shit.

The water wasn't much better either. Sasha was positive they fished it out of a muddy puddle and then tried to pass it off as fresh clean water. There was nothing fresh or clean about any of it.

Finally! Sasha shouted in her head as a hole appeared in the magic containing her.

The instant the spell broke, her magic came rushing

back, filling her to brim.

"Keep your nasty ass food and water," she said. "It's time to play."

With a flick of the wrist, the cage doors swung open. Sasha stretched her muscles before stepping out.

"Ready or not, here I come," she said.

A wicked smile on her face, Sasha rubbed her hands together as she made her way out of the room. She was going to thoroughly enjoy what was coming next.

Chapter Thirty-One

Swallowing down the bile that wanted to escape, Nessa directed Kellen to the place where she'd been held captive. As they drove closer to the building, she couldn't stop the images playing out in her mind of her time as a prisoner.

Her hands shook uncontrollably as they turned the last corner, and her heart was racing so fast she thought it might explode from her chest at any moment. It was the last place Nessa wanted to be, but she owed it to all the other prisoners there. She owed them the same chance at freedom as she's had.

The only thing that made this trip even slightly bearable was the fact she wasn't alone this time. Not only was Kellen, Aidan, Connor and Anya with her in the car, but they were also followed by a long train of cars.

Each one was packed full of wolf Shifters, and at the back there were a couple of vans large enough to fit three dozen people.

Nessa couldn't give the wolf Shifters an exact number of people that were being held there; she could only go by what she'd seen. Rush had taken that number and tripled it.

She understood why, he didn't want to leave anyone behind, so wanted to make sure there was space for everyone, but she still thought it was more than they were going to need.

"It's just at the end of this road," she told Kellen.

Nessa remembered this road all too well. Hiding in the shrubs at the side of the road whenever she heard a noise, then running for her life when they realized she'd escaped. It felt like only yesterday, when in fact it was weeks ago.

"Okay," he said, nodding.

A moment later, Kellen pulled the car over to the side of the road and switched the lights and engine off. Everyone else followed suit behind them, switching off all the lights until they were completely surrounded by darkness.

"There's still about a mile to go," Nessa told him. "You didn't need to stop yet."

"That's okay," he said. "We'll walk the rest of the way."

"That way, we can sneak up," Aidan said.

"We stand more of a chance if they don't see or hear us coming," Kellen said.

"It's a good job we arrived at night then," she said.

"Yep," Aidan said. "We can use it to cover us."

It took Nessa a couple of tries before she could grip the handle, her hands covered in sweat kept slipping. Eventually, she managed it and followed Kellen and the others over to the rest of the group.

Rush was already barking orders as they walked up, and before Nessa knew what was happening, they were splitting up into smaller groups, all heading towards the building.

This was the hardest part of the journey, following her footsteps back to the place that changed her life. Nessa still wasn't sure if her life had changed for the better or not.

Yes, there were upsides to being a Shifter. But even surrounded by others that could shift she was still alone, still that scared girl from before. Only now she was heading towards danger instead of running for her life.

"You can hang back if you want," Rush said, making her jump. "We can find our way from here."

She hadn't even noticed that he had joined their group as they walked through the dark woodlands surrounding the building. But then, she hadn't really been paying much attention to what was going on around her.

Nessa knew she should be paying more attention, but the darkness in her mind kept taking over, showing her everything she wanted to forget.

"No, it's okay," she said. "I've wanted to help those people from the minute I escaped, but I couldn't, not on my own."

"Well, now you can," Rush said. "I'm sure they'll be grateful to you either way."

Nessa wasn't so sure, but it was kind of Rush to say so. She wouldn't even blame them if they hated her for leaving them behind.

"If you do hang back, keep Anya with you," Connor said. "I would rather her not be in the middle of a fight."

"And I've told you, I'm going," Anya told him sternly.

Looking around at all of the other female Shifters with them, Nessa could see Anya's point of view. Why should it be acceptable for others and not her? Nessa would understand if Anya was a Human, but she wasn't.

"Sorry," Nessa said. "I'm with Anya on this one."

"Kellen," Connor said.

"What do you want me to do about it?" Kellen asked. "She's your mate."

Connor opened his mouth as if to say something, then thought better of it as he closed it again.

"Thanks," Anya said, linking her arm with Nessa's. "Us girls have got to stick together."

"You're welcome," Nessa said. "Though, I don't see what the problem is, there are other women here as well."

"Yes," Anya said. "There are plenty of female hunters here."

"Exactly," Connor interrupted. "Female Hunters," he said, dragging out the word 'hunters'. "It's part of their job to do this sort of shit. It's not yours."

"It could be," Anya said.

"No, it couldn't," Connor said.

"Why not?" she asked.

"Because my heart can't cope with seeing you near danger," he told her. "Let alone heading straight towards it."

Anya melted at his words. Nessa had to admit, he did choose the right things to say, even she melted a little.

Nessa would love to find someone who loved and cared for her as much as Connor did for Anya. She stupidly thought she could have that with Kellen, how wrong she'd been.

Since she told him everything this morning, he'd barely been able to look at her. It wasn't just when he was driving either. Even now, he was walking with them, but he was keeping his distance from her. Nessa couldn't deny that it hurt, but she refused point blank to let him know it.

She had decided on the drive, that once they were back in the Shifter realm, she was going to collect up all her belongs and then go back home in the Human realm. Nessa didn't belong in his world, never had and never will. So, it was best for both of them if she just leaves before it becomes even more uncomfortable between them.

"We're not far now," she whispered as they closed in on the building.

"Right," Rush said. "Everyone be quiet now. If you must talk, talk telepathically only."

A chorus of okays went round their group. Nessa assumed Rush let the other groups know the same thing because all of a sudden it was silent.

The only sound was the rustling of leaves under their feet, or was that just hers? She couldn't tell over the pounding of her heart in her ears which seemed to get louder the closer they came.

A few seconds later, the building came into view. Nessa had to fight her instincts; they were telling her to run away from this place as fast as she could. It was either that or throw up, neither of which would help the people inside.

Refusing to do either, Nessa took a deep breath and pointed to the building.

"I escaped through a door on the roof," she whispered. "Then I climbed down that ladder."

Rush opened a telepathic link with her before replying. *"Whereabouts in the building were you being held?"* he asked.

"I was held somewhere in the middle of the building," she told him. *"But there could be people on other floors as well. I didn't see much of the building, most of the time they kept me in a cell on my own."*

"Did you see any other exits apart from the one on the roof?" he asked.

"I know there is one," she said. *"But I don't know where it is."*

"That's okay," Rush said. *"One of the other groups have just pointed it out."*

"Where is it?" Kellen asked, making Nessa jump.

She hadn't realized Kellen had joined the conversation. Nessa wondered who else was listening in, but she wasn't about to ask. She was sure she'd find out sooner or later.

"It's on the left side of the building," Rush said, nodding in that direction. *"And I've just been informed that there's another one at the back that appears to be a loading bay."*

"So, what's the plan?" Aidan asked.

Before Rush had a chance to say what the plan of action was, an almighty bang came from inside the building, followed by flashes of light on the third floor.

"What the fuck was that?" Aidan asked out loud.

"I don't know, but it can't be anything good," Connor said.

"No, it can't," Rush agreed. "Come on, there's no point hanging about. Let's get in there and find out what's going on."

On mass, every group made their way towards the building. It was then that Nessa noticed the Shifters had completely circled the building. Until then, she thought they were just dotted around the perimeter.

A couple of windows were blown out as one of the groups approached the building. Glass rained down on the unsuspecting Shifters underneath.

"Watch out," one person shouted as another said: "Heads up."

Brushing off the broken glass, the Shifters involved continued on their paths. Some were climbing up the fire escape, but most were heading towards the doors at the side and back of the building.

Nessa followed her group to the side door. She was

told to stick close to them, so that was what she was doing, even if it meant running towards danger. She knew what she was getting herself into when she offered to show them the way here, she couldn't abandon them now, no matter how much she wanted to.

It seemed to take forever to make their way inside, when in fact it was only a matter of seconds.

Before she even made it through the door, a fireball flew past her, barely missing her head.

"Duck!" Aidan shouted the warning a second too late as the next one hit the side of her head, knocking her off her feet.

Crouching down next to her, Anya held out her hand to help Nessa back to her feet.

"Fuck!" she said. "That shit hurts."

"Yep," Connor said from behind Anya as he guarded his mates back. "I wouldn't recommend getting hit while in animal form, it takes ages for the fur to grow back."

"Thanks, I'll remember that," Nessa said.

Jumping to her feet, Nessa surveyed the room. Everywhere she looked, Shifters were fighting with Demons. Most were still in their Human forms, but she could see the odd one here and there fighting as wolves.

She quickly took stock of their fighting techniques of the ones in Human form and then tried to copy what they were doing. But no matter how much she tried, Nessa just couldn't fight as well as the others. It didn't help that this was the first time she'd actually been in a fight.

Nessa didn't see what Connor was worried about with Anya. She was holding her own as well as the rest of them, even in Human form. Whereas, Nessa was completely useless. The only thing she seemed able to do in this form, was dodge fireballs.

Deciding to try her luck as a panther, Nessa shifted forms. Instantly, it was like a red neon sign had lit up above her head as a barrage of fireballs headed in her direction.

Shit! She thought, doing her best to avoid them all.

What she didn't realize until it was too late, was that the Demons were doing it on purpose to separate her from the rest of the group.

When the fireballs finally stopped, Nessa quickly realized she was in deep shit. She was completely surrounded by Demons.

Chapter Thirty-Two

All hell had broken loose by the time Kellen and the rest of them made it inside the building. Covering at least six floors, the place wasn't exactly small, but it definitely felt that way with all the Demons and Shifters inside.

Some of the Shifters were fighting in wolf form, but most were still in Human form. There was no way Kellen was shifting with so many Demons in there. He'd had his fur singed once before; he didn't want to go through that again. It itched like mad until all the fur had grown back.

Kellen hated the fact Nessa was with them. He would have much preferred it if Nessa wasn't here with them. Having her so close to the evil bastards made him anxious.

When he'd seen her knocked off her feet by a fireball as soon as she stepped through the door, he instantly regretted bring her along with him. What made it worse was Kellen had seen the Demon throw the fireball, but he hadn't noticed Nessa coming through the door until it was too late to do anything about it.

Luckily enough, Nessa seemed fine when Anya helped her back to her feet. The Demon however, lived for another two seconds before Kellen snapped its neck.

He tried to keep her close to him, but she disappeared under a barrage of fireballs just after she shifted into a panther. From where Kellen stood, it appeared they were waiting for her to shift, but why?

When the fireballs eased off slightly, Nessa was nowhere in sight.

"Where the fuck is she?" he asked aloud.

"Who?" Aidan answered.

"Nessa," he said. "She was here a second ago."

"Well, she can't have gone far," Connor said, fighting a Demon behind him.

"I think I see her," Anya said.

"Where?" Kellen asked.

"It looks like the Demons have her backed into the corner over there," Anya said, pointing in the direction.

A large group of Demons were slowly closing in on Nessa as she tried to fight them off. His stomach dropped at the sight of her trying to defend herself while also avoiding the fireballs thrown her way.

"That don't look good," Aidan said, stating the obvious.

"We need to help her," Anya said.

Just as Kellen was about to start making his way over to Nessa, a loud *Boom* came from somewhere inside. Whatever the cause was, it shook the entire building, raining down bits of ceiling plaster on everyone in the room.

"What the fuck is doing that?" Aidan said.

"I don't know, and don't care at this moment in time," Kellen said, ripping the heads of two Demons blocking his way. "Nessa's in trouble."

He could see her energy starting to wan as she tried her hardest to keep the Demons back. He could see that she was also missing patches of fur along one side.

Doubling his efforts, Kellen wasted no time in tearing apart any Demon that stepped in his way. Nothing, and no-one, was going to stop him from reaching Nessa.

Aidan and Connor were right there next to him, taking care of any that came at him from the sides, and Anya was tucked in behind him. All the time they'd spent training Anya was paying off, as she held her own against the Demons.

Nessa, on the other hand, was now lying motionless on the floor. Kellen hated that there was nothing he could do to stop the Demons from getting their hands on her, but he was still too far away from her.

Just as they were about to lift her up, there was a massive explosion next to her. Chunks of brick flew out as the wall exploded, hitting most of the Demons surrounding Nessa. Then a cloud of dust swallowed the room.

When the dust cleared, Kellen looked over to the newly form hole in the wall in time to see Sasha walk through.

Sasha waved the dust away from her face. "I thought I heard more fighting."

Everyone in the room, including the Demons, stared at her with open mouths. As soon as Anya caught sight of Sasha the biggest smile Kellen had ever seen crept across her face.

"Sasha!" she squealed before racing over to her.

"Anya!" Sasha shouted, climbing over the rubble. "It's so good to see you."

"It's good to see you too," Anya said, throwing her arms around Sasha when she reached her.

Taking advantage of the distraction, the Demons tried getting the upper hand by throwing fireballs simultaneously at the Shifters.

With one flick of her wrist, Sasha extinguished every last fireball as it flew through the air. When she was finished, she turned to the Demons.

Sasha wagged her finger at them. "I don't think so boys."

With that, the last of the Demons quickly disappeared one by one.

"Yeah, I didn't think they would stick around," she said. "It was hard enough getting any of the others to stay long enough for me to kill them." Hands on her hips, she said dramatically. "It's hard to find a good fight these days."

"What the fuck are you doing here?" Rush demanded.

"A 'thank you' would have been nice," she told him. "But if you really must know, I was being held captive."

"Well, you don't look like you're being held captive now," he said.

"Of course not, hence the word *was*," she said, making air quotes with her fingers for the last word.

"Nessa!" Kellen suddenly remembered he was heading for Nessa when the wall came down.

"Who's that?" Sasha asked.

But Kellen was ignoring her now, his solely priority now was finding Nessa amongst the rubble.

"She's another Shifter," he heard Anya tell her. "She was recently turned, like me."

"Ah, I see," Sasha said. "She wasn't the only one either. There's quite a few others as well."

"I had a feeling that might be the case," Rush said.

Sasha shouted over her shoulder. "You can come in now."

A moment later, people started appearing through the wall.

Kellen didn't bother looking up to see how many people there were, not when he still hadn't found Nessa.

"I see her tail," Aidan said, grabbing his attention.

Removing the rubble from where Aidan indicated, it was only a matter of seconds before she was finally free. But she still wasn't moving. Kellen knew there and then that it had definitely been a bad idea to bring her along.

It would have been great if they had seen the last of the Demons, but they weren't that lucky. Just as Nessa was starting to stir, more of the despicable creatures turned up.

"Don't these bastards ever give up?" Connor asked.

With evil grins on their faces, one of the Demons replied to Connor's comment. "No, we don't give up."

"We'll see," Sasha said, stepping away from Anya so she had room to move.

After seeing Sasha fighting last time, he was glad she was on their side. Sasha whipped two blades out of thin air, and as graceful as Kellen remembered, she decapitated the Demon standing in front of her.

Kellen didn't have time to stand there watching Sasha all night. He needed to protect Nessa, especially since the bastards seemed hell bent on getting their hands on her.

Taking up position in front of her, Kellen along with Aidan, were able to keep the Demons at bay long enough for Nessa to regain consciousness. Once she was awake, it took her a couple of minutes to get back on her feet.

"Stay there," he told her. "We'll protect you."

He could see her out of the corner of his eye as he fought against two Demons, she was looking over to the hole in the wall and the people hiding there.

"They'll be fine," he told her, but she wasn't listening to him.

Before he could say another word, Nessa leapt past him. With claws out, she landed on top of a Demon heading towards the released prisoners.

"Fuck!" he swore.

"You really need to train her," Aidan said. "She can't just go around jumping on the enemy and hope for the best."

"Yeah, I know," Kellen said as he pulled the head off a Demon and threw it at another.

Punching through another Demons chest, he grabbed hold of the blackened heart and ripped it out.

Holding the heart up to Aidan, he said: "She's going to give me a fucking heart attack."

"Dude, that's gross," Aidan said, grimacing. "Make sure you remember to wash your hands after touching that."

Kellen couldn't help himself. He burst out laughing, garnering the attention of several Demons and Shifters, even Sasha paused to see what was so funny. When she spotted the heart in his hand, she gave him a thumbs up before turning her attention back on her assailant.

Kellen dropped the heart on the floor. "Don't worry, I will."

"Heads up!" Connor shouted from across the room as a fireball came flying towards them. Both he and Aidan leaned to the side so that it missed and hit the wall behind them.

"I think we're all going to need hosing down before going through the portal," Kellen said after decapitating another two Demons.

Kellen didn't have a clue where all the Demons were coming from. Every time they cut one down, another two appeared to take its place. It was like there was a never-ending supply of Demons, all ready and waiting to take their turn.

"Nessa's going to need more than a hosing down," Aidan said, a look of disgust on his face as nodding towards her. "She's gonna need to scrub her teeth as well."

Kellen looked round just in time to see her sinking her teeth into a Demons as Anya hit it over the head with a piece of rubble.

Aidan laughed. "At least they're working well together."

"Yeah," Kellen agreed. "That's one way to look at it, I suppose."

As soon as the last word left his mouth, a strong blast of air radiated out from Sasha, knocking everyone back a step.

She screamed "Enough!" as she sucked the air back towards her again.

Stood in the centre of a swirling vortex of wind, she looked ethereal as her pure white hair whipped around and her eyes glowed.

Before anyone could say a word, Sasha suddenly pushed outward with her hands, shooting small blades out of the vortex as she did so. Like bullets being shot from a gun, the Demons didn't stand a chance in stopping them.

Every single one of the blades hit its mark. One after another, the Demons lifeless bodies fell to the floor.

"What the fuck?" Kellen heard several people say when the last Demon fell.

"Sasha!" Rush shouted at her. When she turned her

glowing eyes on him, he added in a calm voice "It's over now."

It took a moment for Rush's words to sink in, but as soon as it did Sasha returned to her normal self and collapsed to the floor.

Rushing over to her, Anya knelt down next to Sasha and brushed her hair back from her face.

"Are you okay?" Anya asked.

Breathing heavily, Sasha managed to get out. "Yeah, I'm good now, thanks."

"Fuck me," Aidan said into the ensuing silence. "Remind me never to piss you off."

"Aidan!" Rush said sternly.

"What?" he said innocently. "I meant it in a good way."

"I'm with Aidan on this one," one of the female hunters said. "I wouldn't want to piss her off either."

"Right?" Aidan said, nodding his head. "Me and Krystal can't be the only ones."

All of the other hunters around the room voiced their agreement as well. It was a good job she was on their side because it appeared that nobody would fight her. Which would leave it down to Rush since he was alpha.

Not even Kellen was stupid enough to think he could stand against her, not after everything he's seen her do.

"Looks like you're on your own," Aidan said, slapping Rush on the back.

Aidan soon stepped away when Rush growled at him.

"Is it safe to go now?" came a timid voice from the hole in the wall.

"Soon," Rush said before barking orders at everyone.

He sent several Shifters back to collect the cars and vans. Kellen and Aidan, along with a few others, were sent to search the building to make sure they didn't leave anyone behind by mistake.

What they were going to do with all of the prisoners, Kellen didn't know. They couldn't exactly take them back to the Shifter realm if they were Human. But then, where could they take them that was safe in the Human realm until they found out who had been turned?

This was one of those times that Kellen didn't envy Rush his job. He would hate to be the alpha, having to make the difficult decisions.

At least when he left here, things could go back to normal for him. For Rush, there was going to be a lot of headache while he sorted out the mess Nash had gotten them into.

And there was still Nash to deal with at some point as well. Kellen didn't have a clue what Rush was going to do about him, but something definitely needed to be done. They couldn't have him running around ruining people's lives the way that he had been doing. The sooner they dealt with him, the better both realms would be.

Chapter Thirty-Three

Nash had watched from a distance as the wolf Shifters fought with the Imfera Demons. He knew it wouldn't be long until they found this hide-out, especially with Nessa showing them the way. But they weren't the only ones who had been fighting.

The magic no longer contained Sasha. She had fought side by side with the Shifters, even more aggressively than she had the last time. Any who stood in her way, soon fell to her feet as she cut them down.

It was always a pleasure to watch Sasha in action. She was graceful as a dancer, a deadly dancer. With a blade in each hand, she had moved seamlessly between victims, slowly making her way towards the main group of Shifters in the middle of the room.

He'd told the Queen that she would have to move

Sasha soon or risk losing her again, and he'd been right. If she expected him to capture Sasha again, then she was going to be sorely mistaken.

Nash had better things to be doing other than chasing after the same person continually. Who was to say if he caught her again, that the same thing wouldn't happen?

No, if the Queen wanted her that much, then she can chase after Sasha herself. Nash didn't care what anyone said, he'd already wasted more than enough time on the Fairies.

After tonight, Nash had a feeling he was going to have enough on his plate. There was no doubt in his mind that the Shifters weren't going to leave until they released all of the prisoners. They had already taken over half out of the building already, so it was only a matter of time before they released them all.

He wondered absently what Rush planned on doing with all of the people he was rescuing. It wasn't like he could take them all back to the Shifter realm without giving away the location of the portal to the few Humans left in the group. So, what was his plan?

"What do you want us to do?" one of the mercenaries asked as he walked up behind Nash.

"Nothing," he said.

"But the prisoners?" another mercenary asked.

"Let the wolves have them," he said. "We can always get more."

"Yes, sir," both men said in unison before leaving him alone again.

What the two mercenaries didn't know, or the wolves,

was that this wasn't his only hide-out.

Take as many of the prisoners as you like, he thought gleefully. *Because there's plenty more where they came from.*

Chapter Thirty-Four

Heartbroken, Nessa made her way back to the Shifter realm with some of the survivors, the ones that were no longer Human anyway. The rest were taken to a safe place in the Human realm until Rush knew for certain that they hadn't been turned into Shifters.

Anya had told her it was to protect the Shifter realm from the Humans, and Nessa completely understood. She knew exactly what would happen if Humans found out about Shifters, which was why she couldn't have stayed in the zoo for much longer, so she would do the same if she was in his position.

Nessa was happy, and relieved, that they were able to save so many people, but that didn't change the guilt she had at leaving them behind in the first place. That wasn't why her heart was breaking though. No, that was all for Kellen.

He had barely been able to look at her since she confessed what had happened to her. Deep down, she knew it was coming. After all, nothing good ever lasted long for her. Sooner or later, Nessa always ended up on her own, so she shouldn't have expected it to be any different with Kellen.

Nessa hadn't thought it would hurt this much though. Leaving without so much as a goodbye, but she had no choice. Kellen's actions made it clear that he didn't want anything to do with her, so she would just be causing herself more pain by staying.

Not wanting to make things difficult or uncomfortable, Nessa didn't tell anyone of her plans to go back home. It was about time she did, and now that it was safe enough, she could.

It was hard to make small talk with Anya on the way back to the Shifter realm. There was a few times Anya had tried to start up a conversation, talking about making plans with her and Connor, but Nessa didn't want to break it to Anya that she wasn't going to be around for long.

So instead, Nessa lied to her, saying that she wasn't feeling great after having a wall fall on her. The caring person that she was, Anya offered her comfort, but that just made Nessa feel even worse for lying.

On top of being heartbroken, by the time they made it back to the Shifter realm Nessa had also come to hate herself for deceiving Anya.

"Are you sure you don't want me to come back to

Kellen's with you?" Anya asked as they walked out of the cave in the Shifter realm.

"Yeah, I'm sure," Nessa said. "I'm just going to have a lie down for a little while."

"Okay," Anya said. "If you need anything though, just give me a shout."

"I will do," Nessa said. "And thanks."

"What for?" Anya asked.

"For everything," Nessa told her.

What she really wanted to say was thank you for being such a good friend, and that Nessa was going to miss her dearly when she leaves. She doubted she'd ever see Anya again, especially since she had no plans on returning to the Shifter realm.

She couldn't, not while Kellen was here. It would hurt too much to see him with someone else, she didn't want him to stay single just for her sake, but she couldn't stand by and watch him be happy with someone else. Not when she loved him so much.

Nessa didn't have a clue when it happened, but she couldn't deny that she loved him, not to herself. If anyone else asked, she would vehemently deny it, if only to protect her heart from being trampled on.

"You're more than welcome," Anya said, breaking into her thoughts. "And don't worry about Kayla disturbing you, I've told her she can stay at my house again tonight."

"Thank you," Nessa said.

Kayla hadn't even entered her mind, so Nessa was glad she was staying at Anya's house. It saved her from having to make up an excuse as to why she was leaving quickly before her brother returned.

Nessa didn't know Kayla all that well, but she had a feeling they were closer than Kellen made out they were. Which meant she would want a good enough reason so she could tell her brother, and that was the last thing Nessa wanted.

"I'll come and see you later when you're feeling better," Anya said.

"Okay, see you later," Nessa agreed before splitting off as she headed for Kellen's house.

She hoped it was the last time she'd have to lie to Anya, but she didn't know what else to say. She didn't think Anya would understand why she was going, and because she was Kellen's friend, Nessa knew Anya would feel obliged to tell him.

Nessa had always known she wasn't cut out for lying, and today had more than proved it. She hated lying, and she hated herself even more so for doing it.

One thing was for sure though, she was going to miss this realm and everyone she'd met since coming here. Everyone had been so kind to her, making her feel like one of them, which made it even harder to leave.

She didn't want to go back to the Human realm, back to hiding her other self, but she couldn't see any other option.

The walk back to Kellen's ended all too soon. Nessa wanted to take longer on the walk, but then she would risk Kellen returning before she had a chance to leave. As far as she knew, he could be back at any minute.

Luckily enough, apart from a couple of items, she hadn't unpacked. It took her less than five minutes to make sure she had everything and then she was ready to go. So, with one last look around the place, Nessa grabbed all of her bags and left.

She couldn't even take her time walking back to the portal. She needed to move fast if she wanted to go unnoticed, especially since the hunters patrolled the area. Nessa didn't know how regularly they patrolled the area, it could be every few hours, or it could be every ten minutes. Either way, she couldn't risk it.

Her vision blurred as tears streamed unchecked down her cheeks, but Nessa didn't care. After fighting back the tears all day, by the time she reached the portal she couldn't hold them back any longer. Once the flood gates were open, there was no closing them again.

Fortunately, nobody was around to see her crying, or her mad dash for the portal. It looked like she managed to get away without being seen by anyone, which was what she planned. At least, nobody that she noticed.

It meant she wouldn't be able to say goodbye to anyone, but it also meant she wouldn't have to face Kellen again. Nessa knew it was for the best, but it still hurt.

Lugging her bags through the tunnels in the cave wasn't as easy as it had been the first time through. It helped that she hadn't been trying to struggle with them all by herself, like she was this time. Since she couldn't ask anyone for help this time, she had no choice but to struggle.

Eventually, after a lot of swearing on her part, she

made it through to the Human realm. Wasting no time, Nessa loaded the bags onto her back again, and hurried down the mountain.

She kept checking behind her to make sure she hadn't been followed from the Shifter realm, but she also had to make sure she didn't bump into anyone on their way back there either.

Because she hadn't met all of the Shifters, and certainly couldn't remember half of the faces of the ones she had met, Nessa hid in the bushes every time she heard someone coming. She knew it was useless trying to hide from them, a Shifter would be able to pick up on her scent easily enough, but she couldn't help it.

Once she was away from the Shifter realm, even if it was just away from the area in Scotland where the portal was located, she should be in the clear.

Her home was nowhere near where she'd been held captive, it was on the opposite side of the country for starters. So, as long as she didn't go in that direction, she shouldn't pass any of them.

Nessa couldn't wait to get home. It had been weeks since she'd last stepped foot inside her apartment. It didn't matter that it was the size of a shoe box, it was all hers and she missed it.

She missed being able to relax at the end of a long day, watching the sunset out of her living room window. She missed saying hello to her neighbour's cat on her way up the stairs. The little tabby cat was always waiting to greet her with a meow.

But most of all, she missed having a place she could

call home.

Chapter Thirty-Five

Kellen couldn't wait to return to the Shifter realm. It had been a long night, but finally he and the others had finished searching the building. They found a couple more prisoners in the basement, but other than that the place was clean.

Just like the other building where Anya had been held, this place didn't hold much in the way of paperwork. Not that they expected to find any. It would be pretty stupid of Nash if he left anything that would give away his plans.

Nash wasn't stupid though, at least, he hadn't been back when Kellen knew him. But that was a long time ago now, anything could have changed in that time. Obviously, something had because the old Nash wouldn't have done what this new one was doing.

Kellen couldn't help but wonder what could have happened to Nash since he left the Shifter realm to turn him into a monster. Because that's exactly what he was now, he was a monster through and through.

Nobody in their right mind would play god with another being's life. And no matter what life throws at you, at the end of the day, it's the choices you make in life that define who you are. Unfortunately, Nash had made some pretty big decisions that were wrong.

"What's your plans for the rest of the night?" Aidan asked as he walked out the portal behind him.

"I need to talk with Nessa," he said reluctantly.

"In the dog house already," Aidan asked.

"Something like that," Kellen admitted.

"That didn't take you long." Aidan laughed. "What did you do?"

Kellen sighed. "I kind of snapped at her when she told me what happened to her."

"Oh," Aidan said, grimacing.

"Yeah, exactly," Kellen agreed. "I've got some serious making up to do."

"I'd say so," Aidan agreed. "But why did you snap at her? It's not exactly her fault, she couldn't have prevented what happened to her."

"It wasn't so much about what happened to her," Kellen told him. "I know she didn't have anything to do with that. What I was pissed off about, was the fact there was still people being held captive and she didn't tell anyone."

"She did tell someone, she told you," Aidan pointed

out. "And she probably waited so long because she didn't know if she could trust us, just like we didn't know if we could trust her."

"Yeah, I know," Kellen said. "But I wasn't thinking properly this morning when she told me, all I could think about were the people still being held prisoner there."

Admittedly, he could have handled it better. But what was done was done, he couldn't turn back the clocks no matter how much he wanted to. All he could do now was apologize and hope that Nessa forgives him.

Kellen didn't know what he would do if Nessa didn't forgive him, and hopefully he would never have to find out.

"Yeah, I get it," Aidan said. "I would have been concerned about those people as well, and I'm sure Nessa was too, which is probably why she told you."

"Not helping," Kellen said, feeling even more guilty now.

"I never said I was on your side," Aidan said. "It was a pretty shitty thing for you to do when she was trying to help those people. She was right to wait until she knew she could trust us. They could have ended up in an even worse situation had she told the wrong people."

"Don't you think I know that?" Kellen snapped. "I know she did the right thing in waiting. I just…"

"What?" Aidan asked when he didn't finish the sentence.

Kellen ran a hand through his hair. "I was just a dick."

"Yep," Aidan agreed, slapping Kellen on the shoul-

286

der. "That you were, but at least you're owning up to that shit. Now go and make it up to Nessa before it's too late and you lose her."

"You're right," Kellen said.

"That's a first," Aidan said.

"What?" Kellen asked, confused.

"You saying that I'm right," Aidan told him. "Can I have that in writing?"

Kellen punched Aidan playfully in the arm. "No chance."

"Worth a try," Aidan said, shrugging his shoulders.

Smiling, Kellen shook his head at Aidan. "See you later" he said before running off in the direction of his house.

"Well, good luck," Aidan shouted after him.

"Thanks," Kellen shouted back.

Running flat out, it was only a matter of minutes before he reached his home. All the lights in the house were off when he got there, making it appear as if nobody was home. He knew Kayla was staying at Anya and Connor's house again tonight, but Nessa should still be here, so there should have been some lights on in the place.

Kellen had a bad feeling in his gut when he entered the house. Everything was dark and there wasn't a single noise coming from any of the rooms. Even their scents were faint, as if nobody had been here for hours.

Heading straight for Nessa's room, hoping to find her fast asleep in bed. His heart sank when he walked in to find the bed empty and all of her belongings gone.

"Fuck!"

He quickly searched the room for any indication to where she'd gone, but there was nothing. Not a single item of hers remained, and there was no note to let him know where she'd gone either.

Kellen checked the rest of the house to be sure, but it was the same there. She'd packed up all of her belongs and left without a word.

He hoped she was still in the Shifter realm at least, but deep down he knew she'd left the realm completely and not just his house.

Frantically, Kellen raced over to Rush's house, not even stopping to close the back door behind him.

Something was wrong, he just knew it. As much as he tried, he couldn't stop the feeling of dread from building as the minutes ticked by without knowing she was safe.

Kellen shouted as he barged into Rush's house. "She's gone!"

"Who's gone?" Rush asked, unfazed about the sudden outburst.

"Nessa, she's gone," Kellen said.

"And?" Rush asked.

"Something's wrong," Kellen told him.

"Why do you think something is wrong?" Rush asked. "She could have just gone for a walk or something."

"Do you seriously think I would be here if she'd just gone for a walk?" Kellen asked.

He was slowly losing his patients with Rush. Why did he always have to ask a shit load of questions all the time?

"She's taken all of her belongings with her," Kellen said. "If she'd gone for a walk, she wouldn't have taken all of her stuff."

"Okay, so she might have gone home," Rush said.

"That's what worries me," Kellen admitted. "She could be in danger if she's returned to the Human realm. Nash is still out there somewhere, and I think he still has plans for her."

"I know he is," Rush said, shaking his head. "But not for long if I have anything to do about it."

"The Demons seemed to zero in on her in the fight," Kellen said. "They desperately wanted to get their hands on her."

"Yeah, I noticed that," Rush admitted.

"Whatever they want with her, it can't be for anything good," Kellen said.

"I see your point," Rush said. "But before we go running off to the Human realm again, we need to make sure she isn't still here somewhere."

"She isn't," Kellen said adamantly.

"How do you know?" Rush asked. "She could have gone to stay with someone else here."

"Who?" Kellen asked. "Apart from us, the only other people she has really met is Connor, Anya, and Aidan."

"Have you checked with them?" Rush asked.

"No," Kellen confessed.

"Don't you think you should have done that before racing over here?" Rush asked.

"Yeah," Kellen said reluctantly, but he didn't think she was with any of them.

For starters, he was with Aidan right before he knew she was missing, and he would have thought Connor would have given him a heads up if she was there.

Still, he opened a link with all three of them and asked *"Have any of you seen Nessa?"*

"No, sorry," Anya said straight away. *"I haven't seen her since we got back."*

"Sorry, I can't help either," Connor said. *"That was the last time I saw her too."*

"Nope, I was with you," Aidan said.

"What's happened?" Anya asked.

"Nessa's gone," Kellen told them.

"Where?" Aidan asked.

"I don't know," Kellen told them honestly. *"But I have a feeling she's gone back to the Human realm."*

"That's not good," Connor said. *"It's not safe there with Nash on the loose."*

"I know," Kellen said.

"Are you at Rush's?" Aidan asked.

"Yeah."

"Okay, we'll be right there," Connor said.

"Thanks," Kellen said before closing the link again.

"Well?" Rush asked.

"No, none of them have seen her," Kellen told him. "Not since they arrived here with her earlier."

Taking a deep breath, Rush exhaled before saying "Okay, give me ten minutes. I'll get everyone together again. Then we'll figure out what to do."

As much as he hated to wait, Kellen knew he needed help finding her. He didn't have a clue where to begin looking for her in the Human realm, she could be any-where.

If only he'd found out more about her, then he might know where she'd go. He didn't even know where she lived. Why hadn't he asked her?

He knew she didn't live at the caravan site where he'd first seen her, it was obvious from the bags of clothes and lack of any other personal affects. So why hadn't he thought to ask her where she was from?

Because he hadn't thought she would go back there, that's why. He stupidly believed she'd stay in the Shifter realm, and she probably would have done if he hadn't lost his temper and spoken to her like a piece of shit.

It was all his fault she left, and he knew it. Whatever happened to her now was his fault because if it wasn't for him, then she wouldn't have left.

"Stop blaming yourself," Rush said, reading his mind. "It's not your fault."

"Yes, it is," Kellen said. "If I hadn't spoken to her like shit, she wouldn't have left. In fact, if I'd just apol-ogized sooner, then she wouldn't have gone. But no, I waited too long," he said, shaking his head. "So, yes, it is all my fault."

Nothing anyone said was going to change his mind either. He was man enough to admit he was wrong, he just wished he'd had the chance to tell Nessa. Hopefully though, it wasn't too late to fix things. Hopefully, he'll be able to find her quickly before any harm comes to her.

If not, he didn't know what he was going to do. He

couldn't live without her now that he's found her. He would follow her into the afterlife if he had to. But that would leave his sister all alone in the world, and he couldn't do that to her.

Kellen needed Nessa, not just for himself, but for Kayla as well.

Chapter Thirty-Six

Nessa was glad to finally be home. It had taken her hours to get here, but she didn't care. She was home at last.

So much had changed since she was last here… she had changed. Nessa wasn't the same person she once was, and she wasn't even talking about being able to shift into an animal either.

With everything she'd been through over the last few weeks, it was no surprise she wasn't the same person. How much she wished she could turn back the time, do things differently, especially where Kellen was concerned.

But she couldn't. No matter how much she wanted to change things, she couldn't. She'd made her bed, so now she had to lie in it…alone.

Being alone wasn't new to her, it had been that way since her parents died. Until now it never bothered her, until she met Kellen, she was content being alone.

That was a lie. If she were brutally honest with herself, she'd never been content by herself. She'd always longed to have someone special in her life. Unfortunately, she managed to screw up the first good thing to happen to her in a very long time.

After a long hot soak in the bath, Nessa curled up on the sofa in her pyjamas to watch TV. As she flicked through the channels looking for something to watch, her mind kept bring up images of Kellen.

It hadn't even been twenty-four hours, yet she missed him so much. It felt like someone had ripped out her heart and trampled on it. As much as she tried to stop the images playing out in her mind, they just wouldn't stop.

Lifting her hand to her face, Nessa felt tears on her cheeks. She hadn't even realized she'd been crying until then. Nessa thought she was all cried out from earlier, but obviously not.

Nessa didn't know how long she sat there with the remote in her hand staring at a static screen, but she decided enough was enough. There was no point moping around the place, nothing was going to change.

Wiping them away, she switched off the TV and was about to go to bed when she heard someone knocking at her door.

Climbing to her feet, Nessa made her way over to door. Without looking through the peephole, she swung the door wide open and instantly regretted it.

Standing on the other side were the same Demons from the fight. She recognized one of them, it was the same one that brought most of her meals when she'd been their prisoner.

"Hello again, kitty cat," he said.

Nessa tried slamming the door closed again, but he put his foot in the way stopping her.

Turning on her heels quickly, she attempted to run to the bathroom so she could at least have one locked door between them. She knew that it would be a waste of time, but she had to do something.

There was no way on earth she was going to let them take her without a fight. If she could avoid the fight part then it would be even better, especially since she couldn't fight for shit. She knew that after the last encounter with them.

If it hadn't been for the other Shifters with her last time, then Nessa was under no illusion that she would be dead already. Unfortunately, her attempts at escape were thwarted just as swiftly as her attempt to close the door.

"I don't think so, kitty cat," the Demon said smugly as he grabbed hold of her hair and yanked on it, stopping her dead in her tracks. "You're staying right here."

Nessa screamed as she was suddenly jerked backwards by her hair. Losing her footing and making her fall into him. Reaching up with her hands, she tried to relieve some of the pain radiating over her scalp, but it didn't work.

If anything, the Demon gripped harder and pulled it tighter.

"We're going to have some fun," he whispered into her ear.

Dread churned in her stomach as the other Demons started to laugh. Holding a hand over her mouth, he dragged her back into the apartment.

Nessa knew she was in deep shit when he finally released her. As soon as the door closed behind them, he pushed her into the middle of the room.

Landing on her hands and knees, Nessa wished she was anywhere but here. Why had she thought it would be safe to return home?

There was nowhere for her to run, they blocked every possible exit as they completely surrounded her. Each one of them had a menacing grin on their faces, exposing their sharp teeth to her.

Before she could climb to her feet, or even get her bearings, one of the Demons kicked her in the stomach, knocking the wind out of her. Nessa didn't stand a chance in defending herself.

One after another, they took it in turns kicking her around the room, passing to each other like it was a game. Which it probably was to them, but not for her. Now she knew what it was like for a football.

Every time they made contact, pain shot throughout her body. They didn't care where their kicks landed. Face, chest, stomach, legs, it was all the same to them.

She couldn't even shift into a panther to defend herself. She could barely breathe let alone think straight

296

enough to call on the change. So, she had no choice but to take the beating and hope that they at least left her alive at the end of it.

Knowing her luck recently though, she'd be dead long before they'd finished having their fun. And through it all, Kellen's face kept flashing in her mind, reminding her of what she'd left behind.

With one final swift kick in the side of the head, all the pain disappeared as everything went black.

Chapter Thirty-Seven

"For fuck sake," Sasha said, throwing her hands up. "Can't any of you Shifters keep a close watch on your mates?"

Kellen growled at her.

"No point growling at me," she told him. "I'm not the one that made her run off now, am I."

She knew he was worried about Nessa, but there was still no need to be growling at her when she'd offered to help. After all, she wasn't the reason Nessa had run off, he was.

"Are you going to help us, or what?" Rush asked.

"Of course, I'm going to help," she said. "But don't think for one minute I'm doing it for him," she pointed at Kellen. "I'm doing it for Nessa."

"Thank you," Rush said, nodding at her.

"So, what's the plan?" she asked.

"I was hoping you'd be able to teleport some of us to her," Rush said.

"Sorry, no can do," she said.

If it was possible, she would have already done that as soon as she heard Nessa had gone. Even though she didn't know the female, she still didn't want anything bad to happen to her. And until the rogue wolf was dealt with, it wasn't safe in the Human realm.

"Why can't you just teleport us to her like you did with Anya?" Aidan asked.

"Because I don't know her," Sasha told him.

"I don't see the difference," Aidan said. "It can't be that hard."

"Can you do it?" she asked angrily.

"Um, no," Aidan said.

"Well then," she snapped. "Don't fucking comment on shit you have no idea what you're talking about."

"Okay, okay," he said, hands up as he backed away.

Sighing, Sasha explained "I knew Anya really well, to the point I could pinpoint her location at the snap of my fingers, but I don't know Nessa. I didn't even get a good look at her in Human form."

"Could you use something that belongs to her to pinpoint her location?" Connor asked.

"I'm not a fucking blood hound," she said, looking at him as if he was stupid.

"I wasn't suggesting that you were," Connor said.

"Yes, you were," she said.

"That's not how I meant it to sound," he told her. "So,

I apologize if that's how it came across."

"Apology accepted," she told him.

"Well, if you can't teleport us to her, we'll have to find another way," Rush said.

Everyone seemed to start talking at once, and before long she couldn't hear herself think.

She watched as Kellen began to pace. Sasha couldn't imagine what he was going through. Other than Anya, there wasn't really anyone she cared about, but Anya was more like a little sister than anything.

Doing her best to drown out the noise, she racked her brain for a solution. There had to be some way for her to find Nessa using her magic. Otherwise, what was the point in having it?

Maybe she didn't need to use magic to find Nessa after all. Or at least, not only by using magic. Maybe she just needed to use her brains because it was obvious no-one else here was. But first, she needed more information about her.

"There might be one way," she said loud enough to grab everyone's attention.

Instantly the room was silent as they waited for her to explain.

"How?" Kellen was the one to finally ask.

"Tell me how you met her," she said.

"How's that supposed to help?" he asked, sceptically.

Sasha sighed. "Just tell me as much detail as you can, like where you meet her for the first time? Do you know where she was staying when you first met? That kind of thing."

"Fine," Kellen said. "But I don't see how it'll help."

"And you won't if you don't give it a try," she pointed out.

Luckily enough, he didn't ask her any more stupid questions. Instead, he gave her every little detail about how they met and anything else she might find helpful.

When he finally finished speaking, Sasha climbed to her feet.

"Right, let's go," she said.

"Where are we going?" Rush asked, confused.

"Back to the beginning," she said. "Where else would you start?"

Just because Nessa didn't leave anything in the caravan for them to find, didn't mean there wasn't anything for her to follow. And since she spent the most amount of time there, that was the best place to look.

"Sounds like a complete waste of time," Kellen said.

"Well, from the sounds of it," she interjected. "You didn't bother to check the campsite office for clues, did you?"

Kellen, Aidan, Connor, and Anya all looked to one another before they said in unison "no".

"My point exactly," Sasha said smugly. "None of you thought to check what details of hers they have on their computer system. That's a rookie mistake."

She could see that they were about to argue their case, but Rush beat them to it when he agreed with her.

"Yes, you should have checked out her info while you were there," Rush told them. "It could have saved a lot of time, time she might not have."

"Well, no point hanging around," she said as she lifted her arms out to the side. "So, if you're coming with, then grab hold."

It was no surprise that Kellen was the first to take hold of her arm.

"Is that it?" she asked when the last person grabbed hold. "Or do you want me to come back for more?"

"That's it," Rush said. "The six of us should be more than enough."

"If not, I can always come back later for more," she added.

Before Rush could agree or disagree, she teleported them to the campsite Kellen had told her about.

Chapter Thirty-Eight

It didn't take long for them to find what they were after, but if it hadn't been for Sasha, they wouldn't have had a clue where to even begin looking.

As soon as they reached the campsite, they headed straight for the main building. Kellen could have kicked himself for not checking the office when he first came across Nessa. It would have saved them a hell of a lot of time.

Using her magic, Sasha unlocked the door leading into the main building and the office where the computer was held.

"Give me a minute and I'll have the info we need," Anya said, sitting down at the desk.

"I've disabled the security cameras and alarm system as well," Sasha said. "So, we shouldn't be disturbed."

"Good," Rush said. "The last thing we need is the Humans on our case."

"Got it," Anya said a moment later.

"That was quick," Aidan said. "I thought it would take you longer than that."

"Piece of cake," she said, shrugging a shoulder. "It's only a simple spread sheet, so it was easy to find, especially since we knew the dates. Plus, there weren't many people booked in on those dates which helped."

After telling them the location, Sasha held out her arms again for them to grab onto. Seconds later they were stood outside an apartment building.

"Why are we out here?" Kellen asked when she teleported them to Nessa's home. "Why didn't you teleport us inside her apartment?"

"Because that's bad manners," Sasha told him. "She might not appreciate all of us appearing in her living room."

"Fine," he said.

Storming into the building, Kellen didn't bother to check if anyone else was going with him.

"What number is it?" Rush asked from behind him as he stopped to check the sign.

"Fifteen," he said over his shoulder, not bothering to stop.

"Third floor then," Rush shouted after him.

Taking the stairs two at a time, it didn't take long to reach the third floor. Within seconds, he was outside her front door.

Just as he was about to kick the door in, Rush stood

in his way.

"Knock first," Rush told him.

"Why?"

"Because she might be sat in there minding her own business watching TV," Rush said. "Or, you never know, she could be fast asleep."

"She's doing neither of those things," Kellen said. "She's in trouble, I know she is."

"Knock first," Rush said again.

"Get out the way then," Kellen said between gritted teeth.

Rush stood there a moment longer before moving out of the way. Kellen didn't waste any time, knocking as loudly as he could.

"Subtle much?" Sasha asked sarcastically.

"If you're not going to help, then shut up," Kellen told her.

"Tell you what," she said. "There's a quicker way to do this. Just wait here a sec."

Before anyone had the chance to ask what she meant, she vanished. A minute later, Nessa's front door opened on its own.

"In here," Sasha shouted from inside the apartment. "And hurry up."

Kellen didn't need to be told twice. He raced into the apartment, not stopping until he reached Sasha in the bedroom.

Stood at the end of the bed, Sasha was looking at something on the floor next to the bed.

Sasha turned to him with sadness in her eyes. "It's

not good."

That's when he heard a faint wheezing sound coming from next to the bed.

Walking over to Sasha, dread churned in his stomach at what he was about to see. Absently, he heard everyone else join him in the room, but he didn't pay them any attention. Everything in him was focused solely on Nessa.

Sasha stepped out the way so he could pass, and that was when he saw her. Sprawled on the floor next to her bed, Nessa was a bloody mess. Every inch of her covered in blood, he could just about make out the bruises hidden beneath.

"Shit!" he heard from behind him.

Kneeling down next to her, Kellen gently lifted her into his arms. Holding her broken and bruised body as carefully as he could, he stood and turned to the others.

"We need to get her to medical," he said.

"Sasha," Rush said.

"On it."

Touching his shoulder, she teleported them straight to medical before going back for the others.

"Candi!" Kellen shouted to one of the healers on duty.

"What's happened?" she said, rushing through the door a moment later.

"She's badly injured," he said, placing her gently on the bed. "I think she's been beaten."

"Right," Candi said. "Help me get her clothes off and cleaned up so we know what we're dealing with."

"Okay," he said.

Following Candi's lead, he removed all of her clothes then started to wash away the blood with a damp cloth.

In some places the blood had already dried, making it harder to wash off.

"How is she?" Rush asked as he entered the room.

"Not good from the looks of things so far," Candi told him, not stopping in her task. "She has several broken bones, some severe cuts, and nearly every inch of her is covered in bruises." Candi shook her head as she added "I have a feeling she has a punctured lung as well."

"Shit," Rush said, rubbing his brow.

"She's going to be in a hell of a lot of pain when she wakes up, that's for sure," Candi said. "I just hope she stays unconscious until we've finished cleaning her up and dealt with her lung."

"I can help keep her asleep," Sasha said from the doorway.

Kellen hadn't even realized she was stood there listening until then.

"The problem is, I need her to wake up so I know if she's got a head injury," Candi said. "Other than what we can see, that is."

"I can check for you without waking her," Sasha said.

"Then, yes," Candi said, stepping to the side for Sasha. "Thank you."

"Anything to help," Sasha said with a small smile.

Kellen didn't trust himself to say anything, so he stood back slightly and watched Sasha closely, making sure she didn't cause Nessa any unnecessary pain. Not that he thought she would do it on purpose, but Nessa had suffered enough, he didn't want her to hurt more.

Leaning over the bed, Sasha loosely held her hands to either side of Nessa's head and then slowly closed her eyes. When they opened again, her eyes were glowing white as she stared at the wall above Nessa's head.

It felt like eternity as she stared unblinking at the wall. Kellen wanted to shake her, he wanted...needed...to know that Nessa was going to be okay. But at the same time, he didn't dare disturb Sasha just in case it caused Nessa pain.

Everyone in the room seemed to hold their breath as they waited for the news.

Closing her eyes again, Sasha removed her hands before standing back.

"Well?" Rush was the one to ask.

"Candi's right, she has a punctured lung," Sasha said.

"What about her head?" Candi asked.

"She has a fractured skull in two places, and a lot of swelling around the brain." Sasha said, shaking her head. "I've mended what I can, there's no more swelling, but it will take a while for the bone to mend completely. I've also made sure she won't wake up until she's fully healed, which for her should be in a couple of weeks."

That was one of the bonuses of being a Shifter, they healed a lot quicker than Humans.

"Think yourself lucky she wasn't Human," Sasha said. "She would have been dead before we got to her. But she's not out of the woods yet, you need to deal with the punctured lung."

"Couldn't you heal that as well?" Kellen asked.

"Sorry," she said, turning to him. "I already pushed my limits dealing with the swelling and fractures in her head, otherwise I would have."

"That's okay," Candi said. "I can sort the rest of her."

"What do you need?" Rush asked.

"For you all to leave so I can get on with my job," Candi said.

"I'm not going anywhere," Kellen said, standing firm.

"I didn't think you would," Candi said, looking at him. "But you will need to scrub up if you're staying in here, and make sure you keep out the way while I work."

Without saying a word, Kellen nodded at her before he walked over to the sink to scrub his hands. He tried his hardest not to pay attention to all the blood…Nessa's blood…as it swirled around the sink before washing away down the drain.

"Okay," Rush said. "Let me know when you're finished."

"Will do," Candi said. "Oh, and send in Willow to help me."

"Okay," Rush said as he followed Sasha out the room.

Just as Kellen was drying his hands, Willow came running in the room.

"What do you need?" she asked.

Candi didn't hesitate in rattling off a list of things they were going to need. Kellen didn't bother listening to what she needed. For starters, he didn't know where half the things she was asking for were kept. He knew what most of them were, but there was a couple that he'd never heard of, so he would probably end up bring Candi the wrong items.

Within minutes, Nessa was hooked up to a load of machines as Candi prepared to fix her punctured lung and set her broken bones. There wasn't much that could be done about the cuts other than cleaning and bandaging them. The bruises would eventually disappear, it would just take some time.

Kellen felt helpless as he watched Candi get to work. He was a hunter, not a healer. So, he was completely out of his depth here, but until he knew Nessa was going to be okay, he wasn't going to leave her side.

Even after she makes a full recovery, which she will because he'll make sure of it, he didn't ever want to let her out of his sight again. Kellen knew he had a lot of apologizing to do first, but he wanted Nessa to live with him and Kayla, and he'd do anything to make that happen.

It took Candi and Willow hours, but they finally stood back after doing everything they could do to help Nessa.

"Right," Candi said, sighing. "That's all I can do, it's down to Nessa's own healing abilities now."

Walking over to the sink, she started washing away the blood on her hands and arms.

"How long will it be before she's awake?" he asked.

"I don't know," she said honestly. "It could be a couple of days, or it could be a couple of weeks. It all depends on how quickly her body can heal itself. The good thing about her being a Shifter is she should heal pretty quickly, but it doesn't mean she will. It all depends on her."

"We'll keep a close eye on her over the next couple of hours," Willow added. "Just to be sure she's healing correctly and that there's no complications."

"Why don't you go and get some rest," Candi told him. "We won't know anything for at least a couple of hours."

"No," he said adamantly. "I'm not leaving her side."

"You really should," Candi said.

"No!" he snapped.

"Okay," Candi said, holding her hands up.

"I'll bring you a chair," Willow said. "There's no point in you standing the whole time. She's going to be here for a while, so you might as well get comfy if you're staying too."

"Thank you," he said, turning back to Nessa.

Seeing her with a tube stuck down her throat and wires attached to her made his heart ache. Kellen would give anything to take her place, him be lying in that bed instead of her. Knowing she wasn't going to wake up until she'd healed was a blessing and a curse.

He wanted… needed… her to be okay. Because without Nessa, Kellen had nothing to live for. She was his life, his love… his mate.

Chapter Thirty-Nine

Nessa pulled the blankets up around her. She didn't want to wake up yet, she was too comfortable and nothing hurt while she was sleeping. She didn't want to deal with the pain that was inevitable after the beating she'd just had. But no matter how hard she tried to avoid it; she couldn't prevent herself from waking up.

Expecting the pain to hit her at any second, she was surprised when there was nothing. Not even a twinge of a headache from where she'd been kicked in the head. There was absolutely nothing.

What the fuck?

Had she imagined the beating? No, that couldn't be right, she wasn't losing her mind. But why wasn't she in pain?

"Are you awake?" she heard Anya whisper.

"Am I dead?" she asked, not wanting to open her eyes.

"No," Anya said. "But you came close."

That got her attention. Finally opening her eyes, she noticed Anya sitting in a chair facing her.

"Where am I?" Nessa asked, not recognizing the room.

"You're in medical," Anya told her. "We brought you straight here. You were pretty beaten up when we found you, what happened?"

"Demons," Nessa told her. "They turned up at my door."

"We thought as much," Anya said, shaking her head.

Pushing herself up right, she moved back so she could lean against the head rest. Still expecting the pain to hit, she moved with caution. She breathed a sigh of relief when nothing came.

"How long have I been out for?" she asked.

"Two weeks," Anya told her. "My friend, Sasha, made sure you stayed asleep until you were fully recovered."

Well, that explains why she'd been asleep for so long, but that didn't explain why she didn't hurt anymore. As far as she could tell, she didn't have a single wound on her, which made absolutely no sense.

"Shifters heal quicker than Humans," Anya said, reading her mind.

"Oh," Nessa said. "I didn't know, but that explains a lot."

"Yeah, it's one of the perks," a young pretty woman with mousy brown hair and warm hazel eyes said as she walked in the room.

"This is Candi," Anya introduced the woman. "She's been looking after you while you've been asleep."

"Thank you," Nessa said.

"You're welcome," Candi said. "But I can't take all the credit. Kellen did most of it."

Now that surprised her. After the way things ended with them, she would have thought he would be the last person to look after her.

"Really?" she said before she thought better of it.

"Yep," Candi said. "He hasn't left your side since we found you."

That brought up another question.

"How did you find me?" she asked. "I didn't tell anyone where I lived."

"You can thank Sasha for that as well," Anya said. "If it wasn't for her idea to check out what details the campsite had of yours, then we'd still be looking for you."

"Yeah, they wouldn't let me book a caravan unless I gave them a home address," she said, glad they had insisted.

Nessa had asked if she could leave that part out of the booking form, but the campsite was having none of it, which she was now grateful for. If it hadn't been for their insistence, there was no knowing how long she would have been laying half dead in her apartment.

"Are you hungry?" Candi asked.

"I'm starving," she said, her stomach rumbling for emphasis.

"Good," Candi said. "Because Willow will be here any minute with something for you to eat."

"Thank you," Nessa said.

"You're welcome," Candi said. "Once you've eaten, as long as you're feeling okay, then I don't see any reason you can't go."

"Um… thanks," Nessa said.

She didn't have a clue where she was going to go because it definitely wasn't safe in the Human realm, so she couldn't return home. There was nowhere here for her either, at least not with the wolf Shifters.

Maybe she could join the other panther Shifters living in this realm. But what was she going to do about all of her belongings? Nessa hadn't even been conscious when they brought her here, so as far as she knew all her belongings were still in the Human realm.

Nessa didn't even feel safe enough to return for them, so she didn't know what she was going to do about it. She might end up having to replace everything she's left behind. It was the safest option, but she didn't want to leave the few items she had left of her parents.

"I wouldn't recommend going back to the Human realm any time soon," Candi said. "Until Nash is dealt with, it's not safe."

"I don't want to," Nessa said truthfully. "But I need to at some point, to collect my things."

"Don't worry about that," Anya said. "Connor and Aidan have brought all of your things here. I hope you don't mind, but they also handed the keys back to your landlord. We all thought it would be safer if you stayed here, at least for the time being."

"Um… thank you, I guess," Nessa said.

She appreciated them looking out for her, but it didn't solve the problem of where she was going to stay. If anything, it made things worse because now she really was homeless.

Nessa had been lucky her landlord hadn't taken back the place after she hadn't been there for weeks, but she didn't think he would give it back to her now. She was probably more trouble than she was worth.

Plus, she didn't know how much damage the Demons had done to the apartment after they had finished kicking shit out of her. For all she knew, the place could have been completely trashed. In which case, she was glad she didn't have to explain to her landlord about the damages.

"Don't worry, though, you're not homeless," Candi told her. "There's plenty of places for you to stay here."

"For starters, you can always stay with me and Connor if you want," Anya offered.

"Thank you," Nessa said. "I might take you up on the offer. But truthfully, it would be nice to spend some time with other panther Shifters. Kellen mentioned that a group lived not far from here."

"That's true," Candi said. "The feline territory borders ours."

"They have some lovely tree houses," another woman said as she walked in carrying a tray of food.

This woman, with masses of curly sun kissed auburn hair and bright blue eyes, smiled warmly at Nessa as she carried the tray over and placed it on her lap. She appeared to be much younger than Candi, the small scattering of freckles across the bridge of her nose added to the perception.

Nessa knew Shifters aged differently than Humans, but it hadn't been as obvious until now. Neither Candi nor Willow looked old enough to be a doctor or nurse, yet here they were taking care of her.

"I can vouch for that," Candi said. "And they're more spacious inside than they look."

"Hi, I'm Willow," she introduced herself.

"Hi," Nessa said. "Thank you for the food."

"You're more than welcome, Nessa," Willow said. "It's nice to finally meet you, Kellen's told me a lot about you."

"Really?" Nessa asked, surprised.

"Yes," Willow said. "He hasn't left your side since you arrived."

"Oh."

"Rush had to order him to go home and get some rest, or at least a change of clothes," Willow said. "But to be honest, I don't think Kellen will be gone too long. He really didn't want to leave you."

That shocked Nessa. Last time she's seen him, she got the impression he couldn't wait to get away from her. She hoped he didn't feel responsible for what happened to her because it wasn't his fault. She should have known to be more careful, and to keep her guard up, but she hadn't done either.

"I wasn't sure what you'd want to drink," Willow

continued. "So, I brought you a couple of options."

"Thank you," Nessa said, looking at the array of food and drink on the tray, but not really seeing any of it.

Her mind was filled with thoughts of Kellen. She couldn't imagine him taking care of her while she'd been asleep for all this time. Nessa couldn't help wondering if he'd been the one to clean her.

Not that he hadn't seen her body before, but somehow it felt different. It felt more intimate knowing he'd been the one taking care of her when she couldn't take care of herself. She knew it sounded strange, but that's how it felt to her.

"Talk of the devil," Anya said as Kellen walked through the door.

"I was wondering why my ears were burning," Kellen said, smiling at Anya before turning that smile on her. "It's good to see you awake. How are you feeling?"

"Um… better… thanks," she stuttered.

"I've said that Nessa can go once she's eaten something," Candi said. "I just want to make sure she can keep some food down first."

"I hope you're not planning on going back to the Human realm," he said.

"Don't worry, I won't be. I know it's not safe at the moment," Nessa said. "Plus, where would I go? I don't have a home to go back to."

"I'm sorry," he said. "But there really wasn't any point in paying rent if you're not going to be there."

Even if she wanted to, Nessa didn't have the funds to keep the apartment. As it was, she was nearly out of money. If they were right, and she'd been asleep for two weeks, then she would have already lost the place.

Nessa had planned on finding a job when she returned home, but the Demons turned up before she'd had the chance to start looking. They turned up before she even had a chance to unpack.

"It's okay," she said. "Honestly, I don't think I would have been there much longer anyway."

None of them needed to know about her financial situation, so she kept that bit of info to herself.

"I'm not sure what I'm supposed to do now, though," she said.

"I'm sure something will come up," Anya said, smiling.

"I hope so," Nessa said.

If not, she might be camping out under the stars.

"You can stay with me for a while," Kellen offered.

"Thanks, but…"

"You don't need to bring your belongings over," he interrupted. "Because they are already there."

Nessa wasn't sure what to say. It wasn't that she didn't want to stay with Kellen. The problem was, she wanted it too much. Nessa didn't know if her heart could take the rejection that was inevitable, but she didn't know how to turn him down without sounding ungrateful.

"We weren't sure what to do with your stuff," Anya explained. "So, Kellen offered to store them at his house."

"I know you were talking about going to the feline territory, but I would rather it if you could wait a couple of days," Candi told her. "Just until I know for sure that you're okay. Staying at Kellen's means I can pop by and check on you."

"Okay," Nessa gave in with a small smile. "Thank you, Kellen."

"You're welcome," he said.

"Good," Candi said, clapping her hands. "Now, eat up so you can go to Kellen's. You're still going to need a lot of rest, so let him take care of you." Turning to Kellen, she pointed a finger at him. "Make sure she gets plenty of bed rest."

"I will do," Kellen said. "I'll make sure Kayla doesn't pester her too much either."

"I bet she's going to love having Nessa in the house," Anya said.

"Oh, I know she will," Kellen agreed.

Nessa didn't pay any attention to their conversation. She was too concerned with how she was going to make it through the next couple of days.

It was going to be hell living under the same roof as Kellen. It was hard enough hiding her feelings for him now, in a room full of people. Nessa was under no illusion that it was going to be any easier when they were alone together.

Nessa knew Kayla was going to be there as well, but there was bound to be times where she's out and Nessa is left alone with him. After all, Kayla was still a teenager, she wouldn't want to be cooped up indoors all the time.

Nessa wished things had been different between her

and Kellen, but they weren't, and she couldn't turn back the clock. All she could do was protect her heart as best she could, and hope that it was still in one piece at the end of the day.

Chapter Fourty

Kellen hadn't left Nessa's side since he found her, wanting to be there the minute she finally woke up. He needed to know she was okay. So why the fuck did he let Candi and Rush talk him into going home for a couple of hours? He knew why, Rush had demanded him to, but it still didn't make him feel any better.

Luckily enough, Anya had offered to keep watch and let him know if there was any change while he was gone. So at least she wasn't alone when she woke up, and Anya had kept to her word. She'd opened a link with him the moment Nessa opened her eyes.

What he was most pissed about though, was he wanted to speak with Nessa before bringing her home again. He wanted to make sure she was fine with it. After the way things ended last time, he wasn't positive she would be happy to stay with him again.

Unfortunately, she had visitors at the time and he didn't think she'd appreciate them being witness to what he had to say. And to be honest, he didn't want them to see her refuse to forgive him.

More importantly, he didn't want Nessa to feel as if she'd been backed into a corner. He wanted her to forgive him, but not because she felt pressured into it. So, biting his tongue, Kellen waited.

It seemed to take forever before she was finally ready to go, it didn't help that Anya, Willow, and Candi kept talking to her while she was trying to eat. Once she had finished, Kellen had been ushered into the hallway to wait for her to get dressed.

Nessa insisted on walking back to his house, saying she needed to stretch her legs after being laid up in bed for so long. Candi didn't think it was a good idea, but Kellen had assured her that he would look out for her, and even carry her if it came to it.

So, after saying goodbye to everyone, they started walking slowly towards his house.

"If you need to rest at all along the way, just say," Kellen said. "We can take as long as you need."

"I will," Nessa said.

Kellen didn't know what else to say, he wasn't one for small talk, so they walked in silence. Every time he looked over to Nessa, she was deep in thought as she took in their surroundings.

Not once did she show any signs in needing a rest, and before he knew it, they were arriving at home.

As soon as the house came into sight, the front door swung open and Kayla appeared.

"You're back!" Kayla shouted.

"I told you I wouldn't be long," Kellen shouted back.

"I'm not talking to you, stupid," Kayla said, making Nessa giggle next to him. "It's good to see you again."

"It's good to see you too," Nessa said.

"Are you staying for longer this time," Kayla asked.

"Yes, she is," Kellen replied for her. "Now get out the way so we can go inside. Nessa's been told to rest."

"Okay," Kayla said, jumping out the way when they reached her. "Is there anything I can get you?"

"No, thank you," Nessa said, smiling at Kayla.

"Are you sure?" Kayla said. "I really don't mind, whatever you want, I'll get."

"No, I'm sure," Nessa said.

"Do you want to go for a lie down?" Kellen asked.

"No, I'm good," she said. "Thank you anyway."

"At least sit down and rest in the living room," he told her.

"Okay," Nessa said, letting him lead her into the living room and over to the sofa.

Kayla looked lost, hovering in the doorway. Kellen could tell she wanted to help, she just didn't know how.

So, taking pity on her, he gave her a job to do. "Why don't you put a pot of coffee on?"

"Oh, that sounds good," Nessa agreed, noticing Kayla hovering.

"Okay," she said excitedly before bounding off.

Taking a seat next to Nessa on the sofa, Kellen whispered so Kayla couldn't overhear him. "Thank you."

"For what?" Nessa whispered back as she turned to him.

"For making Kayla feel useful," he said.

"That was all you," Nessa said.

"But you said it sounded good," Kellen said. "It made Kayla feel as if she's helping you."

"I didn't want one until you mentioned it," Nessa admitted.

"Good job I said something then," Kellen said, smiling at her.

For the first time today, Kellen was rewarded with Nessa's beautiful smile. It was amazing how much he missed seeing her face light up as she looked at him. But all too soon, Kayla came bounding back in.

"The coffee's on," she said with a massive smile on her face. "Is there anything else I can do?"

"Not at the moment," Kellen said. "Why don't you go and see Misti and Caleb for a bit? That'll give Nessa some time to rest."

"I suppose," Kayla said.

"Just make sure you're back for dinner, okay," he said.

"Okay," Kayla agreed after a moment. "I'll be back in a bit."

Thank god, Kellen thought as soon as the front door closed behind Kayla. *We're finally alone.*

"I'm sorry," he said without preamble.

"What for?" Nessa asked.

"For everything," he said.

"You have nothing to be sorry for," she said.

"Yes, I do," he told her. "I shouldn't have spoken to you the way I did, you didn't deserve that, not after everything you've been through."

"It's okay," she said.

"No, it's not," he said adamantly. "If it wasn't for me, you wouldn't have left the Shifter realm."

"It's not your fault I was beaten up," Nessa told him. "I should have known it wasn't safe."

"It is my fault…"

"No, it's not," she said sternly as she turned to face him. "You didn't make me leave, and you didn't beat me up. So as far as I can see, you aren't to blame."

Kneeling on the floor in front of Nessa, he took her hands in his and said "It is my fault, but I promise, if you let me, I'll spend the rest of my life making it up to you."

"Kellen, you don't have to," she said.

"I do," he told her. "I love you, Nessa, I have from the moment I first laid eyes on you."

Tears welled up in her eyes as she whispered "I love you too."

"You do?" he asked, surprised.

"Yes," she said, nodding.

"Will you be my mate?" Kellen asked.

He didn't care if it was too soon to ask, he needed to know that she would be his for all eternity, just like he was hers. He wanted… needed… to spend the rest of his life with her.

Tears now rolling freely down her cheeks, she nodded. "Yes."

Capturing her face between his hands, he wiped away her tears before claiming her mouth with his. Her soft lips parted for his tongue as he gently licked the seam.

Letting go of her face, he traced his fingers down her neck, across her shoulders, and down her arms. When they reached her waist, Nessa's arms lifted to encircle his neck, stopping him from moving away.

Hands on her hips, Nessa shuffled to the edge of the sofa, pressing her core against his hardening cock.

Kellen wanted so badly to rip their clothes off and bury himself deep within her walls, but he couldn't. Candi had told her to rest, and she wouldn't be doing that if they carried on any longer.

As much as he didn't want to, Kellen broke the kiss. "You need rest," he told her.

Cheeks flushed, and lips swollen from the kiss, Nessa looked at him with desire in her eyes. "I need you."

Kellen could see desire swimming in her eyes as she said those three little words. Both together weakened Kellen's restraint.

Growling, Kellen reclaimed her lips in a fiery kiss. Nessa lifted her legs and wrapped them around his waist. Even through their clothing Kellen could feel her pressed against him.

Unable to hold back much longer, Kellen slid his hands under her perfect ass and lifted her up. He couldn't stop what was about to happen, only Nessa could do that, but he could choose the place.

Carrying her, Kellen didn't break the kiss again until

they were in his... their... bedroom. Nessa unwrapped her legs so he could lower her to the floor when she realized where they were.

Kellen pulled off his shirt and throw it to the side as he kicked off his shoes, but stopped instantly as Nessa's hands gently caressed his chest and stomach. His cock twitched as he watched her tongue peek out to lick her lips.

When she finished her inspection, she stepped back. Locking eyes with him, she began to slowly undress.

"You're so fucking beautiful," he told her.

All the bruises and cuts had healed perfectly, leaving not a single mark to show what she'd been through. That wasn't to say there weren't any emotional scars, Kellen would be there to help her through them when she was ready, but at least she wouldn't be reminded every time she stripped.

Nessa blushed at his words, but she didn't stop until she was stood before him in a skimpy pair of knickers. The small piece of fabric barely covered her, and when she turned her back to him, he realized there was even less fabric at the back.

Moving sensually, Nessa crawled across the bed, tormenting him with the sight of the thin piece of fabric covering her core. When she reached the head of the bed, she turned back to face him.

Sitting on her heels with her legs spread open, Nessa cocked her finger at him. Kellen didn't need to be told twice.

Leaving his jeans on, Kellen walked to the end of the

bed. Stopping for a second to take in the sight of her on their bed before joining her.

"So beautiful," he said, kneeling in front of her.

Softly tracing his fingers over her hips, he followed the gentle curves up her body and across her ribs. Her nipples peeked and she sucked in a breath when his fingers brushed against the underside of her breasts.

Reaching up with her hands, Nessa ran her fingers through his hair and then pulled his face down to hers. Taking his mouth in a fiery kiss filled with passion.

Cupping her breasts, he gently rubbed his thumb over her peeked nipples, making her moan.

Moving his hands to her back, he pulled her towards him, so her breasts were pressed up against his chest. It had the added bonus of lifting her off her heels so she was now kneeling on the bed, her legs still spread open for him.

Sliding one hand down her back, he squeezed her ass before following the line of fabric between her cheeks to her core.

Nessa gasped in his mouth when his wondering fingers found her entrance. Moving the fabric to one side, Kellen dipped the tip of one finger inside, coating it in her juices before pulling out and sliding it over the bundle of nerves a bit further forward.

Nessa rewarded him with a moan, widening her legs at the same time.

"So wet for me already," he murmured against her mouth.

Kellen circled the bundle of nerves a couple of times

before sliding his finger inside her again, repeating the movement until Nessa was squirming in his arms.

Slowly shifting position on the bed, Kellen gently lowered Nessa on to her back. Lying down next to her, Kellen leaned on one arm, leaving the other free to roam.

Using one finger, he traced a line from her neck all the way down her body. When he reached her pelvis, he veered off to her leg furthest from him, gently pushing it open wider before retracing the line to the other leg to do the same.

Keeping his eyes locked with Nessa's, as Kellen's hand made its way back to her core, he was slowly leaning towards her breast. Finally, breaking eye contact, as his finger slid between her folds he leaned in and sucked one of her nipples into his mouth.

Swirling his tongue around the tip as his finger copied the movement around her entrance before pressing inside. Taking it in turns, he paid both breasts equal amounts of attention while his other hand played with the bundle of nerves.

Every time his finger came close to her entrance Nessa lifted her hips, trying to take him inside her.

"Please!" Nessa begged.

Releasing her nipple with a pop, Kellen asked "Please what?"

"More!" she said.

"More of this?" he asked, dipping a finger inside her.

"Yes!"

"Your wish is my command," he told her.

Moving further down the bed, Kellen settled between her legs. Using his thumbs, he spread her lips, exposing her entrance to his hungry gaze. Kellen licked his lips as he took in the sight.

"So wet for me," he said, dipping his thumbs in on either side.

Nessa lifted her hips, trying to take more of him inside, but Kellen moved his thumbs instead.

Before she had a chance to complain, Kellen leaned in and began to feast on her.

Chapter Fourty-One

Nessa was on cloud nine. There was no other way to describe how she was feeling right now.

Not only had she survived the beating, but Kellen had confessed his feelings for her. Never in her wildest dreams did she ever think he would love her let alone ask her to be his mate.

To go from thinking he didn't want anything to do with her, to being in his bed making love within the space of a couple of hours was a complete turnaround. Nessa wasn't complaining though.

How could she possibly complain when the man she loved was pleasuring her body? She couldn't. It also might have something to do with the fact she could barely form two words together in her mind.

Nessa was so close to the edge, tittering on the verge

of climax, and Kellen had only used his mouth. His very talented mouth.

She could feel his fingers circling her entrance, Nessa tried shifting her hips to take them inside but Kellen kept moving them out the way. She was about to scream her frustration when he finally breached her.

Just what she needed to tip her over. Nessa screamed as the waves of pleasure washed over her. Kellen slowly pumped his fingers inside her, dragging out her orgasm.

When she finally finished, Kellen pulled his fingers out and climbed off the bed. As he was about to undo his jeans, Nessa placed a hand on his, stopping him.

"Do you want to stop?" he asked, concern replacing the desire in his eyes.

"No," she told him. "I don't want to stop."

"Then…" Kellen didn't finish because he didn't have to.

Brushing his hands out the way and replacing them with her own, she looked up into his eyes as she began undoing his jeans. When she was done, Nessa didn't hesitate in pushing them off his hips and down his legs. His large cock stood proud as soon as it was released from the confines of his jeans.

Kellen kicked his jeans off the rest of the way and then climbed back on the bed. Nessa pushed him to his back so he was leaning against the pillows, then straddled his legs.

Hovering over his erect cock, she took hold of it with one hand and began stoking. Eager to pleasure him as he had her, Nessa leaned over and lightly licked the tip of his cock before taking him into her mouth.

Nessa lost herself as she licked and sucked at the same time as working her hand up and down his shaft. She slowly built up speed as she got into a rhythm she was comfortable with.

Kellen suddenly spun her around so she was kneeling on either side of his head.

"That's better," he growled.

Using his hands to massage her ass cheeks, she could feel him opening her up even though she was still wearing the thong. Kellen didn't seem bothered by the thin piece of fabric. Hooking one finger underneath it he moved it to one side so it was out of his way.

"Yes," he said huskily. "Definitely better."

Nessa gasped as he slid a finger deep inside her, his cock twitching in her mouth as she did so.

"And so wet," he murmured, adding a second finger.

Nessa could feel her walls squeezing his fingers as he pulled his fingers back out before slowly pushing them in again. She tried to concentrate on what she was doing but it was becoming increasingly difficult as he built up speed.

Eventually Kellen took over control, sliding his cock in and out of her mouth in time with his fingers as they invaded her pussy. His hair tickled her thigh as his head tilted to one side so he could flick the bundle of nerves with his tongue.

Nessa was so close to the edge again, but this time she didn't want to go over alone. She wanted Kellen to come as well.

Placing all her weight on one arm, she reached over his leg and cupped his balls in her hand, gently massaging.

"Fuck!" Kellen said.

Before Nessa knew what was happening, Kellen had pulled out of her and flipped her onto her back. In one swift move, he had her legs wrapped around his waist as he slid his cock deep inside her.

Nessa gasped at the sudden change in position, and the sudden feeling of fullness. Kellen held still while she adjusted to his size, only beginning to move when she started to relax around him.

Balancing on his arms, Kellen gently brushed the hair out of her face. His touch was gentle as he cupped her face that she closed her eyes, savouring the moment.

Warmth spread through her as she lay there in his arms, completely surrounded by him. Having his weight on top of her made her feel safe and protected, cocooned in the luscious scent of sandalwood and vanilla which was Kellen.

"Look at me," he said, slowly moving in and out of her.

As she opened her eyes to look into his, she was instantly lost in a deep blue sea filled with lust and desire.

"Are you sure about becoming my mate?" he asked, gazing into her eyes.

"Yes," Nessa said without hesitation.

"Good," he said. "Because there's no going back once it's done."

"I don't want to go back," Nessa said. "I want to be

your mate. I want to spend the rest of my life with you."

Kellen lightly kissed her lips before looking in her eyes once again.

"Don't look away," he said huskily.

Keeping a slow pace Kellen didn't once look away from her, and like he asked, she kept her eyes locked with his. Nessa never imagined something as simple as looking into each other's eye would be so intimate, but it was. Gazing into his eyes, she felt like she was the only person in the world he had eyes for.

Nessa could feel Kellen nudging her mind with his. She didn't hesitate for a second to open a link with him. Even though she'd only done it a couple of times, it was as if she'd always been able to. Opening a link with Kellen was like coming home.

Instantly she was flooded with emotions... Kellen's emotions. He didn't hide anything from her, showing her how he felt about her. He wasn't only sharing his body with her; he was sharing everything that he was.

Man and wolf, both in agreement, freely giving her their heart and soul. Nessa could do no less in return, opening herself up to him, heart and soul. Showing him how much he meant to her, how much she loved him.

She was surrounded by Kellen, inside and out. Nessa didn't know where she left off and he started. Mind, body, and soul, they all mixed together and making them one.

Nessa couldn't hold back the tidal wave any longer. A shower of colours rained down in her mind as they tipped over the edge together.

As she blissfully drifted in a rainbow of colours, she heard him whisper in her mind *"Mine."*

"Always and forever, yours," she whispered back.

"Always and forever," he agreed.

Epilogue

Kellen was setting the table for dinner when Kayla walked through the back door.

"Just in time," he said. "Dinner will be ready in a minute."

"Good, I'm starving," she said.

"You're always starving," he told her.

"No, I'm not," she denied. "Anyway, where's Nessa? Is she still here?"

"Of course, she is," he told her. "I told you she would be."

"Is she upstairs resting?" she asked.

Kellen couldn't stop the smile from creeping across his face. "No."

It was a good job Kayla hadn't come home early. Instead of resting, Nessa had been very much occupied all afternoon, but he wasn't about to tell Kayla that.

"Hi," Nessa said, blushing as she walked in the room.

With one look at Nessa, a knowing smile crept across Kayla's face until she was grinning from ear to ear.

"There's a coffee on the side for you," Kellen told her, ignoring Kayla's stupid grin. "Dinner will be ready in a minute."

"Great, thank you," she said, grabbing the cup of the side.

Kayla didn't say a word until they were all sat around the table about to eat. She just kept looking between them, that silly grin in place the entire time.

Kellen knew she was eager to know if Nessa was going to be his mate, she already told him that she thinks Nessa should be. He hadn't told her that he agreed with her because he didn't want Kayla to get her hopes up.

It had been the two of them for so long, he didn't want her heart to break along with his if Nessa had turned him down. So, he'd tried to keep his feeling quiet from her.

"Did you ask her to be your mate?" Kayla finally asked. "Did he ask you?"

"Who said I was going to?" Kellen asked.

"Oh," Kayla said, waving her hand at him. "I know I'm young, but I'm not stupid… or blind. Anyone with eyes could see how you feel about her."

Kellen didn't think it had been that obvious, but apparently it was.

"Well?" Kayla prompted.

"Yes, I've asked," he said.

"And?"

"I said yes," Nessa said.

"Yes!" Kayla said excitedly.

Both Kellen and Nessa smiled at her.

"I can't wait to tell everyone," Kayla said. "They're going to be so happy for us."

"Us?" he asked.

"Well, yes," Kayla said, grinning from ear to ear. "I've got a sister. I've always wanted a sister."

Kellen had to admit; it was going to be great for Kayla having another female in the house. Growing up with only a brother was hard on her, he knew it was. There were certain things she wouldn't want to talk about with him, so it was good she now had Nessa to turn to for advice, or even just a listening ear.

Kellen didn't think it was possible to love Nessa more than he already did until she spoke her next words.

"I've always wanted a sister as well," she told Kayla.

His heart burst with love and joy. For the first time in a long time, Kellen was looking forward to the future. A future filled with love and laughter.

***

Rush didn't know what he was going to do about Nash, but something needed to be done about him. He couldn't be left to run riot in the Human realm, turning whoever he wanted into Shifters.

Unfortunately, none of the other Shifter species were prepared to get involved, saying it wasn't their problem.

Which was utter bullshit. Nessa was proof that it wasn't only the wolves' problem.

The last thing they needed was for the Humans to realize they weren't alone in the world. And they definitely didn't want the Humans to find out that not only were they not alone in the world, but there were whole other worlds.

So far it hadn't been too much of an issue. Wolves and panthers were already a part of the ecosystem in the Human realm, so those Shifters could blend in easily and pretend to be just another animal.

Some of the other species weren't so easily disguised. If Nash decided to turn the next Human into a dragon for instance, then they were going to have a lot of problems. There was no way to hide a fifty-foot dragon.

No, Nash couldn't be allowed to carry on. He needed to be stopped and now, before he caused any more damage… before he destroyed anymore lives.

Darkest Bane

Prologue

Ebony slammed the front door shut. She was glad to finally be home after a long day at work.

"You're back late," Tasmin pointed out the obvious as Ebony threw her bag and coat on the sofa.

"Tell me about it," she said, grimacing.

She kicked off her shoes and headed into the kitchen to grab a glass of wine.

Pulling out the biggest glass she could find, she filled it to the rim and downed half of it in one go. She topped it up again before returning to the living room with the bottle of wine in hand.

She planned on having a nice hot bubble bath and a chilled night on the sofa in front of the TV. Looking after a bunch of toddlers all day long was hard enough, but then having a staff meeting afterwards that lasted for two hours was just taking the piss.

Two whole fucking hours!

Don't get her wrong, she loved her job, but she didn't like her boss. The woman could talk the ear off an elephant, she talked that much. What made it worse, it was mostly crap she'd been talking about.

Nobody wanted to know about her family holiday in a staff meeting. That shit was meant to be kept out of work. After all, it had absolutely fuck all to do with the nursery or the children.

"Long day at work?" Tasmin asked as she eyed the bottle in Ebony's hand.

"You could say that," Ebony replied.

"Are you going to keep on with the cryptic answers, or are you going to tell me what happened?" Tasmin asked.

"Just that silly cow talking about shit again." She didn't need to say who she was talking about, Tasmin already knew who it was. "Can you believe she called a staff meeting and then spent nearly the entire time talking about her holiday?"

"After what you've told me about her, it doesn't surprise me," Tasmin shook her head. "I don't know why you don't just get another job. You're not happy there, and haven't been since you started. So, just get a different job. Problem solved."

"It's not that easy," Ebony said.

"Of course it is," Tasmin countered. "With your experience, you'll get another job in no time. Just go in work tomorrow morning and hand in your notice."

"And what about paying the rent and bills?" she asked. "What am I going to do about money while I'm looking for a new job?"

"I'm sure we can figure something out," Tasmin told her. "I'm more than happy to help you out. All you need to do is ask and I'll help, you know that."

As great as it was for Tasmin to offer, Ebony couldn't take her up on it. She wasn't much better off than Ebony was, so it wouldn't be fair to put all the bills and rent squarely on her shoulders.

She wouldn't be much of a roommate if she couldn't pull her own weight when it came to the finances.

"I'll be fine tomorrow," she said. "I just need a bottle or two of wine to help me unwind."

Ebony placed the bottle of wine on the coffee table and then curled up on the sofa.

"What are your plans for tonight?" Ebony asked as Tasmin sat opposite her.

"I've got a date," she said, smiling proudly. "What about you?"

"I'm just going to stay in and watch a movie," Ebony said.

Other than having a bath at some point, she didn't plan on moving until bed, which probably wouldn't be too late because she still had to be up early for work.

"I don't blame you," Tasmin said.

"What time are you going out?" Ebony looked at the clock.

"David should be here in about half an hour. In fact, I should get ready." Tasmin jumped up and raced into her bedroom.

It was no surprise she'd left getting ready until the last minute. It was always the same no matter what she was doing. Her motto was 'better late than never'.

Ebony was the complete opposite, she hated being late and always aimed to be at least ten minutes early. That wasn't the only thing they were complete opposites about.

Tasmin was a messy roommate, her bedroom floor was barely recognizable through the clothes that littered it. Whereas, Ebony was a clean freak, she hated mess and clutter.

For that reason, Ebony was in charge of keeping the apartment squeaky clean, which she did happily. Thankfully, Tasmin kept her mess in the bedroom where Ebony didn't have to clean or tidy up after her.

She didn't mind cleaning the rest of the place, but Tasmin's bedroom was her own to keep on top of, which is why it looked like a bomb went off in there all the time.

Tasmin ran through to the bathroom just as there was a knock at the front door.

"Grab the door for me!" Tasmin shouted from the bathroom. "Just tell David I'll be ready in a minute!"

"Okay!" Ebony shouted back as she climbed to her feet and made her way to the door.

As soon as she turned the handle, the door was kicked in from the other side. The force was so hard that it ripped the door from its hinges, hitting Ebony in the face in the process. Pain shot through her face as the impact knocked her off her feet.

Her ass hit the floor first, followed by the back of her head as the momentum sent her rolling backwards. As her head bounced off the floor, even more pain shot through her, turning her vision black for a moment.

Before she knew what was happening, a group of men rushed into the apartment. Two of them grabbed hold of her. Viciously flipping her on to her stomach, they pinned her to the floor. The rest of them scattered in all directions.

She could hear Tasmin screaming from the bathroom. She tried to do the same, but one of the men pinning her down quickly placed a hand over her mouth.

Within seconds, the screaming stopped. Ebony's heart sank as she feared the worst had happened to Tasmin, but a moment later relief filled her as Tasmin was carried out of the bathroom.

From what Ebony could see from her position on the floor, a great hulking man had one arm wrapped around her waist while his other hand covered her mouth. Apart from being extremely pissed off, Tasmin appeared to be in one piece and relatively unharmed.

As much as Ebony tried to fight against the two holding her, it was all in vain. She could barely move an inch, the men were just too heavy for her to budge. Even if she hadn't been face down, she would have struggled.

Tasmin didn't have it much easier. Her feet were free, but it didn't make a blind bit of difference. No matter how much she kicked shit out of the guy's shin, it didn't seem to faze him in any way.

"Well, well, well. Two for the price of one," a man said from the doorway.

The sound of his voice sent shivers down her spine. And not the good kind either.

Ebony tried her best to get a better look at the newcomer, but all she could see was the damaged door and the floor.

"So, who do we have here?" he asked.

If he didn't know who they were, then Ebony certainly wasn't going to enlighten him. Tasmin must have had the same thought, as she kept quiet as well. Not that they could speak with the men's hands over their mouths.

Even if she didn't have a hand over her mouth, she wasn't sure she would be able to get a word out. The two burly men were squashing her chest into the floor, making it hard to breathe.

Her mobile phone and house keys, still in her trouser pockets, dug uncomfortably into her thighs as she was pressed tightly against the floor.

Seriously? Do they both have to be on top of me? They weigh a goddamn ton!

"Nobody wants to talk?" the man asked. "That's okay, you can stay silent if you want to. It makes no difference whether you talk or not, you're both coming with me."

As soon as the last word left his mouth, the men holding her down shifted positions slightly. She heard a clanking sound a moment before she felt cool metal against her skin as it encircled her wrists.

Not once in her life did she ever think she'd be in handcuffs. She wouldn't mind if she'd done something wrong to deserve it, but she hadn't.

"Like fuck am I going with you!" Tasmin shouted.

Ebony could just about see her struggling to break free. Not that it did her any good, her arms were pulled behind her back. No doubt she was handcuffed just like Ebony.

"Oh, but you are," the man said calmly.

Tasmin attempted to scream, but it came out muffled as one of the men holding her placed a hand over her mouth again.

The hand was removed from Ebony's mouth long enough for the men to stand up and pull her to her feet. Then it was swiftly returned before she could make a sound.

It was obvious they didn't want anybody hearing Ebony and Tasmin, which could only mean bad things for them. At least she could finally see what she was up against now that she was back on her feet.

"Who are you?" Ebony mumbled. Her words garbled from behind the strange man's hand.

The man who had spoken from the doorway walked over and stopped in front of her, giving her all of his attention. He nodded to the man holding her to remove his hand so she could speak.

"I didn't quite get that," he said. "Do you mind re-peating what you said."

"I said: who are you?" she repeated.

"Ah, I see," he said. "My name is, Mr Smith."

Ebony didn't believe it was his real name, but she wasn't about to call him out on it.

Mr Smith was such a common surname that he probably picked it for that reason. She could be wrong, but she doubted it. He seemed like the type of person who would hide his true identity.

"What do you want with us?" she asked.

Ebony flinched as he lifted a hand towards her face. He gently ran his fingers against her cheek as he brushed the hair out of her way. Ebony couldn't help the shiver of revulsion at his touch, or the look of disgust.

"I want to transform you into a new and improved version of yourself," he said.

"I'm happy with how I am," she told him. "But thanks anyway."

Ebony was proud of herself. Even though she was scared shitless on the inside, she somehow spoke without showing her fear. If she had been one of her students, she'd have given them a gold star.

"I'm pretty sure my friend feels exactly the same," she added, nodding towards Tasmin. "So, you might as well just let us go. I'm sure there are plenty of women out there that'll take you up on the offer, and you won't even need to use handcuffs on them."

He chuckled at her. "I'm sure you're right."

"I know I am," she said adamantly.

"But that still doesn't change anything," he said, turning serious. "I'll still be taking the two of you with me today."

He nodded at someone behind her. Duct tape was slapped over her mouth a second before a dark fabric bag was pulled over her head. Instantly making it so she couldn't see or speak.

"As I said," he whispered menacingly near her ear. "You will be coming with me." He inhaled deeply through his nose. "I'm looking forward to experimenting on you."

Did he just sniff me?

Ebony would have burst out laughing at him sniffing her if the situation hadn't been so dire. As it was, a lead weight sank in her stomach at his words.

As much as she told herself not to, she panicked as they guided her out of the apartment. Having her hands cuffed behind her back and not being able to see made it even worse.

As they led her down the hall towards the stairs, the thought that kept popping into her mind wasn't what she thought it would have been. Instead of worrying about what was going to happen to her and Tasmin, she kept imagining what would happen if she suddenly tripped over and went flying down the stairs.

Would the men holding her arms stop her from falling? Or would they let her go so she face planted on the floor?

Ebony knew it was the least of her worries at that moment in time, but it didn't stop her mind from picturing it. Luckily, she didn't have to find out. With them guiding her way around, she made it down the stairs and out of the building without tripping over.

"One in each," Mr Smith said when they reached the car park at the side of the building.

Her heart sank as she was placed in the back of a car. She had secretly been hoping they would be spotted on the way out of the building and that someone would come to their rescue. But as they strapped her into the car, she realized that wasn't going to happen.

Squashed between two large men, she had no way out. With no other choice, Ebony waited for the first opportunity she had to escape.

Dear reader

I hope you enjoyed reading this book as much as I
enjoyed writing it.
Please could you take a moment to leave a review,
even if it's only a line or two, about what you thought
of the book.
Also, if you'd like to know about upcoming new
releases, sneak-peeks, and special offers you can
sign up to my newsletter. You can also find me on
Facebook, Bookbub, and Goodreads.
Thank you and much love.

Georgina.

www.georginastancer.co.uk
www.facebook.com/AuthorGeorginaStancer
www.bookbub.com/profile/georgina-stancer
www.goodreads.com/author/show/18724439.Georgina_Stancer

Guarded by Night series

Kissed by Stardust
Connor's New Wolf
Midnight Unchained
Darkest Bane

Infernal Hearts series

Heart of the Hunted
Heart of the Damned
Heart of the Cursed (coming soon)

Printed in Great Britain
by Amazon